The Boxford Stories

ISBN-13: 978-0-9907248-1-0

Cover design and book layout: Book Cover Corner, bookcovercorner.com
Cover art by Jacob Dobson

Carson, Kristen

The Boxford Stories / Kristen Carson — 1st ed.

THE BOXFORD STORIES

A Short Story Collection

by

KRISTEN CARSON

Contents

THE GILDED DOOR

It sat on a quiet end of Main Street, just a block down from the Shoreline State Bank and the Sunshine Laundry. Within its dark cavern, you could lose yourself in fantasy. It was the place where Tevye first eyed his sons-in-law, where Herbie squirted oil on the bad guy's shoes, where John Wayne turned Maureen O'Hara over his knee and delivered a good spanking.

Then, when the credits rolled and the lights went up, you were still in another world, gaping at the gilt-edged ceiling medallions and the sparkling chandeliers, at the towering half pillars that bulged from the walls. And even if the place had slipped into a genteel decrepitude, you could still see what the great Gilberto Massanopoli had in mind when he designed it all. It was still a fantasy palace, this place that everyone in Boxford knew as the Gilded Door Theatre.

So imagine the surprise of Boxford's best piano teacher, Ada Runyon, when she walked by the Gilded Door, her arms loaded down with pinch-pleated draperies fresh from the Sunshine Laundry. She saw the poster of coming attractions. "LIMITED ENGAGEMENT!!!: Xaviera del'Abunda, star of *Sky-High Stewardesses*!!! Coming soon in *Amazons in Hard Hats*!!!"

The April-day bliss fell from Ada's face. Whatever happened to the *Planet of the Apes* sequel which had been playing all winter? She emerged from the shadow of the marquee. She walked backward as she looked up at the title trumpeting itself there: Yes, it was true. Even worse, *Amazons in Hard Hats* was no longer COMING SOON! It was *here*. And so was Miss del'Abunda in that poster, where great mounds of her flesh bobbed, barely restrained in their bindings.

The first person Ada called was her best friend, Ruthalin Feldsted. Ruthalin must have talked to her husband, Erval, who went straight to their Mormon bishop. That was why Bishop Keating walked in on Latham Runyon's next Sunday School class. He looked like Dr. Bad News, and the class looked up like all the relatives in the waiting room. He rubbed the bare dome of skin on top of his head. He hoisted the belt around his potatoes-and-gravy paunch. "We've got a problem," he told them. Even his wife looked somber, and Jeralee Keating was the cheeriest person on the planet.

Jeralee wore her entire history on her face. You could see her at age thirteen, dressed in gingham, her hair in a ponytail, as she headed out the back door after breakfast to deliver cantaloupe rinds to the cows. Today, tracks of gray shot through her short little bangs. They ran back across her head, caught up in that ponytail. The figure underneath the gingham had gone all pillowy. But she still looked thirteen.

"Why isn't rating it 'X' enough?" asked Jeralee.

"You wonder," said Ruthalin, "how much worse it can be when they're calling it 'Triple X.'"

"There's a law against that sort of thing!" boomed Erval Feldsted. "Or if there isn't, there oughta be!"

Other voices declared that "We should run them out," or "We should attend a meeting!" But how? And what meeting?

Who in their congregation, their little far-flung Boxford Ward, even knew how the town worked? Half the ward had moved here from the deserts of the West, drawn by jobs at the Crayton Poultry Company (Darold Keating), or Tidewater General Hospital (Erval Feldsted), or Boxford State College (Latham

Runyon, who now shoved his lesson materials aside and sat on the edge of the table).

These transplants filled the center pews each Sunday. Each man wore a white shirt and a look of bemused fatigue. The women dressed in homesewn frocks. They wielded thick, useful arms as they herded their many well-scrubbed children.

A center-pew family could live in Boxford ten years and still not know a thing about City Hall. Who had the time? Fathers worked all day. In the evenings, they taught Boy Scouts how to tie knots, or they drove about seeking lost members. On the weekends, they fixed whatever was broken in the house, unless they were asked to weed melons at the church farm or attend yet another priesthood meeting, where the men met together for instruction and haranguing about their church duties. Which happened often enough that the list of broken house parts never, ever shrank by much.

The women cooked, sewed, gardened and canned. If that did not take up enough time, they cut out flannel board figures to use in their church lessons. And if that did not take up enough time, they looked for somebody who was sick and needed soup and, if no sick person could be found, then somebody who looked a little tired would do.

What you had was a people who believed in civic duty and voting and all that. But when faced with the ballot, they just didn't know whether to keep Joe Green as sheriff, or throw him over for Bill Brown.

In the side pews, folks with tattoos, droopy mustaches and faces deeply lined by hard living filled the rows. These folks were the converts. Native to the county, they straggled in every week or two in family fragments. And even though they had lived around here a long time, they had no idea how to fend off a smutty movie house. The dinette waitresses and the union welders usually saw civic life from the wrong end. Take, for example, Sister Kilby. Didn't her oldest son still have to report to his parole officer? Now, nobody was saying Sister Kilby didn't have a good heart. But what kind of advice could she offer when the Gilded Door turned its back on Disney movies forever and the Sunday School class wanted to fight back? Yes, fight back! They would all write a letter! They would call the ... the ...

"Brother Runyon, can you figure out who to call and get back to us?"

Brother Runyon was a history professor. He knew stuff. Maybe he could figure out what to do.

"Yes, Brother Runyon, we cannot let them get away with this!"

But they were getting away with it. That's the way things were going now. Why just last week, Ada had turned on the TV and there was Woody Allen on *Afternoon with Doug Michaels*. The two of them chatted over Woody's new movie and how it shocked people from Tallahassee to Minot. But why worry? they laughed. The people who didn't like Woody's movie were rubes that probably enjoyed having their teeth pulled by barbers with big rusty pliers.

The sexual revolution was on the march and those who refused to cheer along its parade route felt ... lonely.

* * *

Ada Runyon could see the ladies of the Boxford Music Club through the windows as she walked up the Weston-Welsh's sidewalk on Thursday evening. She paused before the door to shake the water off her umbrella. She barely got the bell rung when Lucy Weston-Welsh opened the door and filled its frame amply. As she smiled, her cheek wrinkles dug deep into her face. "Has it stopped raining out there yet?" *'Esit stawped rehning ought theh yet?'* Oh, that New Zealand accent. Ada forgave Lucy a lot, just because she was fun to listen to.

Lucy moved aside, fluffing at her cap of white hair.

The club ladies clustered here and there in the living room. They were the kind of women you might find in any college town. Most were reasonably slender, because they lived the life of the mind. This fed their souls, so they didn't need cheese puffs and donuts like other people did. And most left the gray strands in their flat hairdos unretouched because, thanks to that life of the mind again, they didn't panic at the first signs of aging.

"You can see, though, that the place is crumbling," said Emily Stinchfield, music instructor at Beaglin Elementary. "The pieces chipped off the columns, the carpet wearing thin."

"Well, I would gladly pay more for popcorn, if it would help," said Rachel Lowenstein, private piano teacher (Ada's competition, actually).

"Are you talking about the Gilded Door?" asked Ada.

"Some people are calling it 'The Guilty Door,'" said Emily.

"And why do we need it here?" said Rachel. "Isn't that what people go to Philly for? To do the things they don't want to get caught doing?"

"You'd think," said Lucy, "that the blokes could get what they needed from those magazines at the top of the rack, far up where the little pikers can't see those girls on the cover and their ..." Lucy fluffed her hands before her chest. Everybody knew what she meant: *And their ballooned bosoms.*

"People! This is 1974!" said Rachel. "Haven't we learned by now to stop objectifying women?"

Ada frowned. She still wasn't clear on the meaning of the word "objectifying." But before the evening ended, Lucy Weston-Welsh said she had an idea that might be worth a try. Relief washed over Ada. Until Lucy pointed around the room at the ladies that would help her. Her finger pointed straight at Ada Runyon.

Who could say no to Lucy Weston-Welsh? Her stout form, her bellowing laugh, her exactitude, which made her just right for playing the grand organ every week at St. Abelard's Episcopal Church, added up to a woman who either got what she demanded, or hung you out to dry. Ada never forgot how, the year Lucy led the Music Club chorus, she cackled every time the pianist made a mistake.

"Ha-ha! I gotcha! I gotcha!"

So on a day chosen by Lucy, Ada found herself in a car parked outside the Gilded Door. She got out when Lucy got out. She looked at Emily Stinchfield to see if Emily had a clue about what Lucy might make them do.

Lucy looked up at the marquee, tightened her lips and set her rudder for the door.

And there, in the lobby of the Gilded Door, stood Mr. Elroy Skibbey, proprietor.

Ada expected some swarthy villain type, a real mustache-twirler. But he was just a homely, ruddy man. He had probably been the homeliest boy back in his grade school, the only sort that ever got crushes on her. He stood there with his hands in his back pockets, looking at the women over his glasses. *You're here to cause trouble, eh?*

Lucy bustled through the introductions and went right into her speech. "Now, Mr. Skibbey, we know that you just want to make money. And we know it's getting harder these days, what with people staying home to watch their color televisions."

"Actually, the twin theatres out at the new mall," he said, but Lucy interrupted and went on about the music club and about Boxford being a decent town and about how she could find things to put on that stage that Boxfordians would pay to see.

And he looked at them through his bifocals. *I'm a really nice guy. I just have to make a living.*

* * *

"Odd man. *Odd* man, that Mr. Skibbey," said Ada.

She and Ruthalin Feldsted wandered among the craft tables at the Poultry Festival. It was their last best chance for a day out together. In another week, Ruthalin's advancing pregnancy would cross the line from evident to huge-and-miserable. Then she wouldn't want to walk around all afternoon anymore. Ada noticed that Ruthalin was reaching the huge-and-miserable stage weeks earlier with baby #10 than she had back with baby #6.

"But what did he look like?" asked Ruthalin, fingering pot-holders laid out on a sunny table.

"Mr. Skibbey? Well, the lobby was dim. And I was hiding behind Lucy ..."

"Whatever for?"

"D'you think I want to be mentally undressed by a man who spends his working hours in a dark triple-X theatre?"

Ruthalin considered this. "I see your point," she said, moving on to a table of wooden toys. "And Lucy would be big enough to hide behind."

"I was just relieved that she didn't pull a bundle of picket signs out of her trunk. I wouldn't put it past her, you know."

"Oh yes, your Lucy would be that sort. Didn't she live through a couple revolutions?"

"Oh, you mean Kenya. She was teaching there when the natives finally got fed up with the British. But she got out before they smashed the store windows beneath her flat."

Ruthalin nodded. "So what happened?"

"Oh. Lucy. She was *so* smooth. 'And we know that the Gilded Door was once a vaudeville house, and the stage is still back there behind that screen, am I right?'"

By now, Ruthalin had arrived at a table of curiously-constructed blouses. She fingered the pleats and turned out the seams to study the workmanship. "So he listened to all this and didn't throw you out?"

"Most people listen to Lucy, if they know what's good for them. And that's how we got two Friday nights a month to use the old stage at the Guilty Door."

"You mean he didn't give up the Triple-X completely?"

"Oh, Lucy's good. But she's not *that* good. We have to prove we can make money for him. She's lining up the shows. We've got a concert pianist coming July 12th, so mark your calendar."

"I see. July 12th," said Ruthalin, absently. She held up a blouse, pointing to the buttoned flaps across the chest. "Are these slits for nursing?"

"That's right," beamed the craft lady behind the table.

"Clever!" said Ruthalin.

"I'll say. With one of these," said Ada, "you could actually sit through Kevin's football games, instead of excusing yourself to feed the baby."

"I could. Though I don't know why I'm hiding *my* bosoms when Xaviera's showing hers off down on Main Street."

The craft lady moved close to her cash box. She beamed as Ruthalin exclaimed over the precision of the zipper installment.

"Well, are you going to buy?" Ada whispered. She could not believe the look in Ruthalin's eye. Was Ada about to witness the county's foremost tin-foil re-user spend money?

Ruthalin held the blouse out for a final admiring look.

"I could make this," she said, and hung it up.

As they walked away, Ada looked back at the craft lady, whose smile had grown brittle but brave.

* * *

"And so, the first will be Mr. Koji Yoshimoto, a classical pianist," Ada told the Boxford Ward.

The people in her husband's Sunday School class broke into a babble of happiness.

"We'll show that Mr. Skibbey a thing or two!"

"He may find out he never needed to go over to the blue movies to make a buck!"

"Yes, well, you can call me for tickets." Ada moved through the room. She passed by Ruthalin's husband Erval as he rocked on his heels next to Bishop Keating. "A thing like this wouldn't happen back home in Cardiff, Utah," said Erval. "Something like this ... well, it's been one of the hardest adjustments, you know? I just think that children grow up better out west. They don't have all the problems you see here."

"You can get away from it there," said the bishop.

"Exactly. I mean, I know we saw it as an adventure, coming back east. But sometimes I wake up early in the morning and I wonder if we did the right thing. I mean, this place is so *old*. It's already made a long list of mistakes."

"Like?"

"Well, the fellas at work say gangsters run all the ports."

"And they say the governor takes bribes."

"Exactly! And now we all have to live with these mistakes. And it's just not like that out there. Boys who grow up out there become *men*."

"They meet better girls too. When Jerry brought home that girl from New Jersey ..." The bishop shook his head.

Erval nodded deeply. "And sure, the kids say, 'It's dusty out there. It's empty,' but ..."

"Empty can be a good thing. It's like a clean slate. Give people a clean slate and maybe they'll get it right this time."

"Exactly."

Ada, who herself had left the desert behind, moved on to where her husband Latham listened to Jeralee Keating. "I told Jerry, 'We used to entertain ourselves. We didn't have all these movie theaters and bowling alleys and spinball arcades.'"

Spinball?

"'And we had more fun then!' I told him. Isn't that right? I told him, 'Why don't you invite your friends over and we'll show them how to have a taffy pull. Or we'll teach them to play Wink 'Em.' And he just can't understand it! Why, I'll bet you remember the days when you pulled back the chairs in the kitchen, invited the local fiddler and had a dance."

Latham nodded politely, even though Ada knew he remembered no such thing.

"It really was more fun then," Jeralee went on. "I tell you, when a town fills up with these places that lure young people away from wholesome, homemade fun, trouble is right around the corner."

What places? Like the paddle boats in the park? Like the concerts in the college auditorium? Like the new mall out beyond the bypass? Why, Boxford was a fine town. Oh, sure, the boulevard was junked up with too many power lines and car lot pennants. And you didn't want to be out on Homecoming weekend, with all the hijinks on the quad over by College Hall. Still, Boxford was getting to be a nice place to spend a Saturday night.

Or at least it was until the Gilded Door started showing Triple X movies.

But Ada envisioned the Guilty ... that is, the Gilded Door's auditorium right now, filled so full that the fire marshal would march in on a gust of importance, plant his fists on his love handles and decree that the aisles must be cleared or else.

And Mr. Skibbey would look through his bifocals and then over the rims of his glasses. He would notice how his naughty movies never packed 'em in like this, no matter how much he might like to watch them himself.

* * *

The Boxford Music Club was a busy crew. They not only had to rent a grand piano and haul it into the Gilded Door. They had to make reservations for their guest, Mr. Koji Yoshimoto, at the Best Rest Inn. Somebody had to pick him up at the Philly airport. When Lucy asked who wanted to do it, a half dozen ladies protested that they couldn't handle all those freeway lanes. So Lucy—confident, fearless, dangerous, if you want to know the truth—took on the job herself. Ada pitied Mr. Yoshimoto.

Then, when he arrived, they fed him a dinner of crabcakes and Emily Stinchfield's famous Grasshopper Pie. They dusted the black lacquer finish on the grand piano and placed a glass of cold water on a little table in the wings and offered their guest a lint brush for his pants. They passed out programs and explained to a stray customer or two that, sorry, it wasn't the usual fare at the Guilty Door tonight. It was the second Friday of the month, given over to classical music and wouldn't they like to come in and give it a try? They found themselves saying all this to the customer's back as he hurried out.

"I hope he finds relief somewhere," said one music-clubber.

"The 7-11's magazine racks aren't but five minutes away," said the other.

Not until Mr. Yoshimoto's opening arpeggio did Ada catch her breath and look around at the auditorium. *Not bad,* she thought as her eyes traveled all the way up to the seats under the balcony. *Not exactly a fire-marshal crowd but ...* Mr. Yoshimoto's Brahms was so beautiful, she looped her arm through Latham's and lost herself in booming, wide-shouldered chords that she would never, ever hear from her students.

When he finished his Brahms, she scanned the half-shadowed faces in the audience again. Did Ruthalin like this? Did Erval?

In his final moment under the lights, Mr. Yoshimoto bowed and bowed. He nodded toward the smiles of these, his newest friends, all of them clapping hard enough to sting their hands. He was the ultimate gentleman—starched, pressed, polite. Blue-haired ladies gathered around him onstage, pumping his hand. Young girls in velvet dresses—Rachel Lowenstein's students, no doubt—gripped their rolled-up programs until it was their turn and their mothers pushed them forward.

Lucy appeared at Ada's side. "I knew we'd forget something. Did we ever decide who will drive him to the motel?"

Ada thought a minute. "I could ask Latham."

Ada found Latham, deep in discussion with Theodore Stinchfield, head of the math department. Latham said yes, he would drive Mr. Yoshimoto. He jingled the keys in his pocket. He looked around for Mr. Yoshimoto, now in the lobby, who bowed and autographed yet more programs.

One young boy stood before the pianist. "Can you sign in my autograph book?"

"Yes, certainly."

"But I left it in the car."

"Would you mind waiting?" asked the child's father.

"Okay. Is okay." As Mr. Yoshimoto looked around the lobby, Ada hoped he didn't notice the burnt-out bulb just over his head, or the carpet threads hanging from the stairs up to the balcony. She hoped he couldn't see now badly little old Boxford needed him. Let him just stand there, wearing his permanent-pasted smile, trying not to eavesdrop on Lucy and the autograph boy's mommy (apparently another good Episcopalian) as they discussed the results of Reverend Anglesey's biopsy.

"Do you know what kind of cancer they're looking for?"

"Nobody's saying."

Mr. Yoshimoto studied the lobby, the mirrors behind the empty candy counter, the dormant popcorn machine stuffed into a corner, the worn velvet ropes lining the walls.

His eye fell on something tucked behind the display case. He cocked his head, reading sideways. Elroy Skibbey stepped forward from the shadows. Mr. Yoshimoto looked up with inquiring eyes. "You collect?" Mr. Skibbey pulled it out—a poster of Xaviera del'Abunda in her hardhat and not much else.

Mr. Yoshimoto gave the poster a long appreciative glance. Even if he only spoke tourist English, he seemed to comprehend perfectly well, as Skibbey explained what went on at the Gilded Door all the other nights of the month. "Ah!" His eyebrows rose up. "I see! I see, yes!"

Skibbey rolled up the poster and gave it to Mr. Yoshimoto, who tucked it under his arm with a secret smile. He signed the little boy's autograph book. He bowed one last time.

Ada's husband broke away from Dr. Stinchfield, shook out his car keys and said, "Ready to go?"

* * *

And he had seemed like such a gentleman. He had seemed like the kind of man that if, say, he were locked into a room at the Best Rest Motor Inn (accidentally, of course) with someone as pretty as Emily Stinchfield, he would never lay a finger on her. He would let Emily have the bed, while he slept upright in the little square chair. And Emily would never wake up to find him standing over her, breathing heavily.

But men could shock you. Latham had. When Ada first met him, he had been one of the most upright young men in her congregation, the kind that took every last commandment seriously, the kind who walked blocks out of his way to avoid a bathing beauty on a billboard.

But when she finally had his ring on her finger, when she finally got him alone behind the door of Room 824 at the Hotel Bonneville, she was shocked at how ably, how eagerly he undid the buttons of her going-away suit.

Not that she minded, oh no! But the next time she sat in church, and saw all those suited men up front, her world had turned so fast that the sun now came up in the west and water flowed uphill. Here were men who delivered thundering sermons to the teenagers, sermons about bridling one's passions. They were so convincing that you were sure these men had no passions at all.

Didn't need 'em!

Bathing beauty on a billboard? They didn't *want* to see it. It was something they didn't *like*, just like they didn't like cucumbers, or Preparation H commercials.

At least that's what virginal Ada thought.

Newlywed Ada knew better. Newlywed Ada understood that it took monumental will for these fellows to stare straight ahead when that billboard loomed.

This morning, as she wiped up an orange juice spill, she remembered Mr. Yoshimoto's delighted face as Xaviera del'Abunda came out from behind the concession counter. As she shook the dust cloth out on the back porch, she pictured him in the passenger seat of Latham's car. And as she sorted socks on the bed, she wondered if Mr. Yoshimoto had tried to share his little souvenir with her husband.

Had Latham looked?

No. She knew Latham pretty well. Ogling the wife was OK. Everybody else was off-limits.

But would he secretly wish that he could look? Did he long, deep-down, for his wife to look more like Xaviera (that is, what little he could see of her as he turned away from Mr. Yoshimoto's poster)?

Ada tucked the folded socks into the drawer, reached down for the laundry basket and caught sight of herself in the mirror beside the door. She stood up straight and studied the image.

The shock of gray at her temple was not that bad. It didn't detract much from her minstrel-boy haircut. And she was still slender, aside from the little pooch-out left over from three pregnancies.

Hers was not the kind of beauty any man would associate with wild midnight fantasy. But maybe she wasn't trying hard enough.

She turned sideways and lifted her chin just so.

She thrust out her bosom until her back muscles complained.

She flared her nostrils and composed her face into its most Xaviera-like pout.

She posed her arm behind her head and stared at herself in the mirror, her body all S-shaped. S for Slithery, for Siren. Then she ...

The bedroom door burst open. "Ada, have you seen my white notebook? I'm late already for pries..."

Latham stopped.

He looked her up and down, his eyebrows jacked up with surprise.

"Don't scare me like that!" Ada undid her pose. "Well, what are you staring at?"

"I wish I knew."

"Oh, this is too much!" She picked up her laundry basket and batted at the air. "Too much Guilty Door! Too much Xaviera! We can't get away from that woman. I just ... well, tell me Latham. Do you ever wish I was more like ... like that?"

"Ohhhhhh," he moaned, low in his chest. He moved close, nuzzlingly close. He looked at his watch. "Darn priesthood meeting," he muttered. "But next time you're wondering," he whispered, "you let me know. And right away."

Then, after one last hungry look, he left.

* * *

The women of the Boxford Ward, as warriors go, were fierce but undirected. They were fierce in the church kitchen on a Thursday morning, with the air conditioning broken and the hot water steaming out of the faucets as they washed up all the sticky utensils and blender parts with which they had conquered four bushels of peaches. They were fierce with the mop and the vacuum, as they cleaned up the morning's food spills in the children's room. They were fierce with a plate of lunch, as each woman ripped into her dinner roll and mopped up every last bit of salad dressing.

They could be fierce about the Guilty Door, too, if they only knew what to do. So, that Thursday morning, when Ada Runyon mentioned that the next show would be the Halifax Fiddle Band all the way from Nova Scotia, they gathered around, these warriors, ready to be told which direction to throw the spear.

The Halifax Fiddle Band was fifteen high school kids, their fiddles, their drums, their accordions, and their keepers. A band like this, Ada told them, didn't have the budget to put themselves up at the Best Rest. They needed homes to stay in, and they must be fed, of course.

The women of the Boxford Ward took them on. Ada scribbled wildly as they volunteered: Galvins, two spare beds; Buckmans, another two. Jeralee offered a potato salad. Ruthalin was good for a cake.

Lucy would be proud. She had an opinion about Mormon women, who knows where she picked it up. When she faced the club and barked off all the tasks that it took to bring in those fiddlers from Halifax, and when the ladies raised their hands and offered this and that and still there were gaps on the list, Lucy looked Ada's way. And that look said, *I know your people will come through.*

So here Ada's people were, coming through. No problem. They changed bedsheets and made cakes all the time anyway. What was one or two more?

Especially when they were still furious about that Guilty Door. Every time they hit the stoplight at the boulevard and Main and saw that marquee, it bothered them like a grease stain on a new skirt. They remembered how things once were, and how they could still be if only *that* hadn't happened.

* * *

It was Ada's job to sweat the small stuff. It was all listed in the carbon-smudged contract Lucy had typed up:

Stock orange juice for a diabetic drummer.

Arrange a hair appointment for the band director.

Provide buttons. One dozen, black, round, 7/8 in., four holes.

When showtime loomed ten minutes away and a costume fell apart, that was no time to knock at the locked doors of Chandler's Fabric, or search the bottom of a purse, or snip what you needed off Lucy's husband's suit coat.

When Ada stepped into Chandler's and found the wall of buttons, she also found Ruthalin, which was no surprise. Chandler's, with its aisles of pincushions and seersuckers, was Ruthalin's guilty pleasure.

Ada sighed before the wall. "Did they used to have this many?" Pearlies. Shiny metals. Buttons big as stethoscopes and small as aspirins. "Where are the plain black ones?"

"What do you need?" Ruthalin looked at Ada's list. "Oh, don't buy those. I have bunches of 'em back at home."

"It's not a problem buying them. No, really! It's in the contract. That means it's reflected in the ticket price."

Ruthalin grimaced. "Why spend money when you don't have to?"

"It's covered. It's not a problem."

"No, I can't let you do this. Well, if buttons were on sale, maybe, but ..."

So Ada found herself standing in Ruthalin's kitchen, while Ruthalin sorted buttons like dry beans and poured all her black, round, 7/8 in., four-holed ones into Ada's cupped hands. It was more trouble than Ada needed, driving all the way out to the Feldsteds' house today. But Ruthalin looked so pleased with herself. *The cause needs buttons. Therefore, I have helped the cause.*

* * *

The cause also needed bodies.

Or so Lucy said one evening as she packed up her music after chorus rehearsal. When the last alto was out of earshot, Lucy leaned close to Ada. "You know, I was surprised to see none of your people at the Yoshimoto concert."

Ada felt like she'd been caught playing with Lucy's baton. "Oh, that can't be," she said, when she could stop stammering. "We're all very much ..." But could she remember where Ruthalin sat? Which aisle she walked down? Whether she wore the blue maternity dress or the peach one? Had Ada seen Jeralee waving across the room at other ward members? Lingering in the lobby after the show?

"Several years ago," said Lucy, "I taught in a place called Idaho Falls—don't know if you've ever heard of it—but it was just crawling with Mormons. And they were the backbone of the symphony there. Wonderful people. And when I met you here, and heard about your ward, I thought the arts in Boxford would be in fine hands."

Lucy picked up her music bag. "But now, I'm just ... puzzled." She walked off to her beater car.

* * *

"As if the whole burden was on us!" Ada dipped her fingers into the cold cream and looked out the bathroom door at Latham. "We're just a teeny part of this town. Yes, there are more Mormons here than you might expect, far off the beaten path and all, but ..."

"But she's right." Latham lounged on the bed. "It should be us filling that theatre."

"There's not enough of us!"

"Oh, come on. Put the Feldsteds in there and you've got a crowd. They even look like more than they are, because none of 'em can sit still."

"No, here's the problem." Ada wiped her face clean. "Does someone like Lucy even understand what it is for Erval and Ruthalin to buy *eleven* tickets? How much money have they got left after the groceries and the shoes? After the tithing and the mission funds?"

"It still should be us."

Ada laid her head on the pillow. "I know. But she can't be unfair about this. I don't know how they did it in Idaho Falls. But, Idaho Falls or Boxford, it's tougher for us than for the average Episcopalian.

That's the part Lucy doesn't see."

"Just go buy a couple dozen tickets and spread them around. We're good for it."

She looked into his face. "Why is it I never think of these things?"

He shrugged, proud of himself.

"All right," she said. "Two dozen tickets. That Mr. Skibbey's not gonna drag Xaviera del'Abunda into this town without a fight on his hands."

"Oh, Xaviera del whatever! She's got nothin' on you. Say, could you do that little pose thing again?"

"No!"

"Come onnnn."

"No, really, I hurt myself."

"Where does it hurt? I'll make it better."

"Stop that!" she laughed. "*Stop that!*" And she was still laughing when the light clicked off.

* * *

On the Friday of the Halifax Fiddle Band's appearance, Ada's phone rang non-stop. If it wasn't seventeen different people wondering when the coffee and barbecue meat were supposed to be at the theatre, it was a host family's bathroom out of order.

Finally, she tucked the extra tickets in her purse. She had promised them all around the ward. Now, it was time to deliver.

She drove through town. Heat shimmered off the sidewalks. She rang at the Keatings' house. When Jeralee's sober-faced eight-year-old daughter answered, music floated faintly through the door.

Inside, Jeralee sat before a reel-to-reel tape recorder. She pressed the off button. "I don't like the scratchy sounds," she told her teen-age son.

"That's just you, handling the microphone."

"Well, I have to hold it."

"No, you don't. You can put it here." He planted it on the coffee table. "It'll pick up."

"Oh, hi!" Jeralee stood up. "I was just recording some songs. I've been procrastinating this for years. But this week I said to myself, 'Jeralee, They'll be lost! Lost! Your little granddaughter will never hear the songs your grandmother sang.' Sometimes, you have to put aside the dusting and the green-bean canning and just do what's really important! Isn't that right?" She walked into the kitchen. "The potato salad's in here." She raised a foil-covered bowl from the kitchen counter.

Ada took the bowl. "And I brought those tickets I promised. I don't want anybody breaking the bank or anything."

"Oh, we won't be needing them."

"Really? Well, good, you got your own then."

"No."

"No?" asked Ada.

"Um ..." Jeralee fingered some loose hairs that escaped her ponytail, "Are you aware that the Guilty Door is still showing those other movies?"

Ada studied Jeralee's face, where Doing the Right Thing did battle with Being Nice. "Jeralee, that was part of the deal. Mr. Skibbey has to make money. We're just trying to show him that he can make more with our kind of show than with his."

Jeralee knitted her brows. What a world! Good and evil were so marbled together that a spoonful of one picked up a stripe of the other. "Well, I couldn't feel right about going there. Someone might see. They might misunderstand."

Ada gripped the bowl of potato salad, an edge of foil jabbing into her finger. She left Jeralee's house, with Jeralee singing something about "Old Uncle Ned" into a microphone that her teenage son would not let her handle, for a granddaughter who was – what? – six months old?

Ada rehearsed, all the way down the Feldsted's road, how

she would tell it to Ruthalin: "*Someone might see. They might mis-understand.*" *Can you believe that, Ruthalin? Let's just lock up and go home now!*

When she arrived, their garage yawned open. Erval puttered in the dark. He emerged, shaking out a rope.

"Good news, Erval!" Ada sang out. "I finally brought your tickets."

"Tickets for what?"

Ada stopped. She stared at him and his rope. "You're kidding me, right?" She watched him toss the rope into the little trailer attached to his van. A tent, a Coleman stove, a couple ragged lawn chairs sat packed into the corner. "Okay, I can see you're going camping. But you're leaving after the show, right? You remembered the Halifax Fiddle Band is playing tonight, right?"

"Is that so?" He dropped new batteries into a big yellow flash-light, clicked it on and watched the bright new beam of light dart around the rafters.

"Yes, that's so. You and Ruthalin remembered, didn't you?" She followed him around like a child whining for ice cream money. The very idea, a grown woman pleading like this!

Giving up on him, she stepped through the door to the hall, pick-ing her way between the bedrolls, the canteens, the mosquito repellent.

Ruthalin, in the kitchen, sweated over a counter of half-made sandwiches. She looked up, shoving back a loose tendril at her fore-head. No, no, she hadn't forgotten the Halifax Fiddle Band, she said, but she had forgotten the Scout camp-out. "You know how these things sneak up on you," she said.

"Maybe the Scouts could skip this time." said Ada. "Wasn't there a camp-out just last month?"

Erval joined them in the kitchen. "There's a camp-out *every* month."

"Well, that's what I'm saying. With plenty of chances to build fires and track raccoon prints all year long, one month off won't hurt."

Erval laid his flashlight on the table. "Those boys need consistency. You haven't got a program at all if one month it's yes and the next it's we'll-let-you-know."

"Erval, we need to fill that theatre tonight. If we don't ... well, Mrs. Weston-Welsh says she's surprised that the Mormons haven't turned out."

"I'll buy a ticket, if that'll help."

Her smile felt brittle but brave.

* * *

Fifteen shadows stood on the old vaudeville stage at the Guilty Door. The lights went up. A hand gripped a drum. Another stretched its fingers before the white of the accordion keys. Another raised a flute to pair of lips. Then the first bow struck the strings and they were off.

Behind the music, extensions cords twined through the wings. Instrument cases gaped open. Up the tar-papered stairs, a lone light shone in a dressing room littered with open garment bags and hair-clogged brushes.

Down the hall, the scent of barbecue slowly died on a long table. Sheets of tin foil, smeared with frosting, potato goo and melon juice, threw light up to the ceiling. Paper plates slouched in the garbage and a small pool of coffee dried in a Styrofoam cup.

And the music reeled on and the dimly lit bodies out in the house seats sat like a wave that had tried for high tide but fallen short of the wet sand line. Toes tapped along helplessly to the beat.

Meanwhile, at the back of the house, dark men straggled in. They stirred in the shadows, too restless to sit. They scowled at the stage.

One made his way unsteadily down the aisle. He found a nice mid-house seat and fell in. The metal fittings wheezed under his bulk. He scratched his lumberjack beard. He yawned the long and thorough yawn of a door creaking open.

His scrawny buddy sat three seats away.

"When do they take their clothes off?" said Mr. Big Beard.

Heads turned. Eyes glared.

"Shut up, Mugly!" whispered Mr. Scrawny. "Gaaa, I can't take you nowhere."

Lucy bolted from her seat and charged up the aisle.

Everybody was too busy being uncomfortable to notice the beads of perspiration growing on a flute player's forehead. Nobody noticed how deeply she swayed or how off the beat she was. Nobody noticed until her wooden flute fell to the floor and she rushed into the wings. Then, before the audience could finish murmuring in surprise, a fiddler ducked through the same gap in the curtains.

By the time Ada arrived backstage, Emily Stinchfield mopped the brow of the waxy-pale flautist. The toilet behind a closed door flushed and platoon of Halifaxers who could not wait for the bathroom retched into cups, shopping bags, and the already pungent garbage can.

Ada surveyed the food table. She stood over Jeralee's glistening potato salad. She laid her hand against the bowl. Feeling its wan room temperature, she counted the hours back to Jeralee's kitchen counter.

Out on the stage, the Music Club ladies laid out the sick. They offered up blazers, stacks of programs, even instrument cases as pillows. Ada walked among the bodies. Even on a night like this, the Gilded Door couldn't help playing like the movies. Scarlett O'Hara in the Atlanta train yard came to mind.

She heard Lucy shouting up in the lobby. "Mr. Skibbey, it's *our* night at the Guilty Door!"

"A man buys a ticket. A man gets in the door."

And, from the orchestra seats, "All I asted was, when they gonna take off their..."

"Cut it out, Mugly! I heard ya the first time. *Ever'body* heard ya."

"I should think, Mr. Skibbey, that you can tell the difference between *your* kind of ticket buyer and *our* kind!"

"I'm a businessman, Mrs. Weston-Welsh. I don't much care where a dollar comes from."

"I'm sorry, ma'am. Mugly, he's had a little too much tonight. He don't know what he's sayin'."

"Well, then, take him home and tuck him in for the night!"

"Right, ma'am. Come on, Mugly. Mugly? ... Mugly? Hey, anybody seen a guy with a big beard?"

Mugly, meanwhile, did his best not to trip over the power cords, the instrument cases, the tar-papered steps.

And when he saw the long table, he found a spoon and dug into the potato salad.

* * *

It sat on an even quieter end of Main Street.

Parents used to drop their children off at the curb on Saturdays. Even when the Disney movies left, the children still came to browse the comic book store next door. But with the likes of Kandi Lotusblossom and Xaviera smirking out over Main Street, the mothers of Boxford feared that comic books wouldn't keep their children's attention. So they didn't bring them anymore.

The comics were a steal, though. "5 cents!!!" said the sign in the window. "Close-out sale!"

At the Sunshine Laundry, smashed cigarette packs and rumpled brown bags blew against the chipped wall. Inside, empty spaces grew on the revolving hanger. The owner spent more time at his new branch out by the mall, where the profits were tidy, and the atmosphere as fresh as a newly starched shirt.

Without customers or a boss to bother her, the Sunshine attendant found time to read each and every story in her *True Confessions* magazine.

And at the Shoreline State Bank, little old ladies pulled up to the teller window, safely encased in their Buicks. They gripped their passbooks, and drove down Main the other way, so they wouldn't have to creep past scowling men who looked this way and that before they entered the Guilty Door.

'ATTA BOY

Latham Runyon wondered what time he ought to close his window. It was going to be a tongue-hanger today. But for now, the morning was still dewy and bearable.

He settled his half-glasses on his nose. It might help him feel more like buckling down to work, because all he really wanted to do was sit in the kitchen with the phone on his lap.

He could imagine what Ada would ask if she found him. *Who are you expecting to call?* And he would not answer her, because this was too big, too sacred to speak out loud. He checked his watch. He wondered what time Elder Sperry's plane would land at Philadelphia International. It'd have to be early, with all there was to do today.

The rumors about Wylie Siltman had flown for months. Wylie Siltman was an important man. Just as the Catholics had their archbishops, the Mormons had their stake presidents, to whom the several wards in their care looked for final decrees on sticky problems. President Wylie Siltman had served long and hard. He'd signed his share of temple recommends, hurried away from the dinner table for his share of stake meetings, sent out his share of missionaries. The local Mormons were sure he was about to stand at the pulpit of the stake meetinghouse for the last time, gripping its routed edge as he dispensed his words of wisdom. Wylie Siltman had upheld his corner of the church just as a tent stake supports the whole. And God was ready to give him a rest.

No doubt this was why Elder DeVere W. Sperry flew from Salt Lake into Philly today. Elder Sperry would choose someone good and wise to replace the revered President Siltman. Well, Elder Sperry wouldn't choose. God would. Latham Runyon knew how these things worked. Elder Sperry's job was to come and stand among the men of the stake, waiting for God to point out the right fellow.

And for weeks now, every time Latham passed Erval in the church hallway, every time he went over to Erval's house, his good buddy joked with him, "Watch out, Latham. You're next. "Or, "Don't plan a vacation this year. They're comin' for ya." Or, "Suits on sale at Penney's, my wife tells me. Better get yourself a good Wylie-Siltman one."

"Wylie's is looking kind of worn," Latham had told him.

"Yes, well think how yours will look if you don't start out new."

And Latham hated to make too much of this, but somewhere in the deepest stem of himself, he felt that the Lord Himself had swept His eye over this sandy spit of land and looked straight at Latham Runyon.

So, even though Latham wanted to sit in the kitchen and hold the phone, he made himself sit at his desk. He looked down through his half glasses at the paper rolled into his Selectric. He pretended he had urgent work to do, even if it wasn't all that urgent. The chapter manuscript wasn't due for months yet. November 15th, 1975, said the contract. And here it was, only August. But this was as good a time as any.

He could hear Ada stacking up the clean plates from the dish-washer. He could also hear Kate asking for the car. She said she'd have it back by something o'clock. All those distractions echoing down the hallway. Now he remembered why he always worked in his campus office, deep in the History Department. But if he went there, how could he hear the call when it came?

He sat back, smoothing down the bristles of his salt-and-pepper hair. The breeze blowing through the curtains carried the zing-zing-scring of Haffner's circular saw next door. Latham didn't know what Pete Haffner was working on over there, but he'd been at it every Saturday for a month now.

Latham himself had been banned from those weekend-home-owner projects. Actually, he kind of liked them. He just didn't know how, once the gutters were hung, they ended up slanted the wrong way. And then the patio door never opened right once he'd fixed it. The last straw was the tree. Was he supposed to know that when you cut a tree, you planned which way you wanted it to fall? Ada wouldn't even let him fix the fence it fell on. She pled—no, she insisted—that he stick to what he knew best. "You just write your articles, correct your students' papers, and leave the handymanning to somebody else."

Like Pete. Whose noise was another reason Latham worked on campus on Saturdays.

Except for today.

Today he worked at home. Where he could hear the phone when it rang. Where he could get to that phone in seconds. He couldn't waste a minute of their time, because he knew they had a pretty full day on their hands.

This eye-of-God feeling came to him one day as he looked up at the door of his cramped office and saw young Divens. Latham had put down his turkey sandwich and invited Divens in. He had taken off his half-glasses and clamped the bows in his teeth as the student talked about the problems on page four of his second draft. And as he handed the paper back to the boy and shook his hand and sent him on his way, and picked up the turkey sandwich again, it just hit him: What he had just done was like old Wylie, welcoming a young missionary home, shaking his hand, sending him out into the world to find a wife and build a life. And he had a vision of himself, rising from the desk in Wylie's orange-carpeted office. Latham didn't know where this picture of himself came from. It just popped up, like a swimmer from the depths. He didn't know whether the picture had *significance*, you know, because not all his pop-ups did. He wouldn't want them to, particularly the ones about crossing the railroad tracks just as the train appeared out of nowhere. Or the ones where he found himself kissing some woman that wasn't Ada.

So when Erval sat beside him in Sunday School and looked over the many red underlinings in Lat's scriptures and winked, "Careful there. Those are the scriptures of a future stake president," Latham could not help but wonder if this vision of himself sitting behind Wylie Siltman's broad, imposing desk, this vision that came out of nowhere, did not have *significance* after all. It matched a feeling of portent. Something was about to happen to him. This feeling came to him lately, like a tap on the shoulder, just before he'd wake up. It came to him when the afternoon sun hit the quad outside his office. Usually he'd look out the window and think of the Snickers bar waiting for him down in the basement vending machines. But lately, he just sat there rubbing his five o'clock shadow and feeling that God had His eye on Latham Runyon. God was telling Latham Runyon to be ready for the thing that was about to happen to him.

It was no use running from the eye of God. Where could you go? Why would you want to get away from God, who saw something in you that He liked? Who whispered your name to the soul of Elder Sperry as he sat on an airplane somewhere above the earth, snapping his briefcase shut just as he was about to land?

At that, Latham looked at his watch. 8:42. Drive time to the stake meetinghouse was two hours. How much gas did he have in the tank? How much time to shower, shave and be on his way? Twenty minutes? But why wait? They hadn't a minute to waste today. Latham pushed the off button on his Selectric and rolled his chair away from the desk.

* * *

The shampooey water ran down his face. He rubbed his head hard to hurry it along. Then there were suds trailing down his back, slow as an elevator at rush hour. He danced in the spray to hurry them along. Here he was, sealed away from the world, away from that phone that he just knew was ringing for him right now. Somebody should invent a cordless phone, he thought, to un-tether him from the one in the kitchen.

When he finally turned the water off and reached for the towel, he had a comforting thought: If he missed the call, they would try him again. Wylie would. Wylie knew Latham and liked him. Now Latham was a realistic man. He knew how these things worked. Wylie would hand Elder Sperry a long list of names—and Latham knew the names on that list didn't just land there willy-nilly, like crumbs on a couch cushion. No. Somebody had to think of your name and put it on there.

And Wylie would think of Latham, because Wylie often pulled Latham aside in the hallways to quip about their common problems. "How are things down at Boxford State?" he'd say.

"Longer meetings, tougher tenure and students that can't spell," Latham would tell him. "And how's it going up at the big U?"

"Three more years and they give me my rocking chair," Wylie'd laugh.

Yep, Wylie'd remember Latham Runyon and put his name down. Then Elder Sperry would call in every man on that list; and while he distracted you with friendly small talk, he sized you up stealthily, trying to feel whether God's finger was pointing right at you.

Now Latham stood before the steam-clouded mirror. He squirted shaving cream into his hand and swabbed it over his face.

It was not the best face, to be sure. He imagined how it would look to those sitting beside him in conference tomorrow. There he'd be, his arms folded as he sat on a hard metal chair way at the back of the gym, looking for all the world like Joe Mormon, with the standard white shirt, the standard wing tips, the standard bald spot, and the standard case of scriptures with a sagging, broken spine.

The young fathers nearby would look at him and think, *I hope I don't become that in twenty years.* Their young wives would study his pocked cheeks and try to imagine just how bad the teenage acne had been. And teenage girls would decide that he was, no doubt, ten times cornier than their own dads.

He would be esteemed as naught, even in his own family. Watching him narrowly as he dozed, they would sit ready to jab him hard at the first hint of a snore.

Then, when his name echoed forth from the pulpit, and he stood up, his seat-neighbors would look up from their chairs, surprised. They would kick themselves mentally for not taking note of him sooner, for not recognizing his eminence.

His children would look up. *Our dad? God wants our dad?*

His wife would bow her head humbly and compose a few eloquent remarks, in case they summoned wives to speak.

And as he walked up to take his new place, people would look up from their seats, squinting at him. And when he reached the stand, Elder Sperry would smile, remembering: *Oh, yes, him. The one that likes Great Biographies, just like me.* Elder Sperry would shake his hand, motion him towards his very own theatre-style seat, a far cry from the metal chairs at the back. Elder Sperry would make him say a few words at the pulpit, where Latham could look down on all those surprised people, who were still taking it in that Latham Runyon was their new stake president.

He could see Ada putting it in the Christmas letter. He could see far-away friends opening the envelope and sitting down in shock when they got to the paragraph about the last stake conference.

People around here would have a new respect for him. He would wear that patina of authority, the one that made people hush a little when he walked down the church hallway. They would part, opening the way. They would listen to his speeches, sure that he had something great and wise to say. They would want to look righteous and dutiful and have no food stuck in their teeth when they met him and he stuck out his large dry hand to shake their small clammy ones.

And with that, he wiped the last bits of shaving cream from the front of his ears. He hung his towel behind the door and marched to his underwear drawer.

Someone knocked at the door. "Lat? You in there?" Ada poked her head in. She looked him up and down with one raised eyebrow. "You have a phone call."

He grabbed her hand and pulled her close. "Do I, now? Who's it from?"

He kissed her and she pulled away, giggling. "I *think* I'd better take a message."

"No, wait!" He jerked open the drawer, pulled out his underwear and scrambled in, hopping across the floor.

But she was gone.

Picking up the shirt he had discarded across the bed, he buttoned it so rapidly, his fingers felt scraped and raw. With one last zip of his fly, he flew out the bedroom door and to the top of the stairs. He was just ready to come down when his wife stared up at him from the bottom.

"That was Lois Kilby."

"What did she want?"

"She didn't say. She just asked for you."

Latham had a dark feeling about this. He trudged back to his room and sat on his bed. It probably had to do with the emergency room. He didn't have time to run off to emergency rooms today.

Like most men of the Boxford Ward, Latham was assigned a roster of families to visit each month, to "home teach." Other men got the kind of families whose houses smelled of Sunday pot roast and fresh-baked rolls, the kind where the mother neatly folded her apron and beamed over her whole brood as they gathered for the official monthly visit.

But no, they gave Latham the Kilbys, with a waifish, undernourished mom who flipped light switches as if she expected that small act to burn down their trailer.

Other men got families with scrubbed children, who answered your questions about how school was going.

But Latham got the Kilbys, whose sons walked, wordless and sullen, through the living room, regarding him like a big, greasy engine block ruining their mother's couch.

Other men got families with fathers that figured their taxes in long-form and fixed their roofs *before* they leaked.

But no, Latham got James Rutherford Kilby, non-Mormon husband of Lois Kilby.

And on the day that they handed him the Kilby's address on a little piece of paper, Latham Runyon girded up his courage and set out to pay his respects to the head of the Kilby household. He wound his way through Pine Meadows, dodging the stares of children out on their bicycles, of young men leaning into their open car hoods. Peering at the numbers tacked on the trailer prows, he finally found #44 and faced two men, sprawled in lawn chairs beside the puny metal steps that led to the front door.

Latham had swallowed hard as he got out of his car. He looked at the scrawny blond man. He looked at the beefy one with the shiny forehead and the lumberjack beard. He looked at the cans of Schlitz on a rusted metal table between them.

"I'm looking for James Rutherford Kilby," he said, fighting down a crackle in his voice.

The big bearded one looked at the scrawny one. "Ruthe'ferd?" He shook, seized by a big, sinus-clearing snicker. "That yer real name, Rut? *Ruthe'ferd?*"

"Shut up, Mugly." The blond one scooted forward in his chair.

* * *

Rut was good for three things in this life:

He could guzzle beer, he could tinker with his candy-red Honda and he could … well, Lois Kilby turned up pregnant last year — surprise!— and out came Rut's first daughter.

In truth, it was the ugliest baby Latham had ever seen, with jowls roomy enough to store softballs. But he chucked her little double-chin anyway because God had sent him over to be nice to the Kilbys.

Maybe God thought Latham, of all the men at church, might understand Rut Kilby best. After all, Latham too had spawned his own surprise offspring. It happened about ten years ago. Ada had barely sent the youngest of their two daughters off to first grade when she got the news and wept all weekend.

And Latham had once owned a noisy little Yamaha back in the summer after graduation, although Ada and grad school convinced him to give it up.

And Latham had tossed back a beer or two himself back in his pre-Mormon frat-boy days. Perhaps God knew that Latham would not only pity Rut's soul, but his tastebuds, too, for if there ever was a lawnmower beer, Schlitz was it.

It was a peculiar friendship. Home teaching always was. Normal friendship grew like a pot belly, fed on things too good to pass up. Like with Erval. Latham and his good buddy Erv sat for hours, asking each other questions like, "If God is omniscient, then how can we be free to act?" Or, "Were the fishes and the loaves invented on the spot, or were they matter borrowed from somewhere else in the universe?"

"Uh-oh," their kids would say. "The dads are playing Stump-the-Rabbi again."

With Erval, there was a give-and-take. *I borrow your ladder, you borrow my book. Memorial Day at your house, Fourth of July at mine.*

But with the Kilbys, it was just give and give and give. Call people who don't call back. Care about people who don't care back, not even about themselves.

And now, today, when Latham prayed nothing would come between him and his phone-that-might-ring, the Kilbys rose up before him, needing ... well, who knows what they might be needing? It could be anything from baby aspirin to bail money.

This was a test. He knew it. God was watching him. God was saying, *Why should I give you the big jobs if you won't do the small ones?*

And with that, Latham Runyon got up from the bed and clumped down to the kitchen phone.

He lifted the black handset and stuck his finger in the first hole.

He paused a moment, just to feel the phone vibes. Anything coming through on this line? Anything quivering with portent?

Was God still watching?

Probably. He swung the dial around and put his finger in the next hole.

When he had dialed all the numbers, he leaned back against the counter and watched the second hand on the clock over the fridge.

Busy signal. Latham dropped the receiver into its cradle, quickly before the busy tone snickered, *Just kidding!* and Lois Kilby's tired and breathy little voice suddenly said hello.

He heard the back door close. In came Ada, shuffling new mail in her hands. "Get hold of the Kilbys?" she asked.

"Couldn't get through." He tried hard to look sorry about it.

He walked back to his desk, settled into the chair and wiggled his fingers over his Selectric keyboard, waiting for the next sentence to clack out.

But nothing came.

And no wonder. It had been a hard morning for a thinking man. Interruptions, distractions—how was he ever going to get this textbook chapter written?

He sat back in his chair. The window before him revealed, beyond the crew-cut edges of the shrubbery, a world lazing its way to lunchtime. The tall oaks across the street waved as if unimpressed by the breeze that pushed against them. A piece of white fuzz, bobbing along like a tiny visiting spaceship, rode that same breeze past the crabapple branches.

He swiveled in his chair. He looked across his broad desk. Beyond the messy part, with the pencil can and the stapler and the yellow legal pad awaiting his jottings, it looked not much different than Wylie Siltman's desk. Latham could almost see somebody like a young Divins, sitting across from him, with his pretty fiancee, eagerly awaiting his wise, stake-presidential advice.

"Now, when Sister Runyon and I got married … "

He sees Divins reach over to the arm of his sweetheart's chair and squeeze her hand.

Pressing his templed fingers against his chin, he looks straight into Divins' eyes and carries on. "Sister Runyon and I made the decision that we'd have a weekly date, without fail."

Divins and Sweetheart look into each other's eyes. A shy smile spreads across her face.

Latham goes on. "It doesn't have to be … "

Just then, Ada burst through the office door. "Well, look what came today!" she said, plunking herself down in the spare chair. She straightened out the folds of the letter in her hand.

Latham quickly put away his templed fingers and his wise face. He grabbed the folder on his desk and lifted his reading glasses up to his nose.

"Do you remember my old roommate Helen?" said Ada.

"Mmm." Latham frowned at the folder as if pinning down a thought blown wild by the gust of Ada's interruption.

"They're coming here!" She squinted down at the letter, mumbling its handwritten words: "'Baltimore … Washington D.C… seeing the sights. Philadelphia around the fourteenth. Love to get together… .' But of course! What day is the 14th?" She got up and squinted at the calendar on Latham's wall. "That's a Thursday. I don't see why not. I'm sure we could go out to dinner or something. What do you think, Lat?"

Latham looked up from his folder. "A Thursday?" His mind raced. But what if the call came today? His life could change in a minute. Suddenly, that calendar would overflow with meetings and church visits.

And weren't all the stake presidency meetings on Thursday nights? How could he tell his own new high council, "Sorry. Can't be there. Friends in from out of town." Obscure friends. People he barely remembered and whom, if he never dined with again, he would not miss.

"Latham? That Thursday looks good to me. Shall I call her?"

He looked at the calendar again. Why couldn't that call have come already? How much patience could God wring from a man who only wanted to know what was about to happen to him?

He looked at Ada. "I don't know."

"What? Why don't you know?"

"I'm not sure what I've got going then."

"But there's nothing on your calendar here."

Latham peered at it over his half glasses. He might need a bigger calendar. He might even need a big spiral-bound date book like his wife's.

She gave him The Look. Oh, but he knew why all her little piano students faithfully practiced their lessons! Under Mrs. Runyon's Look, one's intestines shifted around like cats in a burlap bag.

"Latham, don't you like Helen and Bob?"

"I like them fine."

"Then what's your problem going to dinner with them on the 14th?"

"Nothing! I just don't know if I can or not. Now, I've got work to do, Ada."

She stared, the letter hanging from her hand. Then she left the room.

He turned back to his typewriter.

But he couldn't work.

He rose up out of his chair. He stepped into the hall and opened the front door. Then he burst out of the house and into the August heat of the day.

It could be the last great thinking walk of his life, if that call came today. He circled the block, plucking a leaf or two off the neighbors' hedges, staring back at small dogs yapping from behind picket fences. He nodded to men pushing lawnmowers, to women standing before their flower beds with their hands on their hips, to Pete Haffner, standing in a little pile of sawdust, peering up through his safety goggles.

He returned with arcs of sweat seeping through his shirt. And in the cool murmur of his house, as he approached his study, he glanced down the hall where his wife stood in the kitchen.

"Lois Kilby called again," she said.

"Did she say what the problem was?"

"Something about water on the kitchen floor."

Latham frowned. That should be simple. Let Rut crawl under his kitchen sink and ruin his pipes himself.

Ada stood at his study door. "Are you going to see what you can do to help the Kilbys?"

"I don't know, Ada."

There was The Look again. He forged on, in spite of it. "I don't know if I will have time to get to it today," he said.

"What is this 'I don't know' business? How can a man not know his day is free when there's nothing on his calendar here to say it isn't?"

Latham sat back in his chair and studied the visible will working itself across his wife's face. The last thing he needed right now was a wife glaring at him, her dark eyebrows raised in puzzlement, her arms folded in a way that said, *you're not the man I thought you were.* The last thing he needed was a wife who could say so to Elder Sperry.

Latham sat there, squeezed between that big, empty space on his calendar and the nagging little secret that ate at him like a chigger under his belt.

He would have to tell her the secret.

"Come on in, Ada," he said, motioning her to the spare chair. "Shut the door."

She looked at him, puzzled. She pushed the doorknob until it clicked shut. She sat in the chair. He could see the wheels in her head working, guessing. *Dread disease? Pink slip? Midlife urge to chuck it all?* She studied his eyes like a doctor checking pupil dilation.

He went on. "I could get called today. Elder Sperry is in town, you know. Interviewing for the new stake president. I have a feeling I could be called in."

By now, her jaw hung open. She looked as if she remembered something from far away and long ago, something like faint warning bells he had set off back in their dating days, warning bells she should have heeded, warning bells that, at this moment, clanged like fire alarms. She looked away at the far wall, rose slowly from her chair and reached for the doorknob. Looking back at him one last time, she opened the door and left the room.

Latham stared at his typewriter. *She needs some time, that's all. Let her get used to the idea.*

Just as he finished a new paragraph, she poked her head in the doorway again. "What kind of people are they calling in for interviews?" she asked.

"Oh, bishops. High councilors."

"But you haven't been any of those."

Latham's hands froze over the keyboard. "Gosh darn it, Ada! I've got work to do!"

She disappeared.

So, it was going to be one of those days, was it? His woman thought he was a fool? And this was the woman he depended on and loved, in spite of having to part curtains of her drying hosiery in the bathroom?

If he was a fool, then what of all those premonitions? He hadn't asked for them to wake him up at four in the morning, to sneak up on him as he leaned over to tie his shoes, to breathe down his neck as he stood before his bookshelf, fingering the spines until he found the book he wanted. What was he to make of thoughts that whispered to him, *Maybe you shouldn't start an article right now because you won't get to finish it very soon.*

Huh? Where did all this come from?

Why would his mind play tricks on him like that? Why would God send premonitions that were useless and cruel, actually? Why would Erval see greatness in him that wasn't really there? Why would they call only bishops and high councilors and not him? If God wanted him, He could bypass a little protocol. Was anything impossible for God?

Ada appeared in his doorway again. "Lois Kilby's on the phone."

Latham slunk to the kitchen, despairing. Elder Sperry would never get through to him today. He held the phone to his ear. Sister Kilby's thin little voice came over the line. "Could you please come and have a look at where this water's comin' from?" she pleaded.

Latham hung up the phone with the frown of a man who just learned his car was $3000 sicker than he thought. "I don't know why I should worry myself about the water on Rut Kilby's kitchen floor when Rut himself isn't home to worry about it."

"Oh?" said Ada. "Where is Rut?"

"Off at Mugly's. She says they're barbecuing a billy goat."

Ada's eyebrow shot up. "People do that?"

Latham nodded his head slowly. Nothing Rut did surprised him anymore. "And Lois can't get him there because Mugly's phone is cut off again. Oh, what's the use of all this? I go out there every month and they stand on their little trailer steps and they look so sincere and tell me, 'We're planning to come to church next Sunday. Sure thing. Oh, yes, we'll see you there.' And Sunday rolls around and where are the Kilbys? Sitting in the row next to us? Sitting in any row at all?"

"Coming in late?"

"Hah! They're too shiftless to even come late! And there I am, the chump that believed their promises for the 473rd time."

"How much water are we talking about here? Where's it coming from?"

"I didn't ask. I didn't think. Why would I? I'm Mr. Oops, remember? I'm the husband that doesn't know an elbow joint from an elbow ache. I'm the guy you've told," he imitated her high voice, "'Please, Lat, don't patch that nail hole.'"

"OK, maybe these people deserve you. They make promises they don't keep, so God gives them a home teacher who can't help them." She beamed over her own logic.

He looked at her miserably. Then he lapsed into her voice again. "Please Lat, let's just call somebody who knows what they're doing."

"That's it!" She snapped her fingers. "Why don't you call Erval, Mr. Fix-It himself. He'll know how to help the Kilbys."

Latham just stared at the phone. Would it ever ring for him today? Would it ever ring and not be the Kilbys?

"Never mind," said Ada. "I'll call myself. I've got to ask Ruthalin something anyway."

Latham unfolded himself from the kitchen chair. He shuffled into the living room, fell back into his La-Z-Boy and stared at the ceiling. By now, he couldn't even remember what Elder Sperry looked like, even though he had seen the man's picture dozens of times.

"Uh-huh.... Really?" said Ada, in the other room. "I see. Well, yes, I know, uh-huh."

She poked her head into the living room. Holding her hand over the receiver, she whispered, "Guess what Erval's been doing today? Waiting by the phone just in case Elder Sperry calls!"

Latham sat up in shock. They couldn't want Erval! What about his own premonitions? What about Erval kidding him that "it's gonna be you, Latham. You watch out"? After good buddy Erv's gentle kidding, Latham couldn't take it if he had to watch Erval walk up to the stand tomorrow, grip the pulpit, and pause to take control of his emotions. He couldn't take it, watching all of Erval's ten kids troop into the office with the president's big desk where, with a ceremonious laying of Elder Sperry's hands on Erval's head, they would watch their father become the new stake president. Why, the room wouldn't hold them all. That was one reason to reject Erval right there!

But what if it was Erval? Who would Elder Sperry and God like better? Didn't DeVere W. Sperry have something like ten kids himself? Yes, Latham had seen the picture in the magazine, published when the man first ascended to his position: the wife with her new perm; the handsome older sons in their blazers; the thirteen-year-old son trying to change a smirk into a smile: the older daughters, their souls aged from washing loads of dishes and braiding many, many heads of hair; and the youngest daughter, her hand resting on her father's knee, her smile revealing a corn row of baby teeth.

Somehow the photo looked so right, so authoritative. So much like Erval's family photo, with its fresh-scrubbed, frame-filling look.

That would impress Elder Sperry. Not that he'd see the picture, but he'd hear about all those kids. It'd come out in the interview. "Ten? Why your wife's got her ticket to heaven for sure!" he'd tell Erval.

And Erval'd get the job, because he was so right for it. He'd get the job, all because of his wife's willingness to be pregnant for 64 percent of their sum total married life, so far.

And what had Latham's own wife done to distinguish him? Well, after two kids, she had told him it was fine for him to have his premonitions of six children, but he wasn't the one throwing up here.

But now he saw that he'd been had. His phone hadn't rung yet. It might be ringing at Erval's house now.

No. Wait.

It couldn't be. His wife was tying up Erval's line just now, talking to Erval's wife. "Yes, the store in Brandywine said they sell it, but not in bulk."

Suddenly, Latham's mouth stretched into a villainous grin. He'd make sure Erval never got that call. He'd drag him out to Rut Kilby's house where Elder Sperry could never find him.

He rose up from the chair and walked to the phone. He twisted the pushpins in the bulletin board while Ada finished talking to Erval's wife.

Then he took the phone. He composed his face. He cleared his throat. He licked his lips. "Hello, old buddy," he said. "Whatcha up to today?"

* * *

The deed was done. The phone cord hung there, swinging a little until it came to a rest.

Deception left him limp, famished. He opened the fridge. He took out a plate from the cupboard and began to make a sandwich. As he layered the lettuce over the meat, he felt his wife behind him, puttering over the mail on the table. She was awfully silent back there.

"Well, go ahead. Say it." He spackled brown mustard over his bread. "Go ahead and tell me that every fool between here and the Delaware River is waiting by his phone today. And I'm just one of them, right?" He turned to look at her. She pressed her lips together. She had words there, he knew it, but she held them back like drift-wood against a dam.

"Every guy with a mostly-good home-teaching record and a white shirt ran out and got a haircut, in anticipation of sitting in front of Elder Sperry today, right?"

"You did the haircut too?"

What? She hadn't noticed the white walls he'd been wearing for two days now? Yes, he did the haircut! And took his white shirt into the cleaners. Heavy starch, please. He took it himself because he didn't want to tip her off. This was too big, too sacred.

Too stupid.

He tossed the knife into the kitchen sink, letting it clatter violently.

He sat down with his sandwich. It was altogether too quiet in here. "Well, say something, will ya?"

She pulled out the chair and sat across from him, looking at her folded hands. "Well, I do have a little theory about this," she said, rubbing at her knuckles.

He put the sandwich down and shoved his tongue against the bread stuck in the roof of his mouth. He wasn't sure he wanted to hear it. He looked at the bulletin board, the fridge magnets, the cupboard handles, anywhere but at her, afraid of what she might think of him right now.

That didn't stop her. "I'm thinking there must be an awful lot of men out there that want an 'atta-boy from God."

"Humph."

He stood and put his plate in the sink.

He plucked the car keys off the hook.

He trudged out to his Impala, opened the door and sat on the hot seat.

An 'atta-boy from God, my eye.

He backed out of the driveway.

He didn't need any 'atta-boy. Maybe some other fool out there did, but not him.

Maybe the guy that counted the money at church needed one. He was the one who stayed long after everybody else went home, and rectified the accounts down to the last penny, and never embezzled any of it.

Or maybe the scoutmaster, the guy that dodged the mis-aimed arrows of inexperienced little archers, and rubbed down bad cases of poison ivy, and gave the hot dog off his roasting stick to some kid who dropped his own into the ashes.

Or maybe the church custodian, the guy that shined the glass on the door for the seventy-ninth time that week, complaining that nobody listens when he tells them to push the door open by the handle, not the glass.

Yes, it was true Latham wished God would notice that, every time they assigned him to home teach, they gave him the bush route, sending him out to find the folks that didn't want to be found.

But that didn't mean he needed an 'atta-boy.

No, just because he wished God noticed how he knocked himself out to be nice to Rut, even following him out to Mugly's house to look at his pet rabbits, that still didn't mean he needed an 'atta-boy. But since we were on the subject, didn't God know how tough it was to stand in a rabbit hutch on a hot day in July, willing yourself not to faint dead-away and end up with your face lying in the packed dirt, just inches from the rabbit raisins?

Didn't he wish God noticed him bringing M&Ms to Rut's teenage sons? Or swallowing the sour taste in his mouth every time Lois held her baby out for his admiration? Or listening to the Kilbys promise, for the 473rd time, that they really would come to church next Sunday?

Nobody knew what Latham had to put up with! But God knew. And couldn't God just let everybody else know by having Elder Sperry call him today?

Latham guessed not. Not when so many other chumps with raw haircuts were bugging Him about it, too.

And he swerved in to the Pine Meadows trailer court.

* * *

Erval was there already, tucked under the sink, his hammer-looped pants and his work boots sticking out. Yep, tucked into a tight little place where Elder Sperry could never find him.

And he was singing. At the top of his lungs. "Whut shall we dooo with the drunken sailorrr, whut shall we dooo . . " His work boots gripped the vinyl floor as his tools clanked and his flashlight beam jiggled and his lips whistled all the parts where he didn't know the words.

What was it about Erval, always singing like a goof, as he worked? He sang when they fixed widows' roofs. He sang in the van on the way to the temple site. He sang when they pulled weeds in the church flower beds. With his mouth open and his face all sincere, it was, actually, less like singing and more like yawning *waaay* too loud.

And furthermore, what did Erv, the Mormon farmboy from landlocked sagebrush, know about drunken sailors?

No matter. Erval was the kind of guy God liked best, because Erval sang while he worked, like people in Disney movies. And Erval hurried out here. And Erval could torque a wrench. He knew what to do about things. He could help people.

All Latham could do was profess. Now if Latham had been trained in a nice, practical, close-to-the-earth subject, like Wylie Siltman and his chicken genetics, then he would be as useful as Erval. But no, he professed history, which meant idleness, and reading stacks of books, books with possibly dangerous ideas.

Yep, Erval was the kind of guy God would invite up for a weekend at His lake cottage. As for Latham, God would merely wave in the hallway and say, "How's it goin'?"

Just now Erval scooted out from under the sink. "Well, hello there, Lat!" He ran his hand through the last-stand hairs at the top of his head. He considered the piece of pipe in his hand. "I thought the joint was just loose, but the pipe's eaten away." He looked at Lois. "Your husband's gonna need to get some new pipe."

"I wonder if Rut's coming home soon," said Lois Kilby. She picked up the phone, then stopped in mid-dial. "I keep forgetting. Mugly's phone is cut off."

Latham stood there, watching her hold the phone to her little caved-in chest. Suddenly he knew that if God had wanted Erval, He could've tracked him down, all the way out here to the Kilby's house.

And if God had wanted Latham, He could have done the same thing. All those hours wasted, sitting by the phone. He had failed to see the beauty of being found here. Why, if the phone had rung for him while he sat in Rut Kilby's kitchen, the whole room would have waited in suspense while he answered. They would have seen his face blanch and his breath catch and his posture straighten. Had somebody died? Been in a terrible accident?

And he would've hung up the phone and said, *I'm sorry. I've got to go now. Erval, will you be all right, finishing up here?*

Is something wrong? Lois Kilby would've said as he reached for the keys in his pocket.

And he would've smiled warmly, his kindly leader's smile. His Considered One, maybe even Chosen One smile. And she would've known when he walked away that something indeed had happened, something that elevated him off the ground and made him special and he was *her* home teacher and she and Rut really would show up at church next Sunday, just to see what had happened to *their* home teacher.

Except that nothing *would* happen to their home teacher, because God liked Erval better.

"Well, what do we do now?" said Erval as Lois left to fetch the crying baby at the back of the trailer.

"We hope Rut gets back here and buys some new pipe for his sink."

"But when? We can't leave Sister Kilby without water."

Oh, yeah. God liked Erval best.

But Latham couldn't stand him.

"I guess we better run to the hardware store for some pipe," said Erval.

We? Latham looked at Erv, at the sweat beads on his brow, at his twisted tuft of hair. The last thing he wanted was to go anywhere with Erval Feldsted. Latham would just stay right here where …

He looked around him.

… where three greasy griddles poked up out of the sink and spots of ketchup scum stuck to the Formica table and the newly-wakened baby rubbed her eyes and glared at him and —

Oh, never mind! He'd go to the store with Erval!

But he didn't want to.

He didn't want to listen to Erval talk about tubing and flux and goose-eggs gotten under other sinks. He didn't want to trail him down the aisles of True Value like a seven-year-old following Daddy, scared of getting lost. How could anybody lose Erval? His whistling betrayed his every move.

On the way back to Pine Meadows, Erval pointed up the street. "Tell you what! Let's stop for a root beer float."

Latham Runyon peered through the heat waves rising up from the asphalt. He saw the Tastee Freez sign blinking up ahead.

"Don't bother," he spat out.

Erval looked at him, whistled notes dropping like shot birds.

"Let's just get this over with, OK?" said Latham.

"Ohhh-kaay." The Tastee Freez passed by, and Texaco station and the Aqua-Marine Boats. Erval slapped the steering wheel. "It is gettin' kinda late, isn't it? I sure let the day get away from me, sittin' by the phone, waitin' for that call. You know how it is, dontcha?"

"Oh-ho-ho, not me! You'd have to be *crazy* to want that job."

* * *

They rode back to #44 Pine Meadows in blessed, non-whistling silence. They tromped up the steps. They laid the new pipe on the sticky table.

Lois Kilby appeared with her baby on her hip.

"Won't be long now and you'll be all fixed up," Erval chirped. "Wellll, look who's here!" He bent down to the baby. "Is dat a good thumb you got dere? Do you like dat thumb? Yeah? Yeah?" And he smiled and rubbed on the barely-blond baldness of her head, loving that baby even though it was the ugliest baby on earth.

That was the last straw.

Latham slapped Erval on the back, a mighty, body-staggering blow. "Gotta go, old buddy! Good luck."

As he stomped down the trailer steps, he shook off his brittle smile. He kicked Erval's tire. He drove out of Pine Meadows, fast, with the speed bumps clacking his teeth together, hard.

When he reached the main road, he turned for the woods instead of town. Something about the woods felt snug and private, and as he guided the car around the curves, he waited to feel hidden.

All week, he had felt the eye of God upon him. He had felt on display. He had felt spoken to. *Be ready for the thing that is about to happen to you.*

Right. *Sure.* The eye of God was upon him, all right. And it was *amused.*

He could see God telling His friends, *You wouldn't believe how these conferences light a fire under the unlikeliest fellows. It's like they all want to be an Elder Sperry.*

Well, yeah, who wouldn't? The Elder Sperrys were so fun, so off-the-cuff with their sermonizing because they knew their scriptures well and they injected real personality into the characters.

And you knew God liked the Elder Sperrys of this world. Why else would an Elder Sperry have been called to travel the planet, doing God's work?

And when he landed at your pulpit and he spoke in his fun,

off-the-cuff way and his eyes swept the room and looked right at yours for a moment, you felt you had made a special connection with this man that God liked. Oh, how you would love to play Stump the Rabbi with an Elder Sperry! And you knew he would love to play it with you too, because when he caught your eye a second time, that connection told you that you could be like him, that you had what it took, that he detected it when he smiled in your direction.

And remember: he hadn't always been an Elder Sperry. He had once been a man like yourself and some other Elder had flown into town and turned Brother Sperry into President Sperry. It happens to the least among us. It could happen to you.

So you did the kinds of things the Elder Sperrys did. You wore a white shirt without fail. You did your home teaching every month, even if they stuck you with the bush route. You underlined stuff in your scriptures and made notes in the margins. Then you gave really good talks at church, flipping your scriptures willy-nilly, as ideas came to you on the spot, because you knew them so well. That's what you did so you too might be an Elder Sperry someday. It could happen. It really could. You had the goods. You felt it.

And so did everybody else.

Latham sped along the pavement, under the arching trees that blocked the waning sun. Something about the road looked familiar. Wasn't this the way to Mugly's place? Yeah. Backbone Road.

He came to a cut in the woods. There it was, Mugly's grubby white house back there. Crawling to a stop, he rolled down his window and sniffed.

The tang of campfire rode in the air. A wisp of smoke rose behind the house. He wondered: what does barbecued billy goat taste like?

Not that he *really* wanted to find out. He eased off the brake and reached for the window handle. Looking down at the next bend in the road, he put the car in gear.

Then he heard the dog barking.

It appeared from around the corner, a loping thing, yellow as a sweat stain. It moved like the Secret Service, spotting a gleam of gunmetal.

Latham gripped the window handle, pumping hard, rolling up as the dog ran down the rutted dirt apron surrounding Mugly's house.

"Gyp! Gyp! Shut up!" Rut, straddling his Honda, rolled around the corner.

Latham fumbled for the gear shift. He could still get away, unrecognized, he was sure.

Rut squinted down the drive at Latham's car. "Get back here!" he called to the dog, following, staring.

Latham watched him come closer, paralyzed.

"Oh! It's you!" Rut's smile uncovered his spacey teeth. He looked down at the dog. "Stop that, Gyp! Get back there! Well," he rested his hand on the roof of the car, "what are you doin' all the way out here? Come on in! Don't be a stranger!" He waved heartily toward the plume of smoke in the back.

Latham's stomach fell to the floorboards. But he turned for Mugly's dirt yard. He heard the hootings of the forest through the window that he never quite got closed up.

Mugly, sprawled in a lawn chair, tossed a branch in his hands and leaned forward to poke the coals. And there, above the glowing ash, hung the goat, trussed up by its legs on a surprisingly sturdy-looking spit, considering who built it.

Rut was as busy as a picnic committee, setting up another lawn chair beside the campfire. "What have you got for the man to drink?" he asked Mugly.

Mugly leaned over the arm of his chair, the aluminum squeaking and groaning. Digging through a small cooler, he pulled out a can of Schlitz. It hung there from his paw, dewy and dripping.

"He can't have that," Rut stage-whispered. "He's from church! What else ya got?"

"How the hell would I know?" Mugly, scowling, dropped the can back into the ice and settled back in his chair.

Rut sprang away to the house.

Latham sat down, his chair tilting on the uneven ground. He looked at the clearing around him, at the dog curled up now in a bed of dried pine needles, surveying all with a blinking alligator watchfulness. He looked at Mugly, twirling that stick, scowling at the carcass before him.

He swallowed. "Did the goat do something bad?"

Mugly slowly rolled the stick in his hand, staring into the flames. "He ate my tombstone," he finally said. And he poked the stick into the side of the goat. Pink juices dribbled out, falling to the fire below with a hiss and a cloud of steam.

Latham pulled at his shirt where it stuck to his skin. He'd welcome a little breeze right now, but the tall pines guarded the air here, keeping it all rabbit-hutchy and close.

Mugly looked him up and down. "What're you out here for, anyway?"

"Uh, I was just at Rut's house, fixing his sink."

"You? Fixing his?"

"Well, not me really, but my ..."

Mugly snorted. "That's Rut all right. Useless as tits on a boar."

Latham heard the slap of the screen door behind him. "Look what I found!" Rut held a can of Coke aloft. "'Course, it's still warm." He held it out to Latham.

Great. Another thing he didn't drink. Maybe Rut's wife was one of those caffeine-as-long-as-it's-cold Mormons, but Latham had kicked the habit right after joining.

He took the can. Not knowing what else to do with it, he rolled it between his hands.

"Here, let me stick that in the ice for ya." Rut shoved the Coke into the cooler. He stood up, thumbs in his belt loops. "How much longer, Mug?"

"Five minutes less than the last time you asked."

"Oh, I'm goin' for a ride. Hey!" He looked at Latham. "Why don't you come along? Be near midnight, I guess, before old Bill here is cooked."

Mugly spat, insulted.

Latham gaped at Rut. No way was he going to stay around here 'til midnight, or eat any of that goat, or — he glanced under Rut's lawn chair and counted the empty cans. Three.— or get on that bike with the grinning Rut. "Nah," he held up his hand.

"Ohhh, what's the matter? You don't like bikes?"

"On the contrary. I had one once."

"Well!" Rut looked him up and down. "Well, be my guest." His arm swept across his bike. "Take her around the block."

Latham climbed on. He kicked the starter and the bike roared to life. Rut nodded, impressed with his home teacher's bike-man prowess.

Latham rolled on down the dirt. He wobbled toward the road, nosed the tire onto the pavement, picked up speed. *Around the block,* indeed. How about all the way into town? And then, how about not coming back? He saw himself roaring up his own street, cutting the motor a block from his house, rolling the bike quietly into his garage. He saw Rut, waiting, mystified out in the woods, hot-wiring Latham's own Impala when he caught on. (*Be my guest, Rut. Take her around the block. Anything. Just let me out of here.*)

Or maybe Rut would catch him before he got out of the woods. Then he and Mugly would handle it all themselves. Oh, Latham had a good idea what the two of them would do to anything that "ate their tombstone," whatever that meant. Rut and Mugly had probably seen *Deliverance.* Heck, they might've inspired it.

Yep, this had better be the end of the block. Latham swung the bike around in a wing of gravel and turned back.

But as the fat little front tire rolled over the patch veins in the pavement, as the faded center lines whizzed past, something old in Latham Runyon woke up. How long had it been since he felt the breeze on his face? Why didn't he do this more often? This must be what other men felt like, men who spent their weekends in duck blinds, on trout streams, in speed-boat races.

And why did he never get a chance to feel like other men? He was part of the White Shirt Army, that's why. The Stump the Rabbi crowd. His weekends were all booked up, slinging applesauce at the cannery, riding in the van to the temple site, fixing widows' roofs (or, at least, looking busy beside the real fixers).

Back at the clearing, he gunned the bike and rolled up beside the campfire. Rut rose from his chair, shaking a bottle of ketchup. "Hey, there. I thought you'd come back through the woods. There's a way around, you know." He reached into the cooler. "It's ready now." He handed Latham the can of Coke.

Latham held it, cold and dewy, in his hands. As a dribble of sweat ran, tickling, down his back, he felt the can's evil caffeine rays taunting him. He sat in his chair, bracing against the slope.

Rut nodded toward the can. "At least old Bill here didn't get all the groceries, right, Mug? But he sure made a bad habit of it."

"That he did," Mugly grunted.

"How many times you suppose he broke into your kitchen, Mug?"

"Too many, that's how many. And this time he broke off the doorknob."

"Aw hell, what do you care? Now it matches the rest of the house!"

Mugly glared from under the doughy wrinkles across his forehead. "He ate my tombstone, that's what I care."

"Oh, it was just an ol' pizza. You can get another one."

"Uh-uh! It was the last one at the Quikmart."

Latham wiped his hand from the shine on his forehead down over the late-day stubble on his chin.

Mugly arose from his chair with a mighty man-of-the-woods groan. He unsheathed a knife hanging on his belt and cut a hunk of goat-flesh. "Looks all right to me." He poked the knifed meat into his mouth, then sawed away another piece.

Another thread of sweat bathed Latham, in front this time, sliding until trapped by the hairs above his navel. He yanked at his stuck shirt, fanning himself. He tugged at his collar.

Rut shook the ketchup bottle and squirted it along the summit of the trussed-up animal. He took the next chunk of speared meat from Mugly, swirled it in the dripping ketchup and held it out to Latham. "Eat up."

Latham took the knife. Pepperoni-flavored perhaps? No, old Bill here was probably murdered too soon for that. "I've never had goat before." He stuck it in his mouth.

"Me neither."

"Yep."

"What's the weirdest thing you ever ate?" said Rut.

"Muskrat," said Mugly.

"I had shark once," said Rut.

Latham chewed up, swallowed. "Mexican food," he said.

They stared at him.

"On the Mexican side of the border." He pointed south.

Rut frowned. "Yeah, but what was it?"

"Beats me. But it was weird."

"Hear, hear!" They raised their cans.

And Latham Runyon raised his can, his sealed-up virgin can of Coke, and clinked it with theirs. It felt good in his hand. Very good. Very different from his body, which felt like it he'd dressed in rubber gloves straight from the cannery. And he held that can aloft and aloof while they took a swig from theirs.

And he remembered how, all these years, he'd carefully avoided The Bad Red Can at the department picnics, even at his own family reunions. He'd always reached for the 7-UP, even though it tasted like gum just before the flavor wears off. And all for what?

So he could sit before an Elder Sperry someday, wearing his

white shirt, carrying his worn and well-underlined scriptures, and claim that his lips had never touched the bad stuff. Or even the half-bad stuff.

He looked at his watch. 4:38. Surely Elder Sperry had his man by now. And that man, whoever he was, wouldn't have time for years hence to sit in the woods like this. He wouldn't even have time to look at a picture of the woods.

Well, too bad for him.

Latham gripped the can firmly. He pulled the tab. He poured the cold brown brew down his throat.

And he sat in the woods, laughing at Old Bill stories as Old Bill disappeared, chunk by chunk.

"So dumb," said Rut, "he couldn't sleep on a hill without rolling down it."

"Ugly too."

"I wouldn't talk ugly if I was you. Have another bite, Runyon. And then I'll show ya that very hill. You'll see what a … Hey, Mugly, where'd my bike go? Oh, there it is. Come on, I'll take ya."

Latham counted the empty cans under Rut's chair.

Five.

"I don't think so."

"You don' wanna … ?"

"Just tell me how to get there."

Rut grinned. He slapped Latham Runyon on the back. Down the road thataway, he said. Left at the chain between the posts. Latham nodded amiably, already losing track of the swoops and swerves of Rut's hands. Yeah, yeah, something about the fence line, and going right at the fork in the path.

Latham gunned the motor. He lifted his legs from the ground and rested his feet on the little pegs. He looked back at Rut Kilby and grinned.

And as he roared away, it seemed to him that this was the best he had ever gotten along with Rut Kilby, and yet the wildest, most removed from the White Shirt Army he had ever strayed. He knew what might happen next: Some sort of genuine buddyship would blossom, despite Latham not trying hard anymore. And then Rut Kilby would make good on his threat to darken the church doorway.

And Latham could see his own reward: God calling him aside in heaven and saying, *Thank you for saving the soul of James Rutherford Kilby. As a token of my appreciation, I'd like to invite you and Rut to a little picnic.*

And Latham would say, *You and Rut go on without me.*

That's right. Latham Runyon didn't need an 'atta-boy from God.

He guided the bike behind the chained post. Trees sailed past. Low branches snapped him on the forehead. Gnarled roots bumped under the front tire. And the wind sheared his face and dried his smiling teeth as the fence posts whizzed past.

At the fork in the path, he frowned. Right? Left? Oh, what did it matter? He'd find his way back to Camp Deliverance.

He hung a left.

He rode along, where greenery crept over trail and the lush mayflower leaves reached across for their neighbors and the tips of baby boulders humped out of the soil.

He loved the speed, the feel of his loafers resting in the notches where the big boys tucked their leather boots. He wanted leather boots, with mean square toes. He wanted to grow a beard. He wanted to wear a plaid shirt to church tomorrow, to say "bullcrap" in front of Erval.

He loved the noise. Still grinning, his forehead warm with a low-grade rebellion, he racked the gears till they rang out through the woods. And he sailed on.

He did not see the stump.

It was once the base of a mighty chestnut. Broad enough to air out a sleeping bag, it sat behind the fronds of a proud little sapling. It sat there, flat, with weathered edges, waiting.

And when Latham Runyon blasted through the proud little sapling and met the stump and left the bike and whirled through the air and widened his eyes just like Evel Knievel when he knows he won't make the landing ramp, the stump swore that it heard Latham Runyon cry out, "Dear God! Help meeeee!"

* * *

He was a small man, salt-and-pepper hair, close-cut. He rose up from his metal chair, just seconds after Elder Sperry called his name.

Latham Runyon adjusted his cast-bound arm and turned his head—well, not far; it still hurt too much—and watched the man walk up to the stand and grip the pulpit and struggle for words.

And Latham looked across the room. He saw Erval's upturned, awe-struck face, one in a sea of upturned, awe-struck faces, all of them wondering why they had not noticed the man before, why they had not studied him long enough to detect the secret burden he carried up until Elder Sperry called his name. All of them wondered what this man had that they lacked.

And Latham looked at the man. There were plenty of things this man didn't have. No scrapes on the side of his face, for one thing. No sling cradling his arm. No bruises.

And Latham felt the eye of God, before it turned away to rest on the man at the pulpit. That man would need His help, looking after the likes of Latham Runyon.

GYPSY HOLIDAY

The bird was still icy inside.

Amid the clatter of her family's self-serve breakfast, Ada Runyon reached into the cavity. The moment she found the bag of guts, she felt the cat snaking around her legs. Ada glanced down at Lulubelle's tortoiseshell face. "You didn't like them last year." She held her chill-stiffened hand under a stream of warm water and stretched her fingers. "And you won't like them today."

The previous year, she had roasted the turkey with the little bag of giblets inside, and had taken such ribbing for it that, all last night, she dreamt of pulling livers and gizzards—even a set of owl book-ends—from dark orifices.

Turning, she collided with Douglas.

He looked up at her, his cowlick aloft, a baseball card album clutched to his small chest. "When will they be here?" he asked.

"The Feldsteds aren't coming today," she told him.

He sank back against the counter crowded with pies. "Huh?"

Ada knew how he felt. Just weeks ago, when she had mentioned the A&P's turkey prices to Ruthalin Feldsted, Ruthalin said, "Oh, I've been meaning to tell you. We've been invited to Doyle and LeWanna's this year."

And just like that, a twelve-year tradition—gone.

Ginni, her long hair frowzy from sleep, opened the fridge. "Didn't Mom already tell you, Douglas? About them going to their cousins' in Baltimore?"

"The ones we met last summer," said Kate, still flush-faced from her morning run. "Remember? The woman with the Stepford lipstick?"

"Excuse me?" said Ada.

"Yeah, she ate her entire ice cream sundae without losing a speck of pink."

"A stunning performance," Ada's husband Latham agreed, looking up from a delicate jam-spreading operation at the kitchen table.

Ada remembered nothing about pink lipstick. All she remembered was the leaden, sundae-spoiling feeling that hit her when she faced these new people across the Feldsteds' table and heard Ruthalin say, "It's so nice now to have family nearby." *Just moved out from Denver, blah, blah. Doyle works at the home offices of Struckle and Lutz, the big department store, blah, blah, blah, so nice, isn't it nice, awfully nice.*

Nice for you, Erval and Ruthalin Feldsted, Ada thought now. But then, that sounded so poor sport. And anyway, here was little Douglas looking up at her like she'd announced they were all going on a diet together.

"But," said Ada as she unbuttoned the towel from the fridge handle, "we're going to have a happy day anyway, aren't we?" *Aren't we?* Her eyes dared them.

After all, Thanksgiving was the holiday least likely to disappoint. Nobody got upset over the presents not gotten. Nobody checked the Easter outfit and found a run in the tights. So it couldn't be hard to have a happy day now, could it? And, on that thought, she turned back to the turkey.

"Twenty-two pounds?" Latham, dumping his plate in the sink, fingered the label on the crumpled turkey wrapping.

"The smaller ones didn't look right," she said.

"And five pies?"

"Well, any less didn't seem like enough." Ada reached for the towel.

It was a gift from Ruthalin, one of those crafty people who couldn't leave an object unimproved. Ruthalin's handiwork was propped, fastened and hung everywhere in this house. For example, the sampler over the kitchen sink, the one that proclaimed, as in every good Mormon home, "Families Are Forever"—from Ruthalin. The teeny apron that fit the soap bottle?--Ruthalin again. The dime-store towel, enhanced with a little lace-trimmed neck and that handy button--yes, Ruthalin.

Ada reached for her biggest bowl and thought about those twenty-two pounds of turkey. Maybe she had bought too much. But crowds were what the holiday was all about. Anyone who doubted this hadn't been to the grocery store last Saturday. The aisle was jammed with loaded-high carts, pushed by women who considered the gravy packets, thumped the turkeys, rifled in the cooler cases for tubs of Cool Whip. Nobody got out of the A&P on Saturday with fewer than ten grocery bags.

Running water into the bowl, Ada tested it gingerly for just the right warmth.

"So what are you doing now?" asked Latham.

"Since you won't be getting Ruthalin's famous Pinwheel Rolls today …" She set her bowl down next to the pies and sprinkled yeast over the water.

Douglas watched at her elbow. "Do you even know how to make rolls?"

She shot him a look. "For you, it's all about the food, isn't it?"

"Hey," said Latham, "I've got a project, too. That shelf you've been wanting in the basement? It goes up today!"

Her eyes opened wide. Sure, it wasn't Thanksgiving without the Annual Home Improvement Project, except that her husband was not a project man. Without Erval Feldsted's help, Latham's doors hung funny. His paint peeled. His pipes leaked—that is, if they didn't gush.

She looked down at her bowl. The yeast bubbled and spread. As she stirred in the eggs and the flour, Latham navigated his way through the kitchen, carrying the tall shelf box. He clumped down the wooden stairs to the basement.

It's only a shelf, she thought. *Not like a water heater or anything.*

Still, she hurried the dough along, then tramped down to the basement. Passing the laundry and the folded-up crib, she sat on an old bar stool. "I wonder, wouldn't you rather wait until Erval's back in town to do this?"

He lifted his chin in the air. "I don't need Erval. I can handle this myself." He tossed the directions aside, tucked his half-glasses into his shirt pocket and touched the steel beams and the packets of screws as if they might unleash the spirit of Erval on his behalf.

Handle this yourself, indeed. She pushed off of the stool, peered into the dryer and retrieved a tablecloth.

At the top of the stairs, she stepped into her broad, shiny-floored studio, opened the closet door, and tossed the folded tablecloth on the high shelf. Her eye caught the collection of card tables and folding chairs, all stowed neatly below.

Ada shut the closet door, fast.

But it wasn't fast enough to stop her from remembering how she'd collected them over the years, enough to seat the entire Feldsted family, which just kept growing until Ruthalin had borne her tenth child a year ago.

Returning to the kitchen, Ada reached for the sack of potatoes and wondered if Ruthalin would give cousin Doyle, someone she'd met all of two times in her life, a big old Ruthalin hug. Just what were the Feldsteds doing while Ada scrubbed dirt out of the potato dimples? While Latham pretended he knew all about home improvement down there in the basement? While the TV in the front room blared at her children?

"Gentlemen," Ada heard the announcer say, "for five points please, what will your wife say is the strangest place you've ever 'made whoopee'?"

That's it! Ada slapped the scrub brush down and marched to the living room. "Is this how we're going to spend our happy day? Watching the dumbest show on TV?" She flashed her withering gaze at the announcer and his newlywed contestants. Then she turned the same eye on a slouching Ginni and a chubby Douglas. "Come on, I need help in the kitchen."

When Ada needed help, she wanted Kate, her oldest, most clued-in child. But Kate wasn't available at the moment; did Ada hear the shower running upstairs? "Ginni, let's do the potatoes."

The teen slowly peeled herself off the upholstery, scratching at her oily head.

"You can catch a shower later," Ada promised.

"I don't need one."

Ada stared.

"I'm tired today," said Ginni.

"Aren't we all? I stayed up late to read, and I still woke up earlier than a dairy farmer." She handed Ginni a peeler. "You use this one."

The peeler clinked slowly as Ginni shaved away at her first potato. "Ow!" she cried. "My fingernail!" The girl examined the damage, then stroked the nail against her lip to feel for snags. "I hate this peeler."

"Here, then. Trade with me. Come on, now. And I don't know why you care about a fingernail when you don't even care about getting a shower today."

"Why do you care whether I take a shower or not?" The girl frowned and threw Ada the cold shoulder.

Ada clinked away with her own peeler. "I'm just surprised at you, that's all. You're the one that won't go to the mailbox without all your makeup on. And our mailbox hangs just outside the front door."

"Well, the mailman's on holiday today. And so am I."

Latham's footsteps echoed in the kitchen. His hands gripped Ada's waist as he looked over her shoulder into the sink. "The whole bag?"

"Any less doesn't look right," said Ada.

"Oh, br-rother!"

She looked at the growing pile of skinned potatoes. Had she forgotten that she wasn't feeding football hulks like Marc and Tom Feldsted today? The mound would spawn leftovers that the Runyons would be sick of by tomorrow night.

Suddenly the peeler went still in her hand. She turned to Ginni. "You aren't taking a beauty vacation just because Marc isn't coming over today, are you?"

"Mom! As if!"

And with that, one potato peeler landed with a clatter in the kitchen sink and Ada Runyon lost her kitchen help.

It probably didn't matter. As she looked at the two piles of potatoes, she had to agree with Latham. *Oh, br-rother.*

Still, she felt in her bones as if she had barely a half hour before she heard the knock at the door, and everybody letting themselves in. That's how the Feldsteds did it, being practically family and all.

Like family, Ada could predict which children would hover and beg as she opened up the cans of olives. And when she wouldn't give them seconds, they would take out their revenge by scampering away to her grand piano and playing "Heart and Soul" over and over again until Ruthalin would mutter through clenched teeth, "That Hoagy Carmichael should be sentenced to homes with children!"

Oh, that Ruthalin! What earthy, funny thing was she saying now as her family pulled up and took a first look at cousin Doyle's house? How big was this house? Would the Feldsteds walk in and crane their necks at the high ceilings? Would they face a long table festooned with linen and china? Would Ruthalin swallow hard and wish she'd staged more let's-play-nice-restaurant drills with her children?

How long before somebody broke one of LeWanna's lamps? Or spilled on her brocade tablecloth? How long before she sent a look across the table: *In twenty minutes, dear, I'm going upstairs to concen-trate on my headache. Then they're all yours.*

Now Ada washed the potato starch off her hands and set the lid on the kettle just so. Feeling the call of the piano herself, she brushed her hands on her apron, stepped down into her studio and strolled to the music cupboard.

Her fingers crept through the thin books until she found her Rodgers and Hammerstein. Seemed like Thanksgiving always included a sing-along of show tunes. After the big dinner, after the couch naps and the TV referees' whistles, after Ada and Ruthalin sat in the kitchen, copying down recipes, everyone would gather in the living room to stare at *South Pacific* on the TV.

Then, when the movie was over, Erval Feldsted always got up from the couch with a groan and blared, "Some Enchann--ted Eeee--vening." He would sit down at the piano and accompany him-self. He murdered the music on purpose, Ada was sure, because he knew she couldn't stand it. He knew she would rush over to play it herself. And she fell for it every time.

Now she opened the book and pressed the spine flat. She fit her fingers over the keys and began.

Yes, once he had her there with a couple of his children hooked in his arms, the crowd always swelled up to caroling-party size, and Lulubelle always laid on the wicker table, trying to nap through the whole racket. Then when Erval hit a high note, holding it out like a factory whistle, the cat would raise her head with a nasty glare in her yellow eyes. *Who is standing on that man's tail?*

Then when it was time for the Feldsteds to go home, Erval would hold out his wife's coat. "You may see a stran--gerrrr." And you knew that the kids clear at the back of the Feldsted van would have to plug their ears against their father's braying all the way home.

Meanwhile, Ada would shut the door and turn off the porch light and feel loved, in spite of the broken basement light Latham would find later. Yes, she would feel loved, and lucky to have spent the day with old friends who …

"Mom! Mom!"

Ada now turned to her children. Their faces glowered like thunderheads. Her hands lifted off the keys.

"Stop playing! We can't hear our show."

Ada clenched her jaw and shut the book.

"As sands through the hourglass," droned the announcer.

She stood before the television, her hands on her hips, watching the actress open her door and greet her guests. They handed her a bottle of wine. They kissed her cheek.

"Well," said Ada, "the folks at *Days of Our Lives* seem to be having a perfectly happy day. And if they can have a happy day in Salem, in spite of all their problems, I don't know why we can't do just as well right here in Boxford. And besides," she looked at Ginni, "they all seem to have fit in a shower."

Ada stared at the TV, at the people in their wool and their gold buttons, at the candles burning on the occasional table, at the twinkle the candlelight made as it hit the camera lens. Maybe, she thought, maybe LeWanna was the kind of hostess who placed a little turkey-shaped package of candies beside each plate and played soft music on the stereo and swabbed her roll in gravy just to cover the gaffe of the guest who did it.

Maybe the whole Feldsted family was sitting in a drawing room just like this one, and liking it. And hoping they would have Thanksgiving like that forevermore.

* * *

"And where does that leave us?" Ada sat in the basement, adjusting her bottom on the inadequate stool, spilling all her fears to Latham as he screwed a lay-flat thingy to a stand-up thingy. "I mean," she said, "we've been friends for twelve years. That's a long time."

"Not when you compare it to people around here who are buddies since high school. Heck, since kindergarten," he said.

"Well, twelve years is a long time for gypsies like us. I mean, Ruthalin and I trade kids every summer. We sweep up crumbs at each other's houses, 'cause I know where she keeps her broom. And when their well pump went out, they camped here. When the last hurricane roared up the coast and knocked out our power, we stayed there. What'll it be next time? We get there and find their house already full of cousins?"

"No, the house will probably be empty. They'll probably go to Baltimore, thinking that it's safer than here."

Ada slumped, brooding. "And I always worried that they'd move on us. Remember the night we went over there and the Sunday classifieds sat right there on the table?"

"Yep. He'd circled something in Allentown."

"How could they do something like that?"

"Erval's got to watch out for his career," said Latham, scratching the back of his head with the screwdriver. "And we've done our share of it."

"I know." Circled ads had led the Runyons, over the years, to Vincennes, Indiana; to Denton, Texas; to East Lansing, Michigan; and finally, to Boxford, to their house just two blocks away from the little college. "I know," she said again. "But it stinks to be the ones left behind."

She thought some more. "Maybe they don't feel the need to move anymore. Now that they have their cousins as a way to get away from us."

"Oh, Ada, please ..."

"No, really. Maybe they've been secretly longing for a polite way to stop going steady with the Runyons. Maybe when I call and she puts her hand over the phone to ask Erval ... Well, sometimes it's a very long pause, you know."

"That's because it takes so long to find him. He could be down in the basement or out in the garage or clear out by his rabbit pens, putting on new chicken wire."

"Or he could be right beside her, whispering, 'Why can't they find other people to do things with?'"

"You don't know that."

"No, but I can read between the lines when they agree to meet us for dinner at Barney's and they're a half hour late. When they 'forget' to invite us to Kevin's mission farewell. How could Ruthalin 'forget'?"

"How a woman with ten kids manages to remember anything at all … I mean, come on, Ada, they'll still come over. You know as well as I do that wherever two or more ice creams are joined together, there Erval will be also. But their cousins moved to town! They're just helping Doyle and LeWanna settle in."

"You don't act like this bothers you. Are you saying you're glad the Feldsteds aren't here? You want to hand them off to somebody else?"

"I don't think," said Latham, "that they're handed off. After today, that woman is going to think long and hard before she invites them again."

"Hey, Dad!" Kate called from the top of the stairs. "Time for the Annual Basketball Game!"

Latham looked at his watch. "Gimme a minute. I need to make the Annual Call Home."

Ada followed him up the stairs. He dialed the phone, then carried it into the dining room for peace and quiet.

Kate shifted the basketball under her arm and stroked the towel hanging from the fridge handle. "Where did we get this?"

"That?" Ada peeked under a lid on the stove. "From Aunt Ruthalin. Her family throws these grand sewing parties every time she goes home."

"Don't the Feldsteds go home every summer?"

"They miss one, here and there."

"Didn't you say her family is real close to where you grew up?"

"Yes. Thunderegg, Oregon. It's not far at all." Ada lifted the cloth over the dough and felt around. Hmm. Not warm at all.

Kate twirled the basketball. "We should go with them sometime."

Ada laughed. "Right. Driving six days across the continent just so our kids can swim in a favorite irrigation ditch from her childhood ..." Ada shook her head.

"Well, maybe we should visit our own cousins."

Ada looked long at her daughter and sighed.

Latham returned with the phone. "I'll get back to that shelf now," he said.

"But, Dad. The basketball game?"

Latham wrinkled his nose.

Ada laughed at him. "Go on. It's a tradition."

"You have to play too, Mom," said Kate. "We're short on people."

"Now wait just a minute here ..."

"Come on," said Kate. "You want us to have a happy day now, don't you?"

"But I have rolls to watch."

"What are they doing right now that they need watching?" Kate asked.

"I think you owe us your presence," said Latham.

And with that, Latham and the kids trooped out to play the Annual Basketball Game.

She could at least put them off. She lifted the cloth and felt the dough again. DOA. She frowned at the clock.

Dumping the old batch into the garbage, she wiped the bowl clean. As she stirred the new dough, she nursed jealous thoughts about all those ladies in the grocery store, ladies whose rolls were probably turning out perfectly by now, ready for all that family just about to come through their doors. Real family. Not the substitute kind which Ada had relied on happily for twelve years.

It's not as if she didn't have real family. *Why don't we visit our cousins?* her daughter wanted to know.

She poured the dough onto the counter. She shoved it and folded it.

Well, why didn't they visit us? It became a stock phrase in her letters. "When are you coming to visit?" They gave her vague promises—*someday, someday*—and she believed them. In her idle-minded moments—driving under the tallest oaks in town, or standing on her front step, calling for Lulubelle—she pictured just how she wanted them to find her: sitting beside the grand piano in her broad, Solarian-floored studio, listening with tented fingers to one of her squinting little piano students.

But they hadn't come.

And why should they? She was the one who left.

She squeezed the dough, turned it, shoved it again.

She had never planned to leave those Idaho hills that rose, brown and rounded, behind the house, or the horses that nickered from the lean-to barn, or the family that laid out picnics under the tall cottonwoods and then hurried inside again when the wind arose, carrying the smell of wet dust. This was country where the men wore billed John Deere caps. Hats off, their foreheads glowed a school-paste white against their sunburned cheeks. This was country where women with tight perms and lost waistlines knew how to can apricots, scour milk buckets and patch overalls. She had presumed she'd marry the son of one of these unions.

When Daddy gave up the dairy farm and moved to town, she sat outside in the evenings on the rock wall that kept the yard from falling onto the sidewalk. She saw the young couples walking hand in hand in the moonlight. When they came closer, she hurried to the screened porch, where she could spy on them undetected. Someday it would be her turn to hold hands with somebody special, out there under the streetlights.

By the end of college, it still had not happened.

All the waiting and hoping narrowed down to one evening when she sat in an overstuffed chair, her head in her hands. She had run out of classes to take, interests to pursue, sights to see. It was time to leave. Alone.

Then someone knocked at her door. It was a roommate's boyfriend.

He sat in the other overstuffed chair. He asked, "Why so somber?"

He had a way of getting the story out of her: Girl Faces World, Hands Over Eyes.

"You're going about this all wrong," he said. "Here you are, totally free. No obligations." He pulled a map from his car and opened it before her. "Where do you want to go? Pick a place."

She traced her finger over the names. Kalamazoo. Tulsa. Valdosta. Massapequa. She'd heard of these towns. But, like everyone else she knew, she had never traveled east of Denver, much less imagined living there. She'd never thought of sending letters home with a return address that would make the mailman open his eyes wide and tell her mother, "Ohio! You don't see that too often around here."

She sent letters, filled out applications. The best reply came from a music school in Bloomington, Indiana.

She put herself and her boxes on a Union Pacific train. After traveling through the night, she awoke somewhere across the Kansas state line.

Outside her window, coated in a fine morning mist and backlit by the rising sun, the fresh green wheat of early June waved gently in the fields. She had never seen that color of green before. A gasp escaped her lips. *I, Ada Flory, am in a picture postcard.*

She gasped like that all morning. The wheat went on for miles. And after the wheat, trees grew on the crowns of the rolling hills. They grew in the ravines. They grew anywhere they pleased.

After only a few days in Bloomington, she understood why this new earth looked the way it did. Rain fell in sheets that blurred the landscape. Then the water rolled down the streets in great swipes, seeking the grated gutters.

There was never a girl so far from home and yet so free from homesickness. She wanted to stay forever, to drive beside the gentle rivers, to look out over the forest-covered hills, to stroll the shaded neighborhoods. Later, when she found Latham—lucky man! He had grown up in this postcard—she tied herself to all things green by tying herself to him.

Even though other Mormon families drove west every summer, she made vague excuses—*too far, too much.* But now and then she gave in. And every time she did, somewhere after Omaha, the trees disappeared and the land turned as ugly as a rat's backside. Road signs done up with abandoned wagon wheels and bleached cow skulls begged tourists to stop in at the local museum.

This landscape of loneliness outside every window oppressed her. Shuddering, she would whisper to Latham, "Let's turn around."

But he would drive on, and she would spend her whole visit "home" remembering a time when the water in the ditches or in the garden rows or even in a cup seemed like plenty of water. Now she could see how precarious it all was.

When the visit ended, she and Latham hurried east again, calling ahead to cancel motel reservations. "Let's just drive straight through." The closer she got to the lush shrubbery and the thick pines of her bonny little Yale Avenue neighborhood, the calmer she felt.

Now here she was, safe in her house, safe from cow skulls and moments of truth in overstuffed chairs.

Sometimes in this life, I get what I want.

And she spanked the bread dough and left it to rise.

* * *

Outside, their shoes shuffled on the pavement. "Finally," said Latham. "You're on Kate's team."

"What?" Bodies swirled around her. And just when she knew where the ball was, it wasn't there anymore.

"How many innings do we have to play?" she asked.

"It's not innings, Mom. That's baseball."

She sighed. If only she could think on her feet like Ruthalin did. When the Feldsted kids badgered their mother about joining the game, she'd call out, "You're doin' fine! Don't let me spoil it." Then she'd whisper to Ada, "With a bladder like mine, you don't run and jump."

But Ada was stuck in the middle of the action, facing Kate, who looked for a clear path to pass the ball. *No, Kate, not to me! Don't!*

Then she felt the ball against her stomach. It ran down her like a spilled drink, eluding her grasp. It rang with a rubbery echo wherever it hit. When Ada turned to follow the sound, it had escaped again.

Life slipped by in fast frames. Douglas squinting up at Latham. The net bulging with ball. The creases of Ginni's shoe. Latham bent over, breathing hard. Kate's lip, grim, determined, stuck on a dry tooth. Loose concrete popping out of a driveway crack. Hair curling on Douglas's dewy forehead.

The images flashed by, but somebody had turned off the sound.

Finally, Ginni dropped out of the game and sat on the car hood. Following her cue, Ada stepped away from the Annual Basketball Game (Eerie Edition), and scurried back to the kitchen.

She barely beat them there. They descended like locusts, gulping water straight from the tap, snitching loose pie crust.

Latham sauntered out of the bathroom. "I might as well let out my belt now, with all this food here."

Ada shrugged. "I know how to feed a crowd." She surveyed the kettles on the stove, the patiently ticking oven timer, the little striped dishtowel blanketing the bread dough. She twisted the button towel in her hands, feeling its growing dampness. She turned toward the counter.

"You know, Latham, I could've handled the extra people just

fine." She looked over her shoulder to see if any children were still in the room. Then she spoke in the hushed tones with which she might confide that grandma's cancer had come back. "If Ruthalin had suggested I invite them, I would have done it. Or if she had said, 'We're having my cousins. Why don't you join us?' … But she never gave me a chance. She just went and said yes to them." She blinked furiously at the tears gathering, blurring her vision. "She didn't even tell them that she already had a standing date for Thanksgiving dinner. No, she just went off and …"

"Mom, where's the olives?"

She dabbed at her eyes, then turned on Douglas. "The olive tray is for company."

"I thought it was for Thanksgiving."

She bunched her apron onto the counter. "Sorry! No olives today!"

She shot out of the kitchen, her shoes clicking down the hallway. "You know, you'd all be less disappointed if you just trimmed your expectations a little. If you realized this is just a day. OK, it's a day with a certain dinner menu, but otherwise," she paused at the bottom of the stairs, "the sun rises. The sun sets. The cat wants in. The cat wants out. *It's just another day.*" Her footfalls on the steps made the purposeful thud of a post hole digger. The bedroom door clicked shut behind her, a very final sound.

She sat on the bed, unmade thanks to Latham rising after her. Yes. That's really all there was to it. Get up. Pay a bill. Dust a lamp. Fold a shirt. Tomorrow will be just like it and none the worse for today having been just … a day.

And what's wrong with that? What's wrong with having an ordinary day here on her street full of town-crier lampposts and soft-fallen pine needles? Ada parted the slats of the blind. See? Just like any other Thursday out there, with the breeze waving the arms of the trees, with the woodpile stacked behind the Northam's fence next door.

But in front of the Northam's: six cars.

And across the street, at the Fricks', cars spilling out of the driveway, stretching down the street. Cars with colored tags, from far away.

So tell me why the Runyons are having just a day when everybody else on Yale Avenue is having a celebration?

Ada drew her finger away from the blinds, letting the slats snap together.

This always happened.

Oh, Ada had landed in some fine-looking towns in her time. She had unpacked the dishes and the towels. She had flattened the boxes. Then she had stepped outside the door to look up and down her new street, feeling all quivery with excitement as she pictured her new life.

She loved being part of this world, where everybody was on the run from dull yesterdays. Everybody was eager to barbecue for the neighbors, to tag along on their husbands' company trips, to enroll the kids in dance lessons, to diet, to do lunch, to do both at the same time.

Ada had inherited enough hail-and-howdy Mormonism to know the rules: Say hello first; Don't wait to be invited.

Say hello to the other mother on the park bench. *I'm Ada. Nice to meet you, Estelle.*

Say it again when you look up from the sale table at Penney's and find Estelle digging for a deal on corduroy pants. *Yes, I remember you. Estelle, is it? Hmm, someone seems to have bought up all the size 2Xs.*

Say it again after the PTA meeting. *Oh, and I was wondering, would you like to come to lunch?*

Estelle couldn't come.

Well, all was not lost. Ada still had a sunshiny, billow-clouded day and shade-kissed sidewalks and the stroller rolling along under her hands and Ginni trained at last to sit in the seat and not lean out where the bushes could whack her in the face.

She still had that delicious knowledge that comes from settling into a place. There in the middle of the block, in the red brick Cape Cod, lived the library's Story-hour lady. Here, weaving down the sidewalk, was the chubby boy straddling his stingray bicycle. He always waited down at the next cross street, dime in hand, as the Good Humor truck tweedled closer. And the truck always played "Do Your Ears Hang Low?"

Over there on the corner of Hillcrest and Panhandle Streets, somebody had a marvelous eye for landscaping. Ada envied the azaleas sweeping away from the front walk, the potted petunias set just so on the second step.

Ada turned the corner.

And there, next to the trellis and the bench, she saw Estelle, sipping iced tea with two other Texas belles. In sundresses. Gesturing with their forks, spearing lettuce on their plates. Laughing.

There and then, Ada lost track of her sunshiny, billow-clouded day, of the small hands that reached up to her from the stroller seat. She didn't walk much on Hillcrest or Panhandle Streets after that.

It took Vincennes and Denton and East Lansing until Ada Runyon finally figured it out. When she moved her pots and pans and pillows to Boxford and looked down her street and saw her neighbors, a cold rod of reality stiffened her spine. *You will have nobody. Get used to it.*

Then Ruthalin appeared. And there Ada was, at Ruthalin's kitchen table, crumbling crackers into a lunch of tomato soup, bursting to tell the latest thing. "You know Cleon, my sister's husband?"

"The fellow that owns the apartments? Rents to the college students?"

Since Ruthalin remembered all the other Cleon stories, since she remembered exactly where he hung on the family tree, Ada never had to explain. That's why Ruthalin felt like family.

Then some cousin came out to Baltimore and claimed her for himself. Real family won out after all.

And that's the way it was. The world's teams were already chosen up.

Now Ada stared at the blinds. She pulled back the bedspread and crawled between the sheets. Something heavy sat in her chest, rolling its dead weight like a tire over a tin can. This was an old familiar feeling. It had visited her in Vincennes, in Denton, in East Lansing. It was her heart all right, but nothing a doctor could fix. He couldn't alter the people of the world and snip them away from their previous obligations, leaving them with a little piece of themselves for Ada, who just wanted someone to talk to when Douglas's principal called on one of his despot days or when her period was late or when she just sat, looking out at snow-covered shrubbery, wondering why saying hello first didn't work?

Suddenly the bedroom door burst open. "I did it!" announced Latham. "Come and see."

She closed her eyes against the bright glare of his jubilance. Rolling up slowly, her back to him, she wiped her wet cheeks and followed him down to the basement.

It was a respectable-looking shelf. She had to admit that much. Giving it a jiggle, she looked around at the rumpled instruction sheet, the multiple screwdrivers, the spare, unused crossbeams. "Well. Congratulations. You win the prize for Best Adjustment to the Post-Feldsted Era."

And while he wondered whether or not that was a compliment, she walked up the stairs. "Wait," he said.

She stopped.

"What do you want me to put on it?"

She pointed to a row of Ball jars lined up against the wall, jars filled with applesauce.

Back in the kitchen, she checked the turkey. Fine Coppertone tan. She checked the potatoes. Fork-tender. Apt to fall apart at the slightest pressure, not much better than some people around here.

She checked the roll dough. Flat and cold. She dumped the

dough on to the counter. She poked it, prodded it, gave it CPR. She stood back, waiting for its chest to rise, for it to sputter or for its eyelids to blink open.

It was no use. She scooped up the entire cold mass. With her free arm, she flung open the door under the sink, dragging the garbage can out from under the pipes. She dropped the dough in, like a boulder over a bridge. The plastic can rocked from the impact.

She did not even bother cleaning the greasy film from the bowl, but just started again with the warm water, the sprinkled yeast, the cups of smoothed and leveled flour. She worked like a short-order cook: rapid and surly. She stirred. She scraped. She sprinkled. She tipped the bowl, spilling the new mound onto the counter.

It relaxed, spreading itself, shining with clamminess. Her hands dove in. As they met the dough and pulled away for the next shove, the dough refused to let go. It clung to her desperately like a shy child at the kindergarten door. She struggled away. It followed her, webbing her fingers. It was not even pleasantly fleshy dough, but more like cellulite, not quite gelled. No matter how much flour she scattered over it, it still stuck. As she attacked it, yanked away from it, attacked it again, her hair shook in her face, her breath came hard and her jaw clenched, just as it did when she spanked her children.

She heard Latham climbing up from the basement. "All done!" he bragged. "Whoa! When did the garbage get full?"

Ada looked behind her, her hands still trapped. "It wasn't that full a minute ago."

"What's in there?"

The family gathered around to stare at what grew out of the can.

"The bread wouldn't rise," Ada confessed.

"Well," Latham poked around, "it's rising now."

Nobody said anything. A low hum of stadium-crowd roar floated in from the TV in the next room. The refrigerator motor kicked on. An oven light blinked. Lulubelle slithered around a corner and looked up at the five hard-to-read faces. She stood ready to flee, if necessary.

"This doesn't feel like a normal Thanksgiving," said Ginni.

Ada broke free of the doughball with a speed that probably stripped the downy hairs off her skin. Little earbobs of dough hung from her hands, which hovered threateningly near Ginni's neck. Ada's face crumpled and her lower lip shook.

Then she thought better of it. She plunged her hands back into the bread-flesh, gasping with effort. *Normal Thanksgiving?* Mushroom clouds of flour dusted the walls and sprinkled the pies. What did it matter? She wasn't one of those ladies at the store on Saturday, frowning over their lists, mentally counting up all the guests. She hated them!

Why doesn't anyone else have to get used to loneliness?

She threw on another handful of flour and wiped the tears rolling down her cheeks.

"Mom. Mom!" Ada felt a hand on her shoulder as Kate pulled a box of Bisquick from the cupboard. "I'll take care of it, Mom."

"Leave her alone," she heard Latham say. "It's a grudge match by now."

She never heard the doorbell ring. When next she looked up through the fine white smog that hung in her kitchen air, there stood the missionaries.

Their smiles faded and their eyes widened as they faced Sister Runyon. The younger blond one looked at his beard-shadowed companion.

"We just wondered if there was anything we could do for you." said the older one.

And as they all stood around staring at each other, a crash—a symphony of metal and glass—thundered up from the basement.

* * *

As the windows of the house turned dark, Lulubelle stood in the middle of the kitchen, sniffing the air, eyeing the turkey carcass up on the counter. Her tongue ran along her dry cat lips.

She looked toward the living room, where blue light from the TV flickered against the wall. That meant the man and the children were safely occupied. And the woman—well, nobody had seen her since she went to her room hours ago.

Lulubelle hopped up on the counter.

After gnawing on the turkey leg, she sidestepped a droopy leaf of sandwich lettuce. She padded past the sink, sniffing at the water pooling around the dirty dishes. Then she sampled a few licks from the empty mayonnaise jar.

Satisfied, she landed on the floor. She scrubbed away at her whiskers, then wandered into the living room.

He snored lightly in his recliner. The children sprawled on the couch like pasta dried to the sides of the pot.

Targeting Ginni, whose hand hung off the couch, Lulubelle wiped her nose on the girl's fingers. Ginni rolled off the couch.

Lulubelle trotted to the front door. Ginni followed.

Ginni opened the door and Lulubelle slipped through. Sitting on the brick steps, the cat looked up and down the street. Colored lights twinkled from the edge of the roof next door. And she heard the strains of "Silent Night" from a car radio.

A Little Five-Minute
Thrown-Together Something

Ginni Runyon is in a hurry today. She looks at the rolled-up poster board on the car seat beside her. The pink ribbon tying it all together is wrinkled, but there's no time to do anything about it. The morning is nearly gone.

Hurry speeds her along under the arching trees of her street. It drives her past the metal fence pickets that line Boxford's college campus, and through the neon jungle along the highway, where bright lights promise burgers and discount oil changes and two-for-one dry cleaning. She bounces over the railroad tracks, then makes a right turn just short of her high school.

She is moved by forces she didn't quite see coming. At least not this fast. They push her past the mailboxes along the road, making her the bait for a radar gun all the way to the Feldsted's house. Even when the car rolls to a stop, with the tires crunching over the gravel and pine cones of their driveway, these forces rock her unsteadily forward to Marc's doorstep.

Then, as she stands at his front door, she is not sure she wants to hurry this.

On any other day, she would press the doorbell twice as a warning, then walk in. That's how you do it when your mother and Marc's are best friends, when you are over here once a week, if not more.

But today …

She thinks she sticks out like one of those Uncle Sams standing on some curb, waving at traffic and pointing toward the mattress sale over in the strip mall. At her height, she already sticks out anyway, towering above every other blow-dried head in any crowd. So here she is, compounding her own awkwardness, her finger poised over the doorbell, her arm clutching a rolled-up posterboard which advertises the very worst part of her soul, which is her fall-hard heart.

Do other girls even have hearts? Was any other girl only a hairsbreadth from bawling yesterday at 11:35, the moment when Mr. McFarland's voice crackled over the intercom and dismissed the Boxford High senior class forever?

The finality of it yesterday hit her like the lurch of an elevator, landing hard. There she stood among her fellow juniors, watching from an open window on the second floor. The horn-honking crowd outside, with Marc somewhere among them, drove out of the parking lot onto College Avenue, where a policeman bossed the traffic with a smart snap of his wrist. *It's over, it's over! He's going, he's going!*

Then, this morning, that sense of hurry drove her to the Rite-Aid, where she's sure she stuck out again. Oh, yes, the lady in the blue smock cocked an eyebrow when Ginni plopped the poster board down at the cash register. The blue-smock ladies at Rite-Aid knew everybody's secrets: who needed prescriptions for pinworms, whose bronze legs came straight out of a bottle. And they knew this customer, this tall girl with a weakness for fruity lip glosses and Herbal Essence Shampoo, had never shown any interest in art supplies before. *So what's up?*

Same thing at the A&P. She saw the look on the assistant manager's face when her nine candy bars rode down the conveyor belt. Nine! She saw the hint of censure behind that for-the-customers smile of his. *Will she be eating them all today?* She felt him look her up and down as she left, as if that was the last he'd ever see of her girlish figure.

But what else can she do? At 11:35 yesterday, life changed.

No one has answered the door yet. Her finger pauses over the doorbell again.

Forget it. She steps off the porch.

Why can't she be like other girls? Why does she always do these things? She is sure that no other girl she knows stands on a boy's doorstep, or imagines dramatic scenes where he catches up to her in the hallway just after the Econ teacher has trashed her report and made her cry, or where he just happens to follow the car of the bad man following her car, or where he waits on the ground below, shouting orders to the rescue team while she dangles above on a derailed roller coaster.

She grips the car handle. It is already warm, even in this patchy shade.

As she opens the door, the ribbon on her poster board comes loose. Fine. Let it. She pitches it over the front seat, towards the back, but it catches on the headrest and falls in front of the steering wheel.

"Ginni?"

It is Derek, Marc's seven-year-old brother. He stands on the stoop, holding a throw rug in mid-shake. Then he drops the rug into whatever dirt and sand lie on the front step and he runs toward the car. He is all lightly freckled cheeks and sweat-stuck cowlicks. Among his seven older siblings, he is a creature who pushes into the throng at elbow level, whether he is wanted or not. To his two baby sisters, he is the sort of tease who shuts them in the bathroom and walks away, proclaiming that, somehow, he locked the door and can't figure out how to unlock it.

Now, he pushes between Ginni and the car door. "What is that thing?" he says, pointing at what lays in the driver's seat. "Is it a present?

"No." Ginni tries to shut the door.

"Who's it for? Can I carry it?"

What? Did Ginni spend money at Rite Aid and the A&P this morning, and did she gather up all her mother's old magazines, and did she haul it all up to her bedroom and shut the door with a click that said, *Stay out or else* only to see it ruined by some kid with a milk mustache and dirt under his nails? "No." She re-ties the ribbon. "That's OK. I've got it."

Well. Ginni can't leave now.

She follows Derek. They step over the welcome mat, over the pine needles lodged against it, and into a house that smells of toast and Lemon Pledge. A brother walks by, carrying a light fixture littered with dead gnats.

"Brett, Ginni's here!"

"Yeah, and tell me something I don't know." Brett brushes past Derek with all the swagger of somebody who's got important things to do.

Well, the rug and the light globe explain the Lemon Pledge smell. The house must be getting a real root-it-out cleaning today, making it fit for Marc's graduation party tonight. This must be one of those days when it's handy for the Feldsteds to have so many children.

Ginni steps into the light of the kitchen. April, bent over the sink, armed with a toothbrush and some Comet, turns to look at Ginni. Dropping the brush and rubbing her brow with her wrist, her face goes from private brooding to company-happy. "Hey!" she says. She exhales as if her rescuer has just appeared on the horizon.

Then she sees the pink-ribboned thing in Ginni's arms and she knows why Ginni has really come. The two girls have shared years' worth of secrets, sitting on April's bed, or on the narrow, windowless staircase that bends up through the middle of the house.

"Of course my brother's noticed you ... "

"He has?"

" … *but knowing him as I do, I'm wishing for you somebody that isn't so full of himself.*"

"*When? What did he notice?*"

Now April just rolls her eyes and turns back to the sink. "This is the curse of the eldest daughter," she says, scrubbing at the faucet again. "I would've been glad to dust, but nooo."

The kitchen is unmistakably party central. Ginni looks for a place to lay her poster down but with bread bags full of cookies crowding the kitchen counter, not to mention stacks of paper plates and a big, cake-sized box from the Sweet Shop, there isn't any room. So she leans against the counter and holds her package. She hears the scritchings of the toothbrush against chrome, and April catching her breath.

Marc stands in the next room, perfectly still, his arms out like tree branches. The jacket over his barrel-like body has no sleeves. Yet. His mother stands next to him, pins hanging from her mouth, attaching blue fabric to the sleeve holes.

Evidently he is getting a new suit for graduation and, judging by the flaps on the jacket, it will be in the snappy new leisure style.

Marc is not handsome. Nature gave him his mother's overbite, his dad's thick neck. Then there is the tuck in his chin, also from his dad. All told, his looks are mostly good for scaring opponents across a line of scrimmage.

Still, he jokes all the time that, when he goes off to college this fall, he is going to date Miss Utah. Or at least a runner-up.

April always laughs to his face when he goes into his Miss-Utah routine. "Hah! You'll be lucky to get the Buford County Corn Queen!"

He is not even that nice. Oh, he seemed nice long, long ago when he agreed to be Captain Von Trapp in her backyard "Sound of Music" wedding. With his little popsicle-sticky hands, he helped trail extension cords out the door and he helped set up the gray record player so they could march to real music.

Then, when she toddled out in his mother's high heels to meet her groom, he ran away.

She had stood in the kitchen then, fuming with rage. Make him play his part! she screeched to the mothers, who sweated over a canning kettle of tomatoes. Holding their jar tongs aloft, they stared down at her hot streaked face. Her own mother attempted to follow her rant, while his mother ran to pick up the baby Ginni had just awakened.

Jilted at the altar? they tut-tutted. Maybe he'll come back and play with you in a little while.

No! She wanted him jailed in his room! She wanted him to go without supper! She wanted him pulled from whatever knot-holed tree he was hiding in and plunked onto a kitchen stool under the stern, law-giving glare of two mothers with hot tongs in their hands. No!

But the mothers just turned back to their kettle of tomatoes.

The next time her family went to his house, she had forgotten the insult. She was the first one in the car, same as always, where she waited for all eternity while the rest of her family put tin foil over the cake, or stuffed a clean hanky in a back pocket, or read the Sunday funnies up to the last second before Dad switched off the lights.

Once there, she was the first one, same as always, to press the bell and walk in to the long table where the two families ate popcorn, or maybe a dump cake, every Sunday night.

After the treats, they ran outside and staged tricycle wrecks. She always connived to be the most knocked-out, best laid-out victim. Then she'd wait, listening for his voice, peeking to see how close he was, waiting for his hands to grab hers and drag her over the twigs and the humpy grass to the "hospital."

But you never knew what was next with Marc.

Ginni and April used to round up the younger children and make them play schoolroom. They'd had the place running pretty good, with pupils who sang when told to sing and pledged when told to pledge.

Or they did until Marc jumped out of the closet, upsetting the makeshift desks, spilling the chalk, breaking it.

After that, she only wanted to hide from him.

* * *

"Why are you here?" says Derek as he drags a broom into the kitchen.

"Just wanted to drop something by," she shrugs.

He peers into the open end of the poster cradled in her arms. She clutches it tightly, wishing it were smaller, more hide-able.

"Is it a present for Marc?" he wants to know.

Ginni pulls it away from him. Isn't Derek right at the age when boys like to upset makeshift schoolrooms or rip up posters someone has spent hours constructing, or even taunt big brothers who receive these kinds of things from *girls?*

Why hadn't she remembered how things were at this house? If what she carries in her arms is a present – not that she's admitting it is – the giving of it should be holy and private, just like the hours she had spent behind her bedroom door this morning, working while a singer on the radio crooned about a girl whose "smile warmed like cabin firelight," whose touch "charmed like a breeze in the night," who came along and since then, the singer "couldn't sleep or eat right." She had scribbled on sheets of paper and scratched out lines and made new scribbles. She had pawed through the magazines and cut out glossy pages that proclaimed "Jello is Kids' Stuff!" Then she had pulled the cap off the felt marker and drawn the first line on that poster board.

She had pictured giving it to him on the front steps. It was supposed to be one of those moments where he would find her sitting there. He would join her and she would ask if he went to Ocean City with the rest of his class yesterday, and did anybody fall off a pier, or get arrested, or find their shorts washed out to sea? And she would ask, *Aren't you just a little bit sorry to be leaving old Boxford High?*

No, he would say, *I think the question is, isn't old Boxford High just a little bit sorry to see me go?* Then he would roll his eyes and smile. *Well, Mrs. Croswell is not sorry. Mr. Jager is not sorry. And Mrs. Martucci and her chemistry lab—certainly not sorry.*

Yes, that was how she pictured it.

Which was a far cry from how things are at the moment, with Marc in a bad mood because his mother wants to know: does he want the sleeves to end at his wrist? Or a little longer?

He looks at Ginni and rolls his eyes.

"Marc, what about the sleeves?" his mother asks again. She flicks a curl off her forehead and straightens her shirt where it always bunches like a drawn-up awning over her behind.

"Cut 'em off up here!" He saws at his bicep. "And how long do I have to stand around like this?"

"Marc!" His mother's face clouds over. "Work with me now!"

Marc sweeps Ginni with let's-skip-the-whole-party look. When it comes to dressing up, he is still such a seven-year-old.

Ginni smiles back as his mother says, "Here is it, already noon and I haven't even gotten to the top-stitching!" No, he's not even close to dreamy-looking, but when he cracks a funny and looks at her to see how it went over, she is drawn into his world and offered the seat at his right hand. She is royalty.

He squints as his eyes travels down Ginni's arm. She knows he sees the poster board. He is trying to figure out what it is.

Ginni is not ready for him to know. This thing in her arms, it's practically an announcement. *I think, all the time, about us leaving the church dance and walking around the building and about you holding my hand and telling me that you understand everything that bothers me.*

Now April stands at the stove, flipping a sandwich. The sweet and tangy smell of bread trapped between hot fat and melting cheese attracts children from all over the house. They wander in, carrying their mop buckets and their rag dolls. They crowd and peer and press. Ginni squirms away from this crowd. She climbs onto the bench running along the table and hides the "announcement" in the draping of the plastic tablecloth.

This is what happens when you do things in a hurry.

Until now, she never needed to hurry. He was everywhere she was. He was at the junction of the science and east hallways after third hour. Or he was in front of her in the line at the church drinking fountain.

He was in her Sunday School class. Were they twelve the year the class met on the church stage? Or thirteen? Anyway, the teacher pushed aside a rear curtain to let in a murky, uncertain light from the little window back there. Then he sat on the corner of a little table, swinging his white loafers back and forth, quizzing them on last week's lesson. In the silence that followed, the boys reared back on the hind legs of their chairs.

Ginni always twisted the little string of fake pearls she wore. They clicked softly as she wound them around her finger. One day, she wound them tight against her throat. She felt a pop. The necklace relaxed. When she took her hand away, little fake pearls dropped to the hard stage floor and rolled away.

She didn't dare look for them. If she did, the teacher, whose searchlight stare missed nothing in the whole room, would know that she cared more for her fake pearls than for his true pearls of knowledge. He might follow her gaze, find out where the pearls were and take them away.

She sat there, aching with loss, mentally undoing that last twist. Then she felt a tap on her shoulder.

She turned. Marc held out a palm full of pearls. He poured them into her hand. He stayed after class, too, reaching under chairs, pushing aside curtains, dropping more into her hand.

He shouldn't have done that. But since he did, she no longer wanted to hide from him. No, she wanted to follow him everywhere.

* * *

She worries, all the time, about other girls getting him.

Like the cheerleaders. Marc lined up with the other football players, all across the gym at the big assemblies. He rippled with pleasure, in spite of himself, as the blondest and button-nosiest of them all handed him a layer cake.

What if he flirted with her after speech class? What if she invited him to one of her parties?

But none of that happened.

So Ginni worried about the Mormon girls at the dances up in Brandywine. They possessed an aura, the Brandywine girls did. And they wore wedgy sandals that hadn't made it to the Boxford mall yet. There was a particular brown-eyed one that he always asked to slow dance.

What if this girl suddenly showed up on those Sunday nights around the Feldsted table?

But she never did.

Marc's world was not Brandywine. It was here, where he had cheerleaders to quip with and not take seriously. It was here where he shot baskets on the square of concrete beside his house, where he turned and saw Ginni sitting on the front step. He always sat beside her and, after they finished her popcorn, they drank from the garden hose together.

And he told her things.

"My dad," he'd say, "he's probably pretty disappointed with his life." And Marc would run his hand through his hair, pulling at the damp parts that clung to his neck. "I mean, what kind of life is it? He comes home tired-beat every night and climbs out of his car, and he says, 'Well, will you look at that. Looks like the mold on the north side shingles has spread since last week.'"

And she would nod. Yes, sadly absurd, such a life.

"You know, normal people play on the weekends," he'd say, nodding toward the house across the street, with its tall fat flowers and its open garage. "They go boating. They go golfing. They pack up and back the car out of the driveway and look across the road at Mr. Feldsted, up on his roof with his north side shingles." He'd roll his basketball down towards his feet. "That's sure not how I'm gonna spend my weekends. And promise me one thing, Ginni."

Yes? Yes, what?

"If you ever see me wearing one of those short-sleeved white shirts like he wears, you just go ahead and slug me, OK?"

And Ginni would laugh and pick up a crooked pine twig and poke at the needles caught in the sidewalk seam as Marc told her, "I've heard Kansas City is nice. But I like the sound of Atlanta, too. But what the hey, I'll do both! I'm going to live in a new city every year. I'm sure not gonna end up in some place like Boxford."

And Ginni would think about how she liked the sound of all that, too, as she drew the letters G-I-N-N-I F-E-L-D-S-T-E-D on the sidewalk.

"And I'm gonna come home with fat commission checks in my pocket and hand them to my wife, along with maybe a nice sweater or something."

And she would picture herself in that kitchen in Kansas City, turning away from the bowl where she tossed a dewy mound of salad greens, and taking the box he handed her and folding back the tissue paper and gasping in surprise at the sign of the lovely pink – no, make it a mint green – cashmere. And she would fall into his open arms and … and …

"… won't spend their weekends pushing brooms through the garage or hacking at the weeds with rusty clippers," he would say.

And she would hurry back from that kitchen in Kansas City and look at him as he leaned back on that porch step, eyeing his dad's old Rambler in the driveway. Who's pushing brooms? Who's hacking weeds? She wanted to know.

Oh, his kids.

Their kids.

Her face would grow hot.

What if he can read what you're thinking? Look away!

These little talks marked him as hers. The trouble was, that mark wasn't visible. Obviously he was a hard case. What would it take for him to wake up and figure out that *she* was going to be the woman he would hand the nice sweater to?

Because if he did not wake up now, this summer, she would lose him for good. There he'd go, off to college. College wasn't like here, where you counted Mormons in parts per million. No. Out there, he would find thousands of them. He would find Miss Utah, or her runner-up.

If Ginni didn't get him now, she'd have to admit that he was never within reach at all. She might even have to admit that nobody was within her reach, that she would become the pitiable kind of girl who'd be the last of her crowd to marry.

Ginni came from a tribe of women who waited like the last cat at the shelter, the one with the "unique markings" and the imploring gaze. It's a wonder Ginni had any relatives at all, what with all their problems getting hitched. Her mother married at twenty-five. What's worse, Ginni counted up three—maybe four … no, five!— sweet, slightly pudgy cousins, girls who looked longingly at babies, who got discussed when Mom hung up after long phone conversations. "They say Rayelle wants to move to Spokane. They say she's discouraged that nothing's happening in her life."

And then, when they found their man, all was well, no? Ha! Aunt Hyla's cowboy husband used to frighten Ginni. But really, after a while, she didn't notice the stump where his index finger once was. Or the cleft palate.

She could feel the same fate coming at her, a rolling dust storm of pitiability. This was more than catching. There were genes at work here, lurking, manipulating, sneering.

Unless she was, somehow, one of the luckier ones. But how

could she tell? What were the signs? Did it mean anything that Ginni had gone on six dates (even if none of them were with Marc)? Six, by the end of junior year. Did that put her ahead of her mom's girlhood record?

Did it help that she read *Seventeen* magazine? Lucky for her that she worked at the library, where she could read every issue for free. She could even get her hands on the back issues.

"Hair Care—Our Tip Sheet."

"Summer's Best Fashion Bets."

"Catch His Eye—The Hair, Make-up and Clothes Guys Find Irresistible."

It was the gospel of self re-invention. Ginni signed on and knelt before its altar. Yes, you could improve on nature, so she pushed back her cuticles and brushed the mascara clumps out of her lashes and checked in the mirror often to make sure that what stared back at her was nothing like Cousin Rayelle.

And every wave of that mascara wand was supposed to change the game. She would no longer be the girl with the fall-hard heart. She would be the girl in the radio song. Wasn't that girl lucky? Did she know someone crooned to the whole world that her smile "warmed him like cabin firelight"?

Yes, when Ginni was done transforming herself, she wouldn't ache when she saw Marc across the dance floor, or blush beside him on the front steps or stand in his kitchen wondering if he would like this ... this thing she held in her arms.

She would take her cue from novel heroines.

When the heroine enters the story, love is the last thing on her mind. Most likely, she has come to reclaim the family plantation.

The hero, always an honorable drifter with sorrows of his own, rides up on a horse just in time to be introduced by her lawyer uncle.

He is gallant, deferential, smitten. When he kisses her hand, the heroine is unimpressed. Though disturbingly aware of the hard broad shoulders underneath his shirt and the powerful agility of those legs hugging the horse's flanks, she pulls her hand away from his knightly lips. She has come to save the farm.

And though he comes around with nosegays and gently cloaked advice that she might want to have a closer look at those papers her uncle just whisked past her, though the reader knows how near our hero comes to sweeping those lips of his across those bare white shoulders of hers out on the balcony at the Christmas ball, our heroine still fights him off like spitfire, insisting that the avenging of her family's loss on that ancient land deal is topmost in her spitfiredly feminine mind. And our sharply rebuffed hero burns for her still, returning again and again like a bird flying at a window.

To cause that kind of torment, while behaving with a pulp heroine's indifference—now *that* would really be living!

* * *

Derek approaches the table. The sandwich on his plate is already missing a bite. His fingers shine with grease. He picks it up and takes another bite as he slides onto the bench next to Ginni. "Is that candy in there?" he asks, reaching through the tablecloth.

Ginni shields it with her body. Circling pack of jackals, this child!

In the next room, Marc hands the sleeveless jacket back to his mother. He crosses the kitchen, headed for the nether parts of the house. He is off to change out of his new pants.

But Ginni doesn't think about that. The room around her fades into a tubular and fuzzy distance. She cannot hear the mother muttering over the sewing machine tension or the children getting milk from the fridge or the voice of Marc's sister April asking, "Want a sandwich, Ginni?" or even the tromp of the father coming in from outside.

She can only climb off of that bench and follow him.

All of this still feels too hurried. This is not the way she planned it.

But there is no front step, no just-the-two-of-us. There is just Ginni following him down the hallway, Ginni catching up to him beside the worn arm of the recliner where his father likes to sit, Ginni forgetting that the boy just wants to get to his room and change his pants before a forgotten pin sticks him.

She holds the rolled-up poster out to him. "This is nothing much," she says. "Just a little five-minute, thrown-together something." All her limbs bobble like she is thirteen again, and stupid, and blushing. She just knows it.

He looks like he does at those big rallies, with the cheerleaders and the layer cakes—pleased, but not sure what the catch is. He loosens the ribbon.

Wait! she thinks as the bow falls way. *Why? Why let him know, when you have managed to hide it for so long?*

His eyes sweep over the poster board as it falls open, heavy, covered with glued-on candy bars and wrinkled magazine snippets. "What's this?" he asks. "You rob a concession stand or something?" His lips move as he reads:

Hey, Marc!
It may have been a ROCKY ROAD, but here are a few REESE'sN to celebrate. Today is your big PAYDAY

He smiles, on one side of his face, as if people all over the living room have just jumped out from behind the couches and hollered "Surprise!" as if he wishes they would go away, but he knows you can't say that to people when they think they've just made your day.

so SHOUT IT OUT! Though you may think all this gradJELLOation IS KIDS STUFF, and I hear you don't CARAVELLE of a lot for MOUNDS of speeches

April walks around the corner. She stands by him and reads silently over his shoulder as he touches the Mounds bar.

it'll be NICE 'N EASY. It'll be lots of SNICKERS. So march down that MILKY WAY. Go ahead, be the HOT TAMALE for a day. DOTS all I've got to say about it.
   Truly, Ginni

Marc looks at April. April looks at Marc. And suddenly Ginni can see that he already knows. He's known all along.

He reaches out. He pulls her into a hug. She holds him hard, the urge of it pulling at her like draining water swirling a hapless ant.

But that look between him and his sister—it hovers before her eyes. What? Did Ginni think brothers and sisters don't talk?

Was it April? *Don't you know she's had it bad for you since eighth grade?*

Or Marc? *What am I gonna do? I mean, I like her. She cracks me up, you know.*

Like an adorable little sister, you mean?

Is that all he thinks of her?

Is that him letting go, right now, while she still hangs on? She backs away, bumping into that recliner, and hurries from the room, not daring to look at him.

Back in the kitchen, she climbs onto the bench and leans against the table.

She is not alone. Derek leafs backwards through the Sears catalog. Chin in hand, his dozy eyes fall on bicycles, ski suits, hospital beds. His breath whistles in his nose.

April, at the stove, finally slides the last sandwich on to a plate.

Their mother's sewing machine in the next room hums, stops, clicks.

Ginni hates seeing these people and their little Saturday

moments as she if never knew how they really lived.

Ginni hates hurry, and change, and big intercom announcements at 11:35 in the morning. She hates what they can make her do. She hates the way she smiled and hummed along with the radio when she glued all that candy on, and the care with which she loaded it into the car.

She hates that he said nothing more than a mumbled "Thanks."

She hates that he knows what he's thinking and she does not. If he were thinking what she wanted him to think, he'd be out here, sitting with her at this table, lamenting how little time they have left together. Instead, he is her Captain Von Trapp all over again, with fear in his eyes as she wobbles across the patio door in his mother's high heels.

Pulp heroines never have this problem. They never watch their hero leave town in a blaze of see-it-all optimism, and wonder if, after he's seen it all, he'll figure out that he had it all right back here in Boxford.

Suddenly, Brett, the next brother up, whirls into the room. Chocolate smears his lips, his teeth. He holds up what is left of a Snickers bar.

Derek looks up from his catalog. He jumps off the bench and rushes toward the living room.

Ginni runs after him.

By the time she arrives, mob rule has seized the room. Fending off brothers and sisters with one arm, Marc holds the poster high in the air. But tissue-thin flaglets curl up where two candy wrappers are already torn away.

Finally, he gives in. He peels off one candy and another and another until the message reads: "don't of a lot   peeches."

When Brett reaches for the last piece, Marc drops the poster and the brothers roll like two lions duking it out on the National Geographic hour. They scoot from the couch to the potted plant, slugging, squashing, grunting.

"I've got it!" Marc's hand shoots up from the melee, grasping a wounded but functional box of Hot Tamales. "Save it, Ginni!"

* * *

Marc bends his rug-burned body until it drops low onto the front step. He pats a spot on the concrete beside him and looks up at Ginni. She sits.

He tosses a Hot Tamale into the air. It sails high, peaks, then falls earthward.

Ginni catches it and drops it in her mouth. She is just about to bite into it when he stands up.

"Got to go," he says. "My mom says my dress shirt's a rag. 'Get another,' she says." He waves the wad of five-dollar bills she must have handed to him.

Why, Ginni is an excellent shirt shopper! She scoots forward on the step, so fast that she wears the thin spot on her jeans a little thinner. She tucks her feet into her sandals and struggles with the worn buckle at her ankle. When she looks up, he has already strolled down the front walk, whistling, not looking back.

The door of the family Rambler slams shut. The motor turns over. He backs out with an easy swing around her car parked behind him. Out on the road, his elbow hangs out the window as the tail fins gleam in the sun, then cloud over in the speckled shade. The warbling motor sound fades off.

The Hot Tamale sits on her tongue, so much cinnamon flavor that there's no flavor at all, just a burning.

THE GOLDEN BOY OF CARDIFF

Erval Feldsted finished his lunch of two cheese sandwiches and some home-canned cherries. He pulled a wintergreen candy from his desk drawer just as the mailroom boy dropped the letter on his desk.

It was from the mayor.

Erval spent his workdays at Tidewater General Hospital straining his eyes over the blueprints for the new addition plans, or rushing off to a meeting of the safety committee, or opening work orders that arrived all day long—THHUUNKK!—via the pneumatic tube. There was nothing about his job that would attract the attention of the mayor of Boxford.

Was it something besides his job? Erval had lived in Boxford for fifteen years now and he still ran afoul of those little unwritten customs that everyone else seemed to know about. Take, for instance, the weeds out back that he had allowed to grow over his head a couple summers ago. Nobody back in Cardiff, Utah, would have marched up to his front door and demanded to know when he planned to trim them back to a more civilized height. Nobody back in Cardiff would have looked, quite frankly, a mite threatened when he offered to take them back and show them how his ten children had beaten paths through the weeds, forming an entire play-town. "See how much fun they're having? I thought I'd give them another week before I cut 'em down." And nobody back in Cardiff would have gasped, "Ten? Did you say ten children?" as if he harbored wet-backs in his garage.

Things were just different here. The land was flat as a floor. It stretched to the east where, a short drive away, the Atlantic Ocean lapped against its sandy edges. It wasn't like back in Cardiff, where the mountains stood around the valley, firm and impassive, keeping out all the troubles of the world.

Back in Cardiff, Erval never had to wave away tobacco smoke. Here, it was the aroma of public life.

Back there, the women buttoned up to their chins. Here, they had Ocean City and all those beaches, where they tied two hankies together and called it a swimsuit.

Back there, nobody swore unless the bull kicked you in the spleen. Here, Erval needed a mental bleeper. "When the /fornicat-ing/ park board found out just how much /fornicating/ money the concessions were making ... those /illegitimates/ decided that we have to fork over a /fornicating/ forty-five percent, since the /Guy-who-made-the-universe/-/cursed/ money is made on park premises. I mean holy /diarrhea/, how can they sit there on their fat /pack animals/ and just hand down decisions like that? Why don't the /diarrhea/-heads leave us the /place-you-don't-want-to-go/ alone like they have every mother- /fornicating/year?"

Yep, Erval Feldsted still felt like a stranger in Boxford. So when the letter from the mayor landed on his desk, a cramp clenched up in his gut.

It sat atop the Waltons mug he received at the last company Christmas party. (He had actually unwrapped a "Charlie's Angel" mug, hurriedly trading it for a trucker one that said "10-4 Good Buddy," then trading again until he got something more Erval-like.) His hands trembled a little as he opened the letter.

Inside it said that George Rittenhouse requested Erval's presence in Room 204 of City Hall, early Monday morning.

Hm. He couldn't think of anything he'd done wrong.

On the other hand, maybe he had done something right.

Erval made a mental note to mention it to his best buddy, Latham Runyon.

* * *

Latham and his family often came over to Erval's house on Sunday nights. All the littlest kids hid from one another in the trees out back. The teenagers lounged in the family room, telling each other which science teacher to avoid. The wives sat in the kitchen, discussing dread diseases. But Erval and Latham dished themselves second bowls of ice cream and played their favorite game, Stump the Rabbi, wherein they asked each other difficult questions like: where were Joseph Smith's Gold Plates these days? And, how did the Book of Mormon's Lamanites' skin turn dark? Was it actual genetics? Or was it more of a water-into-wine kind of thing?

Their little game usually led them straight into their special language. "Yea and verily," Latham would say, "my spoon hath broken. Hast thou another?"

"Yea and verily," Erval would reply. "And lo, let him call unto him a damsel—April, could you bring another spoon in here?—and let all things which are expedient be given unto man." It was awfully patriarchal. And awfully dweeby. Just ask their teenagers.

But what really got their blood pumping on Sunday nights was checking up on whatever the world had said about Mormons that week. Had the newspapers mentioned the new temple in Washington? Did they get the story right? Or did they throw in nut-job phrases like "secret ceremonies" and "allegedly lost truths"?

On this Sunday, Erval handed the *Tidewater Gazette* to his friend and said, "Did you see this article?"

Latham scanned the pictures. "What's this? Sunbonnets and handcarts?"

"Some reporter went to the Pioneer Day celebration up in the Brandywine Ward. I can't believe they let him print some of this stuff."

"'Old fashioned foot-races … renditions of "Billy Boy" … sour-dough baked over a fire,'" Latham read. "'Commemorating the 1847 trek when Brigham Young led the Church of the Latter-Saints'—well, they could stand a fact-check of two."

"As always. But read on."

"'They seem to enjoy this dress-up game, as it reminds them of a time they were at their most heroic,'—What in the world!"

"Keep going," said Erval.

"—'even though, back then, they were a people so desperate that all their worldly goods fit onto a 4x3 cart fit for dragging across a continent.' What?! I hope they didn't feed this guy their best slice of cherry pie only to have him write garbage like this."

"I'm gonna write the *Gazette* a letter! They completely missed the point of that celebration."

And as Erval and Latham spooned up the last of their ice cream, they remembered that bank robber out in Arizona three years ago, "and of course the paper made sure to mention that he was once a *Mormon* Sunday School teacher." Then there was the executive up in Connecticut last year, left his wife for his secretary, took off for somewhere balmy and tropical, no one knew where, really. Company officers were still searching for all his Caribbean bank accounts. "And of course, the paper trumpeted the fact that he was the *Mormon* CEO of National Starch."

They would have remembered a dozen more if Erval hadn't taken their Styrofoam bowls to the sink and said, "I've really gotta to hit the hay. Did I tell you I've got a meeting with the mayor tomorrow?"

"*The* mayor? Rittenhouse the Rotten?"

"Yep. Him."

"Whatever for?"

"I don't rightly know."

"But you can't stand him."

"Well, he's twenty pounds of manure in a ten-pound sack, that's for sure. But I got to be there at 7:30 in the morning."

As Erval's head hit the pillow that night, he couldn't help thinking that it might be nice, just him and George shooting the breeze across the mayor's desk. The mayor would ask get-acquainted questions. "Ten kids?" he would say, his eyebrows shooting up to his receding hairline. "You Catholic?"

"Nope, Mormon," Erval would say, which would lead the mayor to ask about the alcohol thing and the tithing thing, and maybe even the Osmond thing. Erval might even get a chance to pull out the Plan of Salvation chart, his nice little stick figure flow chart on the path to heaven he had drawn up and mimeographed and stuffed into his briefcase for just such moments. The mayor would listen very nicely but, of course, commit to nothing. He could never give up his vices. Still, they would become pals. And next time they saw each other somewhere in town, the mayor would …

No, no, no, wait a minute now, Erval warned himself. *The man is a liar and probably a womanizer too. After he softens you up with his lunch-buddy charm, he probably asks you to do a job that's so dirty, not even his cronies will do it. Well, resist the charm!*

Then again, it could be something important. All his young life, back in Cardiff, Erval and the other children had been told they were part of a royal generation. They were the salt of the earth. They were the city upon the hill. They would be called upon to do important things.

Oh, those important things might look small:

Stick your finger in the hole in this dike.

But they would have far-reaching consequences:

And don't move that finger until we sound the all-clear.

Those things would make everybody admit that Mormons weren't philanderers or bank robbers after all. They were a clean and cheerful people, the kind that make good neighbors.

Erval couldn't help but think that, if the mayor was calling, maybe his time had come. So he stared at the ceiling, picturing heroic acts, until he finally fell asleep.

* * *

Joe Pepper, reporter for the *Tidewater Gazette*, gulped down the last of his coffee and tossed the cup in the trash can just outside City Hall. He wiped his hand over his strawberry-blond beard, just in case it harbored coffee drops. Then he opened the door.

His editor wanted him to follow George the Rotten around for a day. People kept saying that George intended to run for governor next year, and old George hadn't done a thing to quiet the rumors. A little one-on-one, just the mayor and Pepper and the tape recorder, could tease out the man's plans, though Pepper might not find the right moment until some late hour after the meetings and the elementary school plaque-presentings and the poultry-grower dinners wound down for the night.

But for now, Pepper climbed up the marble stairway of City Hall. The place was empty. Not even the water department ladies had arrived to sit behind the frosted glass of their offices yet.

Mayor George was in his office at 7:20, as promised, hanging his suit coat on the back of his chair. "Mr. Pepper!" he said as Joe knocked at the open door. "Come on in. How's Pete these days?" His voice always sounded like a wagon bed dragged over gravel.

"Grouchy as ever," said Joe about his editor. "Gulping antacids like candy."

"Heh-heh. Serves him right." Rittenhouse sat down and thumbed through a pile of papers at his desk. With his round face and a physique that betrayed his fondness for Philly cheesesteaks, he was as much a machine mayor as a man could be in a town the size of Boxford. It was a town with three major employers—Tidewater General Hospital, Boxford State College and the Crayton Poultry Plant. It was a town big enough for a mall, but not a mall with escalators; big enough for every brand of fast food, most of them clustered around the campus, and some of them with a second store out beyond the bypass. Now if George could only get the weekend traffic to stop and spend some of their fun money here in Boxford instead of merely passing through on their way to the Atlantic shore towns thirty miles away, he would be completely happy.

"What have we got first today?" Pepper asked.

"Well, this just in: a memo from the DCD."

"Which would be?"

"Department of Certain Doom," the mayor cracked, handing the paper to the reporter.

Pepper saw that it was from the Department of Civil Defense.

"They want us to empty out our fallout shelters," said the mayor.

"Really. Wow, nobody's thought about—I haven't thought about those since—what?—fifth grade? So why now?"

"Oh, the same old story. Just like that supercollider down in North Carolina. You follow that story at all?"

Pepper had. Scientists wanted to build a donut-shaped tunnel for smashing atoms. They chose a redneck town that could use the economic boost. Scientific types started moving into the quiet little burg. They used eminent domain to move scores of families off the acres above the tunnel. They started digging.

And three billion dollars later, Congress cut the funding.

"It's a mess down there," said the mayor. "Eighteen miles of tunnel so far. And the project stops. Poof! And all the scientists and the construction workers move away. The two new elementary schools they had to build, plus the new drug stores and groceries, all of them struggling.

"Anyway, it's kinda the same kind of story here. After years of spending for enough cots and foodstuffs and gizmotrons to stock these shelters all over the country, suddenly there's nothing left in the government trough for sending any more supplies. Unload 'em, they're saying."

"Even when two countries still have their fingers poised over the little red button?"

Mayor George shrugged.

"So you'll be sending city workers in to empty them out?"

"Are you kidding? There're sixteen of these, all over the city. These people all have staffs. They have dollies and work gloves. Let 'em take care of their own. My guys are busy." The mayor stood up and rolled his chair to his desk. "I don't know how many of these shelter guys will show up this morning. Probably nobody from the college, since they don't believe in anybody using little red buttons over there." He led the way out his office door. "Don't worry, it'll be short. We ordered in doughnuts and when they're gone, nobody will stick around."

Pepper followed the mayor to Room 204.

The room was a few parts dignity and a few parts castoffs. A portrait behind the rollaway podium of someone bearded and solemn and long-dead, lent the dignity. Two spare conference tables sat along the edges of the room, looking jealous of the walnut table in the middle.

Pepper circulated. He already knew a few men in the room—the police officer, the fireman, the school superintendent. He introduced himself to the minister from the Gilead United Methodist Church. Then, as he jotted names in his notebook, he took a seat at the walnut table between Robert Barco of the Crayton Poultry Plant and Erval Feldsted, from Tidewater General Hospital.

The mayor stood at the head of the table. He looked Feldsted's white shirt and navy blue suit up and down. "Goin' to a funeral today?"

"No. No, there's no funeral today, not that I know of," said Feldsted, wiping his palms on his suit coat.

Pepper had vaguely wondered the same thing. Why didn't the man dress in wash-and-wear like everybody else in the room? Except for the suit, he looked every bit the engineer that his job title denoted. A lone tuft of hair sprouted from the bald spot that capped his head. The tuck in his chin looked like four-wheel-drive territory for a razor every morning.

"Got a memo from the Department of Certain Doom," the mayor waved his piece of paper as he sat down.

Old jokes already, and not even 8 a.m. yet, thought Pepper.

Feldsted, and only Feldsted, laughed clear from the belly.

As the mayor went down the list item by item, Barco trumpeted opinions on every water barrel and radiometer and piece of plastic tarp that the mayor mentioned. What they should do with it. Whether it still worked or not. Who invented it and when. Barco, with a spade-shaped beard punctuating his deadly handsome face, seemed like one of those guys who would tell God where to hang the stars, if he could just get past his secretary.

Ignoring Mr. Interjector as much as he could, Pepper felt a story brewing. Boondoggle of Waste. Cold War Era Errors. That sort of thing. He'd like to get a look at these shelters before they cleared them out. He made a few notes, something to pursue after he wrote his story on George the Rotten.

Who now spilled his coffee, a casualty of one of his sweeping gestures. George was an arm-flyer, he was.

Feldsted popped up and left the table. He returned with a handful of napkins, dabbing the table around the mayor's papers. When he looked satisfied with the clean-up, he took the napkins away and came back with a sprinkle-covered doughnut.

"Now, about the food," said the mayor. "Says here that the crackers are rancid and need to be thrown out."

"How does a cracker go rancid?" asked Mr. Police Officer.

"If it has fat content, ..." said the Crayton guy.

"That's what I mean. Where on a cracker is there room for any fat?"

"How many pounds are we talking here?" said Feldsted.

"Well, let me do a little math," said the mayor. He reached for his shirt pocket. "Ooops. No pen. Anybody got a pen?"

Feldsted scrambled in his suitcoat and produced a pen. He looked pleased with himself.

"Take them to the town dump," suggested the school superintendent.

"What?" said the fireman. "And see the rodent population go up?"

"Oh, I hate to see that much food go to waste," said the reverend.

"Can't we just feed 'em to pigs or something?" asked the fireman.

"You're not going find a farmer that will let his pigs eat them," Barco insisted. "Our contract growers feed their chickens a very scientific formula. They're obligated, or Crayton won't buy the birds. It'll be the same with pigs."

"Oh, it won't hurt the pigs," said the suited-up Mr. Feldsted, "and believe me, I know pigs. I used to raise 'em. We fed our pigs crushed corn, watermelon rinds, even leftover hotcakes. Why, they even ate a chicken or two that wandered into the pen looking for scraps."

Pepper had a hard time taking notes just then, for the meeting had broken up into so many conversations. To the man from Crayton, the very idea of pigs eating scraps was as bad as driving north in a southbound lane.

Mr. Police Officer had arrested folks who kept pigs in their yard.

The minister said he has seen pigs at the county fair that year, and was "so proud of the young people and their efforts."

Meanwhile, Feldsted, so long as he had the mayor's ear, offered him a crash course on the finer points of hog-killing. "After that, we dipped the carcass in the scalding barrel, and then we scraped off the bristles ..."

Mayor George winced, even if he was enough of a politician to feed Feldsted encouraging nods.

"... He can think somebody's pigs will eat them," the Crayton guy told the minister, "but we're not in the days of wooden false teeth and privies anymore ..."

" … have to use an ax to chop through the breast bone, then you start pulling out the guts out and cleaning out the inside of the hog."

Okay, okay, they were convinced. The man knew pigs. Give him the crackers.

Or most of them were convinced. "Hundred to one, you won't find a place that will take them," said the Crayton guy.

"Oh, Barco, let him try," said the mayor. "Surely there's some small pig operation out there, trying to make it on a shoestring. We gotta take these things somewhere."

And that was it. Meeting over. Everybody happy. Two last dry doughnuts left, and Feldsted reached for the one with the sprinkles.

Pepper still wanted to see these shelters. He could shadow the police and fire guys. But the public was used to them pointing where to go in emergencies. An ordinary citizen, however—that was a fresh angle. Did Mr. and Mrs. *Gazette*-Reader know that the guy next door stocked latrines that they might have to use when the unthinkable happened? Did they know what they would eat for a week if circumstances parked them down there? Could Mr. and Mrs. *Gazette*-Reader trust this guy? Did he really know what he was doing?

He watched Feldsted brush a sprinkle off his suitcoat. Most people who climbed the ladder from pig farm to navy blue suit took care to hide the part about the pigs.

The freshest angle, Pepper knew, came from the person that baffled you, the one that got under your skin and made you say, *What the …?*

As Feldsted started for the door, Pepper slapped his notebook shut and followed. "Say, Mr. Feldsted," he said, catching up. "I've got a few questions for you."

* * *

Of course, Erval bragged about the whole meeting to Latham the next Sunday.

"Typical city fellows," he said. "Can't solve a problem that's as old as dirt."

"There you have it, Erval. They can take you off the farm, but they can't take the farm off you."

"And the reporter wants to follow me down into the shelter. I guess I can show him. Nobody said it would be giving away national secrets or anything."

"Yea and verily, Erval, many are called but few are chosen."

"Yea, and by small and simple things are the wise confounded."

"And how did you like the mayor?"

"Not such a bad fellow, I guess. He even gave me a friendly slap on the shoulder."

"Yea and verily, thou hast found favor in his sight."

"Enough, guys," said Ada, Latham's wife. "We need to go home now."

Erval thought he detected a new respect from Latham. And Erval liked it. *Underestimated your old friend, did you now? Uh-huh. Thought old Erval knew nothing but steam pipes and temperature gauges while you're over there at the college lecturing about history, huh? Well, how do you like that? Guess Erval gets around town after all.*

"Can I go down in your shelter, too, Erval?" Latham asked.

"You can if you show up on Tuesday at three."

"Yea, and we shall see that which is hidden of mankind."

"Dad, please. Just … stop it."

Erval, waving through the cloud of bugs that swarmed around the porch light, said goodnight to Latham and his family, and he went to bed contented.

* * *

Latham never liked driving over bridges. Or under them, for that matter. Approaching the shadowed arches beneath a passing train, he would murmur under his breath:

The bridge will hold.

It will.

It will!

Unless it won't.

It left him with a seized-up feeling across his back, a feeling he might not notice until five miles later, when he would breathe deep and open his hands to make his white knuckles go away.

Latham had that same feeling on Tuesday, just before 3 o'clock. He shut off his Selectric and turned out the light in his office. Passing the offices of his fellow history professors, he descended the two flights of stairs and walked out into the May sunshine. He passed the library, walked under the Holcomb Gate ("Gift of the Class of '58") and got into his warm car. And that's when he noticed the seized-up feeling.

He turned on to College Avenue. Driving past the iron pickets of the new campus fence, he murmured:

Erval will behave.

He will.

He will!

Unless he won't.

Oh, Erval was a great buddy in the living room. And there was nobody better to sit with on the back row of the Sunday School class, where he and Latham could play a whispered round of Stump the Rabbi while the teacher insisted on sticking with the lesson plan. *So, just how did the ram show up in the thicket?*

But the thought of Erval unleashed out there on an ordinary weekday worried Latham.

If he could trust Erval, Latham would have invited him to Town and Gown ages ago. Town and Gown was the day when Boxford State College professors invited someone from off campus to a catered luncheon in the sunny, window-lined Crayton Dining Hall. Who but Erval would be Latham's natural choice? But how long did Latham put it off every year? Long enough that it wasn't quite right to call Erval up and say, *Hey! You busy? There's this lunch, started about a half hour ago.* And how many years had Latham done this?

With Erval, well, you just never knew what might come out of his mouth. Growing up out there in Cardiff, Utah, left Erval thinking that the whole world understood him when he said, "Seven high priests showed up to pick the watermelons."

He might as well have said, "Aliens from Pluto talked to me on my radio last night." What would all the geologists and the finance profs across the table do? Pause their coffee cups right in front of their mouths and frown in puzzlement? They might not say anything, but they'd probably think, *Did anybody really check into why Professor Runyon left Michigan State and came to us?*

Latham drove up the boulevard to the sprawling Tidewater General. Erval had instructed him to park in the back. No, not in the lot with the Porsches, but the one next to it.

Inside, in the elevator, he pushed B for basement. After he turned the corner and pushed open the door to Erval's office, Latham found his friend handing out flashlights, work gloves, hardhats.

A pudgy-faced man, his limp reddish hair brushing the top of his turtleneck, clapped a hardhat on his head. "Goin' down the mineshaft of the Cold War, we are," he said. He seemed delighted with his costume.

Must be the reporter, Latham thought.

Just now, Erval was playing a role somewhere between General Patton and world's best tour guide. He handed a ladder to Bernie, a bulb-headed lad on his crew. He grabbed a boxcutter and led the three of them—Latham, the reporter and Bernie—out the door. He whistled a tune, stopping only to point out that "This is the morgue... this is the development office," as he led them through a maze of hallways and out into a courtyard. "This," he pointed ahead to a wall of brick and stone, "is the original wing of Tidewater General."

It put Latham in mind of lobotomies and iron lungs.

Erval nodded at an overhead sign, the familiar black-and-yellow shelter symbol. "Capacity: 384," it said.

Erval searched through his key ring. He tossed a fact, even a couple dates—"They stopped sending the supplies in '72,"—to the rapt and jotting Mr. Pepper as he unlocked a scarred oak door and clipped the key ring back onto his belt. Then he whistled some more.

Latham felt that bridge feeling seize his back again. He caught himself looking at this Mr. Joe Pepper, as they all descended the dusty treads of some metal steps. Was the whistling getting on Pepper's nerves? Because if you knew Erval as long as Latham knew Erval, you got pretty sick of it. Whoever wrote "Whistle While You Work" should have to spend an afternoon with Erval in his garage. They would bolt out in under twenty minutes, bug-eyed and gripping their heads.

Of course, they could all be thankful Erval wasn't singing because—Latham forced a deep breath to loosen all that tension in his back, and where was it all coming from?—because …

Wait a minute! What was that tune ringing out of Erval's lips as they all walked past the jugs of de-icer, the spools of cable and the strings of Christmas lights that littered every square foot save for a path down the middle?

Latham knew it. It was "Servants of the King."

And what if Pepper—who was taking tons of notes, remember—wanted to know, *What is that song you're whistling, Mr. Feldsted?*

Then Erval would have to tell him and Pepper wouldn't recognize it and somebody would have to admit that it was a church tune and, of all church tunes, "Servants of the King" was the last one that Latham would want to fall into the hands of some smarty-pants reporter, who would probably write: *With its temperance-march beat and its lead-the-charge lyrics …*

Latham could never croak that song out without a furtive look around the chapel. Anybody rolling their eyes? Smirking? He stood ready to cut them dead with his sternest frown. *Let's be grown-ups now. This song is about zeal for the work, about the honor of doing it.*

It was also a song that could never pass the Dorothy Test.

* * *

When Latham told his sister Dorothy that he was joining up with those Mormons, the look of distaste on her face was so fleeting that he convinced himself he hadn't seen it at all.

When he brought a Mormon girl through Dorothy's door and announced, "I want you to meet Ada, my fiancée," the temperature of Dorothy's hospitality could set jello. *So, Latham's Mormonism is no youthful whim, eh? He's in it for the long haul now?* That made her little brother just as much a stranger to her as this Ada girl.

That's OK. Dorothy could just stay back in Evansville, living her garden club life, undisturbed by her embarrassment of a brother. Except when she decided to visit Boxford.

Actually, Latham was pretty sure Dorothy was more interested in her cottage at the shore. But since her little brother lived so near the rented beach house, Mom back in Indiana would never allow Dorothy any peace if she failed to call on him.

So Dorothy came to dinner.

It went well enough. Ada outdid herself. She borrowed cookbooks from the library. She splurged on the mushrooms that lurked in her sauces, on the doilies that sat under her éclairs. And after dinner? "Well, we know you want to play in the sand this week, Dorothy," Latham told her, "but Sister Partridge's pageant is at the church on Friday night. Ada's the pianist. The little girls are Lamanites. They've been rehearsing for months now. The public is invited and all. Won't you come see Sister Partridge's pageant?

On Friday night, with his sister beside him, Latham smiled encouragingly at the stage. He nodded as his daughters came on. He stole glances at Dorothy. The snifty look on her face as she followed the action up there in the lights made his smile fall off.

The thing is, he already *knew* Sister Partridge's pageant was bad. Her music—every choppy ditty of it—did she just throw notes into the air like cards, writing them in whatever order they came down? Her costumes—you couldn't have the little Lamanite lasses running around in loincloths, like they really did, oh no! So dirndl skirts it was. And her script? Did she really write in all that weeping, and those dreadfully long moments with people holding their hands up, supplicating? Or was that stuff thrown in by all the ham actors up there?

He had squirmed through it all for months of rehearsals, never daring to say, or even think, that it embarrassed him. Nobody dared. Sister Partridge was a good lady, a sincere one. God loved the good and the sincere. If they drew Him a picture, His face would brighten, He would give them a kiss and hang the picture on His fridge. He didn't care if her Lamanites looked like Swiss chocolate-milkmaids, because her goodness and sincerity trumped all, even excellence. Right?

And what was excellence anyway? To a people that once isolated themselves in the desert, who looked back with more than a few bitter feelings at the folks that chased them out, what was excellence but the prideful ways of man? *No, we don't have to meet the standards of a people like that. There isn't one idea of theirs for which we have any use.*

Except if you had a sister named Dorothy, whom you were trying to convince that you had not gone off the deep end.

Yes, his religion was still as true as the law of gravity. But Sister Partridge's pageant was a turkey.

And "Servants of the King" was a turkey.

There were plenty of other songs in the hymnbook that were as rousing as chariot races but, of course, Erval didn't whistle any of them down here in this cavern, overstuffed with cables and Christmas lights, where Joe Pepper looked around and said, "Obviously nature abhors a vacuum."

"Yes," said Latham. "I doubt that 384 people could find enough elbow room to cower down here."

And the whistling Erval led them past concrete posts, pocked cement walls, an office chair, a patriotic wreath, until he stood before a metal door, flipping through his key ring again.

"Say, you are quite the songbird, Mr. Feldsted. What is that tune there?"

"Oh, that is …"

Latham butted in. "He *is* quite the songbird, isn't he? He's been famous for his singing. Why, since he was ten years old, every old lady in town has been coming up to Erval and asking him to sing at her dear departed's funeral." Latham sniffled dramatically. "'Why I just know that's what Hyrum would've wanted. He would've appreciated it.' Isn't that right, Erval?" Latham slapped him on the back. "The man standing before you here is well-known as the best singer in all of Cardiff, Utah, and that's a town of 300 people, mind you. You can write that down in your notebook if you want. Can't he, Erval?"

"Aw, it's nothin'."

"Don't let him give you that. Funerals, Christmas programs, baseball games. Or had they even heard of baseball in little old Cardiff, Erval?"

"Utah? Really?" said Pepper. "Did you know a lot of Mormons there?"

Erval unlocked the metal door. "You might say that."

"Are you one of them?"

Latham saw a brief cautious darting of Erval's eyes. "Yes, I am." He looked over his glasses at the reporter. "Mormons aren't just in Utah, you know."

"Oh, I know that. I did a story on some up in Brandywine. They were celebrating their pioneer week and …"

Erval stopped. "You? You wrote that garb—?" He pressed his lips together.

"Oh, you read it? Thanks."

Erval narrowed his eyes at Pepper. Then, with a glance at his ladder-bearer, he gave the keys a final twist and he opened the door. They all stepped in and stared at the floor-to-ceiling boxes and barrels before them.

Erval reached for a box.

"So," said Pepper, "the crackers are somewhere in here?"

Erval pricked the box with his knife. "I remember that article. Yes, I do. You know the part I remember the most?" He looked off into the distance. "'People who like to play dress-up games because it reminds them of when they were at their most heroic.'" He turned to Pepper. "Tell me, did any of those people write letters to complain about that story?"

"Not that I know of."

Erval turned back to his box. He gave it a good fish-gutting slash. "Did you do any homework so you'd know what their 'dress-up day' was all about?"

"Oh, yeah, I found some good stuff out there."

"Stuff that explained how hard the trip was?" Slash. "Stuff that told the story of a people who conquered a desert in spite of hardships?" Slash. "Stuff about superhuman perseverance in spite of persecution?" He put his knife hand on his hip. Latham watched the flaring of his jaw muscles. "And about how they never complained about their lot?"

"Actually," said Pepper, "they complained a lot. There was a guy named William Clayton who wrote in his journals what he really thought of everybody along the trip ..."

"Oh, no. Not Clayton! He wrote a song that gave them courage along the trail. It's practically our national anthem."

"Well," said Pepper. "That's pretty good for a fellow that was one ticked-off dude most of the time."

"Oh, you guys are always looking for stuff like that, aren't you? Why can't you get the part about Brigham Young being a great prophet who led the people after Joseph Smith was brooootally, viiiiiiolently ..."

"Hey, now, take it easy, Erval," Latham stepped forward.

" ... viciously, savagely ..."

"Is he going to be all right?" Pepper asked Latham.

" ... gorily ..."

"Boss?" said Bernie, "Boss! Could you watch how yer wavin' that flashlight?"

" ... murdered! While he was imprisoned for no reason at all except for the lies by the evil anti-Mormons! And then Brigham led the saints thousands and thousands of miles across a desolate wasteland where no man had ever gone before. He built thousands of cities!"

"Cities?" An inchworm of amusement flexed itself underneath Pepper's blond beard. "And what exactly qualifies as a city?"

"You have to remember," said Latham, "Erval here is from Cardiff. And when he moved to Grand Junction, he was awestruck by the tall grain elevators and the Main Street storefronts. Weren't you, Erval?"

"Uh-huh. OK." Pepper looked from Latham to Erval and back again. "But that part about conquering the desert, well, what else could they do? The stuff I read talked about how they were the have-nots of the world."

"Mr. Pepper," said Erval, "I doubt you got a-hold of the right stuff."

"Well, from what I checked in the notes, a great deal of it was taken from people's diaries."

"Diaries!" Erval humphed. "Diaries are where people go to complain."

"Actually, Erval," Latham jumped in, "they're considered a reliable primary source. Without them, we history professors wouldn't have anything to profess."

"Some of us," said Erval, shooting a poison look at Pepper's notebook, "are too busy *making* history to write it down!"

He directed Bernie to set up the ladder over by the boxes. Then he slapped on his gloves and climbed up.

"So," said Pepper, "how many pounds have you got in these boxes?"

Erval glared down from the ladder. Then he turned away and reached for a box.

Apparently, Mr. Erval Feldsted was no longer speaking to the press.

II

Erval felt cornered. "Snookered" was the word they used back in Cardiff.

Why should he believe that brightly curious act that Pepper was putting on right now, examining the water barrels over there with Latham? "Hey!" said Pepper. "No water in them?"

"Look here," said Latham. "They've got an instruction sheet. Says to fill the barrels 'in case of a rise in international tensions.'"

"Huh? Like, run a hose down here?"

No, don't believe the act. Pepper was capable of spending the afternoon with a bunch of celebrating Mormons, eating their picnic food, then writing what he did. Wasn't he supposed to have a keen reporter's eye, an eye that might notice that they were a clean people, a cheerful people, the kind of folks that gave back change when the clerk handed them too much? Where's the part where he put down his notebook and asked questions that had nothing to do with his newspaper story? Questions like: *Why are you so clean and cheerful?*

That's what they told Erval back in Cardiff: Be audaciously Mormon.

Turn down the Sunday invitation.

Refuse to look at the pin-up.

Decline the coffee.

They'll admire you for it. They'll want to know what makes you so different.

Well, in all Erval's Boxford years, if anybody admired his blatantly Mormon ways, they sure kept it a secret.

Fine.

He didn't need it.

Erval climbed down off his ladder.

In fact, it was okay with him just to feel like a normal guy, somebody with a lunch box and some car keys and, back at home, a lawn to mow. Somebody besides The Boss Who Can't Drink Coffee.

And anyway, after fifteen years at the hospital, the guys pretty much dropped the coffee questions altogether.

Just one o' them things, the shop guys gossiped. *The boss can't drink coffee. Dillis can't get no transfusions. Martin and his new wife couldn't get married at Holy Savior. Then there's Watson, who can't keep his pants zipped. Oh, we got all kinds down in the shop. Hand me that wrench over there, will ya?*

That's right. Live and let live. Normal guy. Well, sort of normal.

You know the boss believes people see angels, don't ya?

Nah, can't be.

I'm tellin' ya, Dillis heard him say …

And how's that for audacious? Really, there was no getting away from it. His known beliefs stuck to him like a giant slogan written across his shirt. They tempted people, made them want to say, *Oh yeah? Prove it!* You never knew which small, daily act they would pounce on.

He could be at the company Christmas party, loading up his plate with chocolate mint meltaways. The pathology chief would walk by the refreshment table. *Hey,* she'd say, *if you can't have coffee, why is it you can have chocolate? That stuff's full of caffeine. That's what's the big no-no is in coffee, right?*

She had smiled when she said it. But behind the smile, the words dripped with challenge. So what was she getting at anyway? Did she want him to put the chocolates back? Or would she rather he crack under pressure, take some more and say, *While I'm at it, I'll have a*

Heineken? And don't tell her what was and wasn't in chocolate, because she knew her way around beakers and molecules.

Who was she to check up on him, when she had no idea what it was like to pick one's way through the thou shalts and the thou shalt nots? It was hard work, keeping oneself a good Mormon boy.

And now, after a lifetime of this exertion, here Erval was, plunged down into a fallout shelter with a reporter who reflected his image back to him, making it pretty clear that Joe Pepper and the rest of the world were not the least bit impressed. Did Pepper think five minutes of flattery could make Erval forget it? Did Pepper, standing here picking through the first-aid kit Erval had just opened, think he could bury his scorn under all the looky-here curiosity that bubbled out of him as he held up the pills and packets?

"Check out this stuff!" said the reporter. "Your garden-variety aspirin. And a little sulfadiazine. A little pheno-barbital."

"Whatever for?" said Latham, digging further. "Oh, of course. Another instruction sheet. Let's see, pheno … pheno …" He ran his finger down the paper. "Here it is: 'Administer in case of emotional difficulties.'"

"Sounds like it was for the people goin' nuts down here," said Pepper.

And, of course, Erval was the bad guy in all this. *Hey, now, take it easy, Erval,* Latham was always saying.

Well, you try defending a story about angels and visions in groves! Try it for years and years! Sticking up for these things did something to a man, to an entire people. It bred a pugnacity deep into the bloodline. Like a lion with a sore paw, you snarled at the gentlest prodding.

Neither was God helping him out especially, letting people write complaints in diaries, complaints that reporters found centuries later, and used to paint a picture that made sensible folks pretend not to be home when their Mormon neighbors dropped by with a plate of cookies.

No, wait. That's what the neighbors had been doing all along anyway. But this just gave them better reasons to keep doing it.

Erval watched Pepper, snooping his way through the shelter, staring at a framed sign on the wall. "Here's the instructions for the shelter manager. That would be you now, wouldn't it?"

Erval shook his head. Boy, but the *Tidewater Gazette* sure sent its best.

Pepper jotted a few more notes. "'Register all shelter occupants on arrival,'" he read. "'Complete the staffing pattern.' So you've got to assign people to do, let's see, 'Feeding, Water. Sanitation. Inventory of shelterees' items. Sleeping arrangements.' Wow. Did you know all this?"

Erval put down his box cutter and straightened up. "What are you gettin' at, Mr. Pepper? Are you sayin' that I don't know my job?"

"Oh, no, no, just …"

"Do ya wanna go up on that ladder and interview Bernie there? See what he writes about me in his diary?"

"Hey, I …"

"Whoa!" said Latham. "Holllld on, everybody. Hold on, here," he took Erval's arm and dragged him outside the shelter room.

"What are you trying to do, Erv?" he whispered fiercely.

"I am trying not to clock the man," Erval whispered back.

"Oh, sure! Go ahead! And *really* give him something to write about! Now why don't you take yourself a deep breath and remember that the man in there is one great big microphone. What do you want him to broadcast next? 'Mormons are an extremely touchy people, prone to blow-ups'?"

"You haven't seen me blow up yet!" Erval growled.

"Yea and verily, Erval," Latham pointed his finger right at Erval's chin dimple, "I tell you that if you do not watch your words and your deeds, you shall screw us all over bigtime …"

"Oh yea and verily, buddy, we hath a cunning one in our midst and if I so much as wipeth my nose on my sleeve, he writeth that we are a desperate people that can't even afford hankies."

Latham cocked his head. "Oooh, somebody's goin' nuts in the fallout shelter today."

"I was provoked!" said Erval.

"Yeah, well…" Latham sucked in air through his teeth. "Your best bet now is to be as boring as possible." He straightened Erval's collar. "I know you can do it, buddy. Now get in there."

Erval got. But halfway through the door, he stopped and blinked. *What does he mean, "I know you can do it"?*

* * *

Pepper didn't know what this Mr. Latham Runyon said to Erval Feldsted out there. But now Feldsted walked in looking as if he thought somebody had hidden his flashlight while he was out.

Pretty soon, though, Feldsted whistled and caught the boxes Bernie pitched down to him. He jumped to pick up Pepper's dropped pencil. When Bernie's ladder slipped a couple inches, Feldsted was the first to steady it.

"You OK there, Bernie?" he chirped.

You see, Pepper, I'm not really a hothead, oh no.

Now he trumpeted a tune as he poised a knife blade over the box of crackers. "Bum-ba-ba-ba-bum!" He punctured. He sliced. He lifted the flaps and dug through the packaging until he pulled out …

A cracker. Finally.

It looked like any off-brand cracker—paler and thinner than the good stuff. He held it out to Pepper. "Go ahead. Report on this."

"Hey, wait a minute," said Latham Runyon. "You've been playing captain of this expedition. You go first."

Feldsted paused. Which Pepper thought was a good idea. That little cracker could be as deadly as strychnine, or as harmless as moldy cheese. But who knew which?

Feldsted bit off a corner and mulled it around. He licked the salt off his lips. "I don't see what the Civil Defense people are so excited about," he said. "All crushed up in a bowl of soup, one cracker's as good as another." He turned and studied the wall of boxes.

"Say, Erval," said Mr. Runyon, "you aren't considering taking some of those crackers home, are you?"

"Can he do that?" said Pepper.

"Erval here's got ten kids," Runyon said. "He's got a lot of tricks up his sleeves for keeping them all fed."

Feldsted glared at Runyon. *Give the man some color details, will ya?*

Runyon put up his hands in surrender.

"All right then," said Feldsted. "We're expected out at Mentzer & Sons this afternoon. Big pork operation. Here, Latham, you carry a sample box for them."

And, with that, he ushered them all out of the mineshaft of the Cold War and turned out the lights.

* * *

Pepper settled himself in the front seat of Feldsted's Rambler. A late afternoon sun did its best to shine around some clouds so fluffy that they looked fake. As Erval maneuvered the car between the fenders and taillights on the boulevard, Pepper watched a couple late schoolbuses, empty, heading back to the garage.

All the crows in town sat together on the letters of the giant A&P sign and, if there wasn't room there, they perched on the powerlines. The Golden Arches loomed ahead in a field of neon signs.

Pepper needed something stimulating about this time of day. He looked at Runyon in the back seat. "Buy you guys a cup of coffee?"

"No, thank y ...!" Feldsted began.

Runyon quickly sat forward and slapped Feldsted genially on the shoulders. "Erval here would probably like a milkshake," he said. "Wouldn't you, Erval?"

As they pulled through the drive-through, Pepper couldn't shake the feeling that he'd said something wrong. That whole shoulder-pat thing felt like someone saying, *Down, boy.*

Pepper watched Feldsted over in the driver's seat, sucking on his straw. In spite of his hot streak, the guy had an innocence that Pepper didn't quite know how to classify.

No, wait, Pepper had seen something like it at that picnic up in Brandywine.

Back when he had hatched his story idea and made his phone calls, Pepper and his photographer had pulled into a white-lined parking space at the Brandywine church. They walked into the Mormon picnic just as a horde of men unloaded folding tables and chairs from the back of a pickup.

Pepper saw right away that they were an extremely cooperative people. His eye had fallen on a tall, pale man, his hair combed straight back, his face, for all Pepper could tell, incapable of anything but an eager smile. The man looked the part of a mortgage-paying, pencil-pushing commuter. And why not? Brandywine, two hours up the highway from Boxford, was a city of bankers, pill-makers and ship-builders. It was big enough place to run buses on the quarter-hour, to have suburbs.

This man threw a manic energy into erecting tables all over that parking lot. Later, he beelined toward Pepper and his photographer, Slick, offering them plastic cups of lemonade. Then, when a pioneer cart tipped, nearly spilling some supplies, Mr. Commuter rushed over and righted the cart. When the blankets and the flour and the "baby" were all set in place again, Mr. Commuter stood up straight with a look of satisfaction on his face. *I'm a good boy. I'm a helpful boy. I am!*

Pepper thought it might have been the presence of the photographer, but Slick was off shooting pictures of a sing-along. And besides, everywhere Pepper turned, he saw the same look: on the face of the woman that gathered up half the dirty paper plates at her table, on the man that fiddled with speaker buttons and dials until the feedback went away, on the man that played semaphore as the pickup backed into place again.

And he had seen it on Feldsted's face back at City Hall, wiping up the mayor's coffee spills. He had seen it in the shelter, when Feldsted steadied Bernie's ladder. You couldn't call this kissing up, could you, not when a guy did it for his inferiors?

Now Pepper watched Feldsted in the driver's seat as the lightpoles of Boxford gave way to the country mailboxes. Could Pepper imagine him speeding? Throwing that milkshake cup out onto the roadside? Is this what it was to be a believer? God was so real that Feldsted and all the others could feel him up there, watching. Was that it? *Daddy, did you see that? I kept the baby from falling onto the pavement. Did I do good? Daddy, do you like me?*

Pepper looked out at the passing boat dealers, at the brick ranch houses with squared-off shrubbery. Was there really somebody up there watching all the time? On earth, you could sue a guy like that, make him stop. But up there ... Pepper shivered.

"Hm. Have they changed these?" Feldsted said. He studied the cup in his hand.

"I don't know. Since when?" said Pepper.

Feldsted thought a minute.

"Erval doesn't eat out much, as you might guess," said Runyon.

"I suppose not," Pepper agreed. "With ten kids and all. Wow. Most people don't have near that many anymore. Do they complain much?"

Feldsted looked at him quizzically.

"You know, about not getting to eat out very often? Or not getting any attention? I suppose the teachers at school help out some, seeing as how they could be kind of disadvantaged."

"Disadvantaged?" said Feldsted. "Why, I can't count how many teachers tell me, 'We can always spot a Mormon kid. They raise their hands to answer questions. They're not afraid to stand up and give a

book report.' Just right out there in front, that's the way they are."
Feldsted looked over at Pepper with a triumphant look.

"Well, how about your wife?" said Pepper.

"Huh? Can teachers spot my wife?"

"No. I mean, how's she holding up? Does she get out much?"

"What in the world?! Of course she gets out. She's got Relief
Society once a week."

And when Pepper asked what that was, Feldsted launched into
quite the speech, something about Spiritual Living lessons and
Cultural Refinement lessons for the women. "Why, in an entire year
of Relief Society," said Feldsted as he pulled up to a country-corner
stoplight, "my wife gets the equivalent of college education!"

"Really? You mean she writes papers and all that?"

"Huh?" Feldsted looked in the rearview mirror at Runyon.
"Papers?"

"You know. Research papers," said Pepper.

"Whu ..." Feldsted frowned at Pepper. "What in the world are
you talking about?"

Runyon sat forward again. "Erval here only got a couple years of
college. He might have missed out on the whole papers thing."

Pepper studied the two men. The churches weren't his usual beat.
They belonged to the reporters clear across the newsroom from him,
reporters who whined about how one little sentence in their story
triggered a mountain of vicious, upset mail. Pepper was starting to
get it now. The picnic in Brandywine, the moment in the shelter
when Feldsted decided to whistle and be sunny and helpful—these
people were knocking themselves out to be on their best behavior. Was it for his benefit? Did they have a little meeting before he
showed up? *Be sure and tell the guy: Our children this! Our women
that! Our pioneers—oh what pioneers they were!*

What kind of sugared-up rocket fuel did it take to sustain this
chipper behavior? How hard would it be to get them to relax? And
where were the grumblers in this bunch, the back-row boys who

made fun of the cheer squad out front?

An announcement interrupted his thoughts. "Erval," said Runyon, "I'm smelling the pigs. We must be getting close."

There it was, up ahead, on the left, a little sign next to the mailbox, "Mentzer and Son."

Feldsted looked at the dashboard clock. "I spoke to Mrs. Mentzer on the phone. She said not to worry about the time too much. She said Herb's usually around."

He pulled into the drive. He passed the main house. Two men in corduroy jackets and mud-caked boots watched their approach. "All righty, then!" Feldsted cut off the motor. "Let's go feed some pigs."

They all got out of the car. Pepper inhaled, then regretted it.

The older farmer wore an enviable head of mostly white hair. His belly hung over his belt. He looked them over as if he'd really rather not deal with city dudes this afternoon. *I'm a busy man, chores to last me six ways to next February. So I hope you're not selling something dumb, like piped-in music.*

Erval explained his cracker problem, the man nodding, the son working at the snuff in his lip. "I brought a box of them in the trunk of my car," said Erval. "You can look them over."

The father sucked in a lungful of air and shook his head. "I'm sorry, we just couldn't. I mean, we got to protect their health, the leanness and all that. We took 'em to market, we wouldn't be paid as much per pound. Sorry," he shrugged.

Feldsted nodded, doing his best to look sporting about it.

The son offered to escort them back to the breeding house. They had sows in heat today. And Mentzer and Sons were the county's leaders in artificial insemination, he told them brightly. "We buy the high-quality stuff. From Germany."

Another day, maybe, said Feldsted, a brave smile still pasted to his face.

"Hot dog, Erval," said Runyon when they climbed back into the car. "You could write about high-quality stuff from Germany in your diary tonight. That is, if you had a diary." He winked at Pepper.

"Hmmp," said Feldsted weakly, staring straight ahead.

It was a quiet ride back to Boxford.

* * *

The next Sunday, the Feldsteds gathered for dinner at the Runyons' house. All together, they filled three tables.

After dinner, Ada Runyon sat at the wicker table in her piano studio, just a step down from the living room. Ada kept a stack of *National Geographics* on the table, to occupy her piano students as they waited their turn. One lay open to a story on New Zealand, left there by Erval's wife, Ruthalin. "This is one place I'd want to go," Ruthalin had said, just before slipping away to change her toddler's diaper.

Ada opened her trusty steno book. *Monday*, she wrote. *Return library books. Buy laundry soap, carrots ...* There was a third item. She clicked the pen in her hand. What was it now?

She could hear the television movie in the next room, *Fiddler on the Roof*, go to a commercial break. She had half-listened to the progress of the movie over the last hour. Motel danced through the forest with Tzeitel. Tevye shook hands with the butcher, then retired with him to the town tavern to celebrate the butcher's new betrothal. The men of Anatevka danced. The Russian soldiers intruded. And a tipsy Tevye staggered home through the streets of Anatevka, meeting the wily constable along the way.

"I'm sure," said Erval, as the next commercial praised Dial Soap, "that the Jewish people don't appreciate being portrayed as drunkards."

"What?" said Latham.

"I'll bet they don't like them showing one of their own drinking like that."

"I don't think," said Latham, "that they have anything against drinking ..."

"Well, sure they do."

"No, I haven't heard of …"

"I wonder if any of them wrote a letter to complain," said Erval.

"Why would they write a letter when they made the movie themselves?"

"Ohhhh, they did not."

"Of course they did. Gosh, Erval, look at the star. He's as Jewish as they come and …"

"Right! Hollywood Jewish! And we know how religious they are."

"Then look at the credits, Erv. You're going to see a long list of Jewish names."

Ruthalin returned to her chair. "Are they at it again?"

Ada rolled her eyes and nodded.

"I had a great idea this morning," said Ruthalin, picking up her magazine again.

"Mm-hmm?" Ada continued with her lists.

"I decided we ought to invite that reporter, Joe Pepper, to dinner."

Ada stopped her pen. She looked at Ruthalin. There was nothing Ada had heard about Mr. Pepper that would make her want to spend an hour eating with him. But why burst Ruthalin's bubble. If she wanted to do it …

"I think," Ruthalin went on, "that if he could see a real Mormon family, sitting around the table, doing what they do every day, then he could write more a little more accurately about us."

"But he's not doing a story on Mormons." Ada clicked her pen with her thumb. "He's writing about fallout shelters."

"Well, he should be writing about us. He messed it up the first time. And now he has a chance to make it right."

"I don't know why he would care," said Ada. "He's a busy man. He's already done that kind of story and now he's moved on."

"I think we could get him interested in doing another one."

Ada forgot all about her upcoming week. She could see the last thing she'd written—*Call Sis. Buckman*—but when she tried to think what came next, her mental film was broken and flapping wildly around the reel. Her thumb click-click-clicked on the pen. She saw Latham walk into the kitchen.

She followed him, catching up with him at the sink. "Lathaaaam," she whined softly, and she told him all.

"But he's not writing …" said Latham.

"That's what I said to her," Ada whispered. "And I just have this vision of Pepper walking into her family room, where the couch needs replacing and one end of the curtain flaps loose from the rod."

"Well, what can you expect, with ten kids?"

"Chaos and ruin, of course. And Erval and Ruthalin take it all in their stride. They're kind of proud that they can handle it, I think. Which doesn't mean that Pepper would see it that way."

She could hear Ruthalin in the living room now, making her case to Erval. "I just feel like he's been delivered into our hands," Ruthalin said.

"It almost sounds like they're plotting a murder," Latham whispered.

"The worst thing would be if Erval made his children sing for Mr. Pepper."

"No worry there. Children usually chicken out at command performances." Latham picked at the frosting bits from one of the cake pans they had just emptied. He stopped suddenly. "But Erval wouldn't chicken out."

"Oh, gosh no!" Oh, sure, that kind of thing was OK when it was just the Runyons and the Feldsteds together, because the Feldsteds were Latham and Ada's *dearest* friends. They were like fellow immigrants. Ada felt comfort in their company because when she blurted out words from the old country, words like "crik" and "cangyon" and "dripper pan," they knew what she was talking about. Yet Ada died inside because Feldsteds refused to cut words like these out of their vocabulary. They refused to blend in. Well, as much as any good Mormon *could* blend in.

"No," Ada said, thinking again of Erval singing. "This dinner idea must die."

They heard Erval in the other room. "I will not have that man in my house!"

Latham raised his eyebrows. "Sounds like it's dead."

They both exhaled and walked out of the kitchen.

But when Ada rejoined Ruthalin at the wicker table, when Ada picked up her notebook again, Ruthalin bubbled over with menu ideas.

Ada glanced over at the men and their TV movie, at the Jews in their scarves and coats, standing on a bleak and wintry plain. "But I thought Erval said no way."

"Oh," Ruthalin waved her hand, "that man can talk! I know, let's do a Dutch oven dinner. Give it that pioneer flavor."

"I think we've pioneered Mr. Pepper quite enough, thank you."

* * *

When the movie ended, Ada slipped into the living room, just as the guys stood up to stretch.

"See?" said Latham, as the movie credits rolled names like Stern and Bonstein and Goldwyn and Perl across the screen.

"Those are German names," said Erval. "What makes you think they're Jewish?"

"Erval, where've you been all your life? Do you mean to tell me that you've lived in Boxford all these years and you didn't know that Goldwyn is a Jewish name?"

"Well, I don't know about that and all, but I'll bet Mr. Goldwyn lays awake some nights, sorry that he didn't stand up and speak out about the drunk scene."

Latham slowly knocked his head against his palms. "Yea, and

verily, Erval, it grieveth me that I must speak unto thee thus, but not everybody thinketh as we do, Erv. Not everybody looketh out for insults and offenses …"

"Oh, yea and verily, my friend, I tell you this that ye may know that the spirit of erroneous storytelling is given to every moviemaker, that he may persuade all men that no good souls walk upon the earth, no not one, and he inviteth all men to join in the carousing, yea, and in the staggering home from the tavern, and he throweth up the stumbling block to the faithful among the Jews …"

Ruthalin stood beside Ada. "Again?"

"Let's have another piece of cake and not tell them," said Ada.

* * *

On this Saturday afternoon, Erval wanted no witnesses, just in case he got turned down a second time.

He dropped his twelve-year-old son off at his baseball game and then he drove far out into the country, where the roads had no shoulders or center lines, where they grew lumpy and uneven from bearing up under loaded farm trucks.

His second farmer was a young one, fresh out of ag school. Bushy-browed, flanked by a sad old St. Bernard, he swept his arm toward the back forty, describing his father's potato operation. He pointed to the long building across the road and explained his ambitions. For now, he ran a little custom butchering operation, a few summer pig roasts. But he was going to buy more equipment, "when I get things going a little more." Pretty soon, he'd have real walls instead of those black tarp curtains in that building over there, he said. "When I can afford it," he said.

This is a man who can't turn down free crackers, Erval assured himself. He threw in some pig-farmer talk, like "corn-to-pig ratio" and "farrowing crate" just to show the young farmer that he knew how it was.

They entered a shed near the house, the dog shuffling along behind. The young farmer showed Erval a bin filled with meal for his pigs. It was corn and roasted soybeans. He had ground it up himself. "I'm sorry," he told Erval, as he combed his hand through the sandy meal. "But I couldn't feed the pigs spoiled food."

* * *

"Spoiled food?!" Erval said to himself as he drove back down the lumpy road. "It's crackers! I ate one. I'm still alive."

He followed the roads back to town. He wished he could go home and bang tools in his garage. But he couldn't. He had to put in his appearance at Duane's game.

So he drove to the middle school.

He found a seat on the bleachers. As he sat in a cloud of his neighbors' tobacco smoke, barely aware of the smack of bats against balls down there on the field, or the smell of concession nachos down the row, a yawning pit of apprehension opened before him.

He was going to fail.

He had presented himself as the know-it-all about pigs. When all was said and done, he knew zilch. He was the town fool who labored away in the basement of the hospital. Boss of the shop crew, who knew so little that when he sent his men out in the hospital truck to pick up paint, they could stop at Bad Louie's for a game of pool and a couple cold pints while they were at it, 'cause he, the boss, was too weak and stupid to stop them.

He was going to fail.

Why hadn't he stayed back in Cardiff, where everybody knew him, where he had a place? It was *his* town back there, that village where he would walk up 2nd East just as Sister Torgerson stepped out her door and she'd say, "Will we see you at the May Day Party? I can't wait to hear you sing!" It was the spot where, all dressed up in his best, he'd turn the corner across from the school, crossing paths with the little nine-year-old gang that played around there. And they would taunt him. "Going to see Velna?" they'd say. Then they'd giggle and make kissy-kissy sounds, which he always ignored.

Why hadn't he stayed where he could have taken his place among the men that gathered at Redd's Store, bought their sacks of nails, then hung around to talk about what the railroad was doing to wheat prices and whether it would rain next week. Or of how quickly old man Weatherly went after he got sick, and what day to bring Heber's bull over to Parley's cow.

Why did he have to be the Golden Boy of Cardiff, the one who took that big job over in Grand Junction, the one who never kissed Velna, but married the out-of-town girl instead? Everybody talked about him. He was Our Very Own Erval, The Boy Who Made Good.

Yet what had Grand Junction done for him but lead him further off course? He remembered the little kitchen there, where he had opened up the newspaper and spotted the ad for the job in Boxford. Yep, there at the little Formica table, Ruthalin unfolded the map Erval had bought at the service station. She squinted at the eastern edge of the country until she found where this Boxford was.

Then, surrounded by their five squirmy little children, they asked each other, "Well, what do you think?"

Erval thought the money was good. Ruthalin thought it sounded like an adventure. They both thought, "Two years. Maybe three. Then we come home."

And now, here he was, sitting in the stands at the seventh-grade game, on the verge of looking like a twit.

Royal generation, indeed!

Good neighbor!

If he had wanted the comfort of his own small, native burg, he should have refused to be their Golden Boy.

But destiny had never let him slink into the background.

Oh, but he was such a long way from Cardiff now, plunked

down fifteen years in a strange town where he still couldn't remember not to talk about the miraculous healing of Aunt Mary's leg, or what his grandpa Gustafson might be doing in heaven right now. He still couldn't get used to the fact that people boated on Sundays here. Without trying to hide it.

He was such a long way from all that royal-generation talk. If there was anything to it at all, then he was exiled royalty, stuck in a strange land until some regime change called him forward and turned him loose.

Meanwhile, where might such a prince throw his energies, his ideas?

What would happen if he offered this world his good old farm-boy know-how?

Failure and disgrace, that's what.

Thank goodness he was a long way from Cardiff now, where they could not see that their Golden Boy had risen to the level of his incompetence.

* * *

At the final out of the afternoon game, Erval paced the borders of the field, waiting for his son to emerge from the crowd of jerseys. When Duane appeared, carrying his mitt and a well-worn gym bag, Erval jingled his car keys in his pocket and started across the sandy parking lot. He passed the moms and dads calling to other cars—"Are you stopping at McDonald's?"—and bore down on his Rambler, parked somewhere over by the pine trees.

"Dad! Wait up!"

Erval looked back. Duane knelt in the sand, stuffing a sock and a bunch of trading cards into the bag. "What's the problem?" he said.

"I told you, I need a new bag. The thin spot is worn all the way through now."

Erval started toward his son. "Just put it all together and hold it like …"

But beyond Duane's crouched body, clear over by the concession booth, Erval saw a spade-shaped beard on a man who collared the back of his son's neck, making a perfect picture of father-son bonding as they strode toward the parking lot.

Erval knew only one man who had a beard like that: Robert Barco, the blowhard of the Crayton Poultry Plant.

His breathing quickened. He looked down at his son. "Will you quit kneeling there and staring at the hole?" he said. "Get up! We got things to do!"

Erval turned for the car again. He walked faster.

"Dad!"

Erval spun around. He saw two cards blowing out of Duane's reach. They flew toward the rear fenders of the next row. "Forget the cards, will ya?" He walked back to his son, his boots pounding. He bent and stuffed and jerked and snapped, "Get on with it! The whole afternoon's lost!" He expected the shadow of Barco to fall over him in 10, 9, 8 … He whispered in a way that threatened, *Listen up, boy, and listen good!* "Do you think I got time to pick up every little thing?" he said.

Gripping the bag against his own chest, he stood and collared Duane, escaping, escaping, not daring to look anymore at the whimpering, stunned boy beside him. Really, when you weighed some twelve-year-old's childish troubles against a father's daily, real-life pressures, who had the right to push who around today?

Erval let go of the boy and squeezed himself between an Impala and a Volkswagen—mirrors too close. He stomped onward, looking back every now and then with a commanding jerk of his head toward the Rambler.

In the car, he gripped the steering wheel, took a deep breath and started the motor.

He kept to the back rows of the lot as he crept along, the motor idling low. Safe behind the glass and metal of his car, he summoned enough manners to nod with passable good will at other fathers that passed his window, until he ended up in a queue of brake lights, with nothing to do but listen to Duane sniffle over the lost cards.

"Oh, stop that, now. We'll get you some more. After all," he grinned, "what's a paper route for?"

"It won't be those cards. They were a Ryan and a Garvey!"

Erval watched his son wipe his eyes and nose and stare out the passenger window. Erval had only the vaguest idea of the Ryans and the Garveys of this world. He let the car creep along, turning back to the dusty bumper before him, pressing the brakes, waiting, looking at open trunks and fathers and sons until one of the fathers stood up straight, slammed the trunk shut and turned around to where Erval could see his spade-shaped beard.

Barco cocked his head in recognition. He walked toward Erval's car.

Erval could not have felt more caught if had it been a state trooper swaggering up to his window. He rolled down the glass, hating the compulsion he felt to do it.

Barco planted his hands on the window frame and peered in. "Any luck yet with your pig farmers?"

"We're working on it," Erval said, putting his on brave and cheerful and trustworthy face.

"I see." A corner of Barco's mouth turned up ever so slightly. "Well. You remember that guy, Joe Pepper? He's been calling me up, wanting to ask questions about my shelter."

Erval rolled up his window slowly as Barco walked away.

Apparently, the press was no longer speaking to the Golden Boy of Cardiff.

III

Latham was halfway through his turkey-and-swiss sandwich when his office phone rang.

It was Ada. From her tone of voice, he could tell he wasn't going to get far through his notes on the McHenry Family Papers.

"Erval has decided that he wants Pepper to come to dinner after all!" she said.

"I thought he shot that particular squirrel out of the nut tree."

"Well, he only stunned it. It didn't die!"

"What made him change his mind?" Latham picked at a loose piece of crust.

"Ruthalin doesn't know. She was about to drop off to sleep last night when he said, 'You know, Ruthalin, I've been thinking …'"

Latham calmed her down, hung up and finished his sandwich.

When he pulled into his driveway that night, brushing past the last piano student scurrying out the studio door, he found his wife in the kitchen, brushing a sauce over some chicken.

"She's asking my advice!" Ada cried. "She wants to know, 'Should I fix the Chinese noodle casserole? Or would the Can-Can Chicken be better?' My advice is to drop the idea altogether, but she doesn't seem to hear that. Even if it was a good idea …"

"What would make it a good idea?"

"If Pepper really were writing about us." She wiped her hands on a paper towel. "Even then, he would get this impossibly homey impression. When Ruthalin thinks 'cooking for company,' she goes after it like feeding the threshing crew or something. I mean," she opened the oven door, pulling at the rack, "there'll be plenty to eat, but it's sort of a big pot of something plus some hunks of bread to soak it up."

"What's wrong with that?"

She stared at him hard. "Latham, are you really that clueless? Would you want me to invite the Dean of Liberal Arts over and feed him beans and cornbread?"

"You wouldn't do that Ada. You'd fix something difficult and Frenchified."

"That's right. I would."

"Then maybe you should offer to have the dinner at our house."

"No!" She tossed the basting brush into the sink. "There shouldn't be any dinner, because Mr. Pepper is not interested in us. Not the Feldsteds, not the Runyons, not the Mormons. Not any of us."

The tangy scent of the leftover sauce pricked at his nostrils.

* * *

The next day, Latham exited the Shoreline State Bank, slipping his receipt into his shirt pocket. He tucked his copy of *American Historical Review* under his arm. It was fresh off the presses, with his own chapter printed inside.

He felt like treating himself to lunch today.

He passed the downtown lawyers, their ties flying in the breeze. He ducked into the City Deli and studied the menu board. The Monte Cristo sandwich sounded good.

He ordered.

Settling into the corner table, he pulled the *Review* out from under his arm and began thumbing through the pages. He ran his finger down the Table of Contents. Ah, yes, there it was, "Power Elites in Piedmont Virginia, 1911-1929" by G. Latham Runyon.

Latham turned to the page and examined his work, printed to margined perfection. Well, let's just see about that. He scanned the all-too-familiar sentences, faintly aware of the deli door's openings and closings, of the dickering between sandwich-maker and customer.

"The usual?"

"Yep. All three. In fact, let's do box lunches today."

The second voice sounded familiar. Latham looked up from his book. There stood Pepper, draping himself over the glass that covered the hunks of cold cuts.

"Which one do you want? We got the mini, the midi, the maxi ..."

"Oh yeah, when did Gino do that?" said Pepper.

"Lady lawyers complaining. 'That's too much potato salad. I don't want to pay for a cookie I can't eat.'"

"Well, which box comes with the cookie?"

Latham debated with himself: Say hello? Pretend he didn't see Pepper? He went back to his book. A peaceful lunch was part of the treat today.

Just as he spotted a page break error in his article—how had he missed that in the proofs?—the sandwich man called his number. He got up.

"Oh. Hello, Mr. Pepper," Latham said, reaching for his plate.

"Runyon! How's your friend? Any pigs yet?"

"Still out there bothering the farmers, as far as I know." Latham returned to his table.

Pepper, the three boxes stacked all the way up to his chin, walked over to Runyon. "Well, he is a pretty determined fellow."

"You don't happen to know any pig farmers, do you?"

Pepper shook his head. "A guy has to shoot somebody or move three hundred jobs outside the county to get on my radar. I'm kind of like the school principal, you know. I don't know the names of the well-behaved ones."

Latham nodded. "I hear they invited you to dinner."

Pepper raised his eyebrows. "Oh, yeah." He sat down across from Latham. "They invited me all right. For next Tuesday."

"You know, you don't have to go. They might have misunderstood what you're trying to accomplish, following Erval around from shelter to pig farm and what-not."

"Oh, no, no! I was flattered. Feldsted, he's sort of a God-and-country, square-the-corners specimen. It'd be fascinating someday to take a year off and find all the Cardiffs out there and what makes these people tick. The Mormons, even. They're kind of shrouded in mystery, an intriguing people."

"Thank you, I guess." Latham smoothed a napkin into the book, to hold his place.

"I mean, they have this fantastical founding story. It'd be a real trip to ask questions of a people who could fall for a story like that. You know, see what attracts them to it."

Latham sat there, ready to be asked.

"I suppose I'd find the whole spectrum, people still in the thrall of it, and others who are starting to see through the whole thing. Yourself, for instance. You're a man with a trained mind. I'm sure you can size it up for what it is. I don't know, maybe you go along with it to keep peace in the family or something. You've got a mess of loyalties there."

Latham ground his jaw. He glanced at his cooling Monte Cristo sandwich, traced his fingers over the bindings of the *American Historical Review*.

Pepper watched him, his chin barely above the top box.

"No, I go along because I believe it," said Latham.

Pepper still watched him, as if waiting for the punch line.

Latham smiled a tight smile and reached for his plate.

"Well," Pepper gripped the boxes. "Deadlines, you know."

Latham nodded.

He heard the squeak of the door from Pepper's leaving. He rubbed his fingers together, greasy from the sandwich, then wiped them on his napkin.

* * *

The Feldsteds took up an entire row in the center section of the chapel. Evidently, Erval's son Marc did not think his share of the space was adequate. He moved into the row ahead. Now that he was eighteen, Marc was full of moves like that.

Erval fumed. Erval stared him down. Erval leaned forward to catch Marc's eye. None of it worked and Erval found no relief until he became caught up in the story from the pulpit:

"We couldn't find the car keys. And my husband had to go to work. And we had already said two prayers, asking for help to find them. We had looked everywhere. We just didn't know what to do. And Calvin said, 'Why don't we pray again.' And I'll admit I was getting a little tired of trying that. But I did and when we finished, I felt an overwhelming urge to make a sandwich.

"And when I opened the mustard, there the keys were. I guess Calvin Jr. had been playing with them ..."

Five minutes later, another story. "The doctor came in after the operation and he told us that he had never seen a tumor shrink like that. He just can't explain it. But I know why."

Five minutes later, another story. The Farrows were pregnant. Finally!

* * *

At the Feldsteds' house that night, Ruthalin mentioned the Farrows as she dished out bowls of ice cream. "They seem overjoyed," she said.

"They seem to want us to know every detail," said Latham, handing the Nestle's Quik over to Erval.

"We certainly didn't need to hear about thermometer readings," said Ada. "And the word 'trying,' in mixed company, has always made me squirm."

Erval masked his ice cream thoroughly with chocolate powder and followed Latham into the front room. He mixed the contents of his bowl, hunting down the hidden white stripes that hadn't yet soaked up the chocolate.

"I think you've beaten it into submission now," said Latham.

Erval stirred some more.

"You're talking my ear off, Erval. I'm going to need an Anacin in a minute, if you don't shut up. Eh? *Eh??*"

Erval took his first bite, the softened ice cream trailing off his spoon. "Everybody gets their little miracle today," he said.

"Not me. Did you hear me get up there and tell a story today? Nope, I'm fresh out at the moment. No cured cancer, no bun in the oven, although if I got up and said so, you'd see the miracle of old Brother Bivins coming back to life."

"Oh, don't make fun."

"OK." Latham took a bite of ice cream. "But someone should make that man move from his seat against to the wall. He gets way too comfy over there."

Erval stared at the floor, stirring absently.

Latham passed his hand in front of Erval's blank stare. "Earth to Erval. Come in, please."

Erval looked up. "Why can't I get any help? I thought we were the chosen people, entitled to some success. It's not as if I'm up to any mischief here. I'm just trying to help out."

"I see. Well, you might have handed God a pretty tall order. Lost keys are easy for Him. Finding willing pig farmers? And you know His rule about not forcing anybody's will."

"Oh, I think if He could stick Daniel among a bunch of lions, who played with them like they was little bunny rabbits," Erval ate another mounded spoonful, "or help him impress the king with his little eating contest...."

"If that's what you want, then you're going to have to change your diet, Erval," Latham said.

Erval dug in his bowl again. "I don't know why this has to be so hard."

"Hey, if you fail, I think the mayor will forgive you."

"And he will think ever afterward, 'Those Mormons, they don't know what they're talking about."

"Waaaait a minute. Where does that come in?"

"I gave him my word. I told him I'd take care of the problem."

"To prove what? 'The Mormon guy found a place to dump the crackers. Therefore, the church is true'?"

"Well," said Erval, "what's so bad about that?"

"I just don't think that's a very good game to play, that's all. I mean, you should listen to yourself, bragging to Joe Pepper. 'My kids are brighter than stadium lights!' then you sit there grinning. You never say the next part, but it sits there like a cue card all the same. 'Therefore the church is true. My wife, she's no poor subjugated slave. Therefore the church is true.'"

"Yeah, well things are what they are."

"And it cuts both ways. Sometimes our kids are stupid and our women look worse than birds with some kind of feather disease. What are people to think of Mormondom then?" Latham scraped up the last of his ice cream. "Come on, you know there's only one reason this church is true. A boy in a grove saw a light, and two personages standing in the air."

"You can't say that to people! It shuts down the conversation. Shuts it down cold. It makes them mad. It makes them say, 'Why does God talk to you and not us? What are we, His red-headed stepchildren?'"

Latham set his bowl on the side table. "Things are what they are."

They heard their wives' laughter from the kitchen. Somebody turned on some water, making the pipes groan and shudder. Three boys raced through living room and got all the way to the other side without Erval hollering, *Slow down! We walk in the house!*

Nope. Erval just sat on his own couch, limp as a tossed afghan. "Then I can't wait for the Millennium," he said. "Jesus will show up and tell them, 'They were right all along. They were telling the truth.'"

"Yeah, well I'm afraid Brigham has some bad news for you. He said there would be people of all faiths there and, as long as they confessed the Christ, they could go on their way and nobody would bother them."

Erval looked so beat Latham wasn't sure he would make it up the stairs to his own bed tonight. He looked at up his friend. "When's He gonna tell 'em that it's us?"

The two men sat, staring, as if a campfire crackled before them. Their weekend was closing down fast. Then it was back to agendas and rush and toil, and no time to think. But sometimes thinking wore a man out worst of all.

Latham sighed heavily. "He tryeth a man's patience."

"Yea."

"And verily."

* * *

It was the sort of Monday when nothing went right for Erval. His hair tuft wouldn't lie down. The leads in his mechanical pencil kept breaking. The chicken in his chicken and noodles had been dark meat, with bloody flecks. And now, as he left the hospital for a quick lunch-hour errand, a bug splat in the middle of his windshield marred his view.

He turned north on the boulevard. He needed more grout for the tub in the kid's bathroom.

In the True Hardware's parking lot, he shut off the car. He hurried past a clerk in a hardware apron and a man in overalls, heaving plywood into a pickup. He walked through the door, ignoring plastic tubing and door hinges and safety goggles, things he would normally stop to examine.

At the checkout, he waited, nervously glancing at his watch, while the clerk called back a price check.

He paid, and burst out into the warming air again as he tucked his wallet into his back pocket. He opened the Rambler door, crushing his sack by the neck as he bent himself into the driver's seat.

Approaching the lip of the boulevard, he sat, listening to the rhythm of his right blinker light. He could be here awhile, since the truck in front of him—the guy with the overalls and the plywood, in fact—waited for a break in the traffic. The driver stuck his arm straight out the window. Erval wondered if, the last time this Gramps came into town, the boulevard had still been a small town two-lane with only an occasional jalopy going by. Today it was a whizzing, noisy, clogged strip that nobody with any smarts tried to turn left onto. *Come on, come on, Gramps! Why doncha go down to the light?* Erval thumped his knuckles on his steering wheel and stared at the letters—F O R D—on the old guy's tailgate.

He saw movement in the truck bed. He sat up, trying to see over the tailgate. Cages. Hmm, the plywood must have hidden them back there in the parking lot. Was that a pig's ear, just under the grid of wire? It moved again.

Erval switched his blinker from right turn to left. The traffic opened up a little. Gramps put-putted across the center line and drove north. Erval waited for a Pepsi truck and a steering-wheel-gripping housewife, then pulled out into the northbound lanes. He dodged and weaved and sped under yellow lights going red, always keeping his eye on that tailgate up ahead. He followed until the neon and asphalt of town changed to flat fields.

The little parade turned, with Erval following the truck into trees tall enough to be called timber. The guy finally turned into a dirt clearing.

Gripped by a wave of timidity, Erval slowed to a roll. He looked at the little brown house, at the trailer, at the sheds that dotted the little homestead. He swallowed the timidity and pulled in.

The man walked away from his truck with the stiff amble of someone sore from lifting feed bags his whole life long, but someone who couldn't stop doing it because it was such a habit. A crescent moon of second chin hung from his face. He watched Erval's approach with a mix of friendly wariness.

"I'm looking for a man with some hungry pigs." Erval introduced himself.

"Any man with pigs got hungry ones, I s'pose."

He said his name was Corky Ferran. "We been here six generations," he said, nodding toward his rotting fence posts, his wife's flowering shrubs, his shed full of old wagon wheels, galvanized tubs and baler twine.

Erval lent him a hand with the tailgate of the truck, and the plywood, yammering on about fallout shelters.

"I don't worry too much about them things," said Corky. He climbed into the truck cab, turned over the engine and backed up against his pig pens.

"But we got all these leftover crackers, see?" said Erval, standing aside as Corky opened the cage and guided his pigs down a plank and into the muck of the pen. "I'm thinking any farmer could use a little free feed," he said as he followed Corky into the shed, where Corky tended to a couple upturned quarts of oil, draining their last drops into a jug. "Makes the ledger come out looking a little better," said Erval, although he suspected Corky's accounting system might be as simple as scooping up whatever was in his pockets.

Corky set the empty quarts upright, scratched the back of his neck and looked out toward the clothesline where Mrs. Corky had hung his work shirts.

"Wellll, I wouldn't mind taking some off your hands. It's crackers, you say?"

Erval was so happy that he shook the man's hand hard enough to make Corky's second chin waggle. And then, after a promise to return soon, Erval drove away.

He beat a drum roll on his steering wheel. He sang a fanfare— Bum-pa-ba-ba-ba bum!—which filled the small cab of the car. He drove past forest and fence post, waving his arms to the beat of the imaginary brass band that accompanied him.

Back at the hospital, the crew stared as he strode through the shop to his office, humming and bah-pa-pum-pa-pumming.

"The boss have a nip at lunch today?"

"He can't do that."

"Well, the man is high on *something*."

* * *

The secret to a successful dinner party was a gal like Ruthalin, yes it was.

Erval was proud of her. He looked halfway down the long picnic-style table to where Joe Pepper sat between Erval's teenage sons. "Eat up, there's plenty," he told Pepper.

Now if he could just get Ruthalin to sit down and enjoy herself. She and Ada kept fussing over all that woman stuff. "I'm getting the plastic cups," Ruthalin told Ada. "I'm sure you didn't bring your goblets here to watch half of them get broken." And she returned from the kitchen with a small stack of faded tumblers, passing them out to the littlest kids.

Erval was just a little proud of himself, too. He was sure he had impressed Pepper, yes he had, as he led him around on a pre-dinner tour of the house. "Built it myself," Erval had told him. "A whole year and a half of coming out here every night after work, measuring and cutting and hammering."

"It's a monument to sweat equity," said Latham, backing up Erval's story.

"Amazing. Absolutely astounding," Pepper said as he examined the ceilings and the entryways.

Erval liked hearing that kind of thing. He liked it very much. But he had just nodded humbly. *Aww, it's nothin', not for the Golden Boy of Cardiff.* Then he had hurried Pepper into the laundry room to show off the shelves he had built there for his wife.

"Look at that," said Pepper.

And Erval had heard, in Pepper's tone, *heroic!*

Pepper had looked at Erval's hands. "And after all that sawing, you still have all your fingers!"

All the praise made Erval even jollier. When he sat down to dinner, his stories grew longer and more effusive. He answered every one of Pepper's questions as if he really knew what he was talking about. It worked, right up until the time he claimed that his Mormon forbears had invented the irrigation that transformed the desert West from a deathtrap to a garden spot. (Sort of. Depends on where you look.)

Joe Pepper looked at Latham and said, "I thought that was invented in Mesopotamia."

"It was," said Latham. "The Egyptians, the Chinese, they were all irrigators."

Erval blinked. Why would they tell him such things? Nobody back in Cardiff had said anything about the Mesopotamians, no they hadn't! "Well," he recovered himself, "maybe so. Maybe they rigged up something primitive."

"Oh, no. These were pretty sophisticated systems," said Latham.

And Joe Pepper nodded.

Erval frowned. Really? But Sister Swenson, the history buff back in Cardiff, always said … Oh, bother! You know, men who made their living dispensing information could be pretty annoying. When were they going to get their noses out of the history books and notice what the Saints had done? All the history book writers had ignored that one, yes they had.

But never mind. Ruthalin saved the moment, offering seconds on the Chinese noodles.

* * *

Pepper dug through the noodles on his plate, searching for the chicken somewhere in the middle of it all.

He had worried that dining in a house full of children would feel a little like a Third World bus ride, sharing seats with chickens and goats. Actually, it turned out no worse than Camp Wee-Wa-Hi-Ya, where Pepper once spent three of his young summers. Yeah, a lot like camp, only better supervision at the tables. And nicer plates and glasses, courtesy of Runyon's wife.

Pepper thought he had about figured out what it was between the Feldsteds and the Runyons. They had a country mouse/city mouse thing going between them. On top of that, Latham Runyon acted like weight in the hem of a curtain, something to keep Erval Feldsted from billowing all over the place.

In any case, Erval's wife sat down again—she'd spent the whole dinner getting up and down—and looked at him. "Now, you were saying? About that fellow who owned half the downtown buildings in Brandywine?"

"Oh, yeah," said Pepper. "So Hyde—that was his name—Hyde had his eye on this piece of waterfront. And the problem with that was that ..." Pepper'd entertained them all evening with his stories. After all, having rubbed shoulders with thieves and arsonists, having interviewed tycoons and champions, senators (minor ones) and wannabes, he had a lot of stories to tell. "Anyway, so Hyde wanted this piece of waterfront and a guy named Giardina from up in Philly had plans for it and the word was that it could be unhealthy to want something that Giardina wanted. But Hyde decides to invite him to a card game and ..." Pepper looked around the table. Many, many faces of children. Little ones with milk mustaches, big ones with downy starter mustaches. "Uh, maybe I'd better tell a different story."

He switched to his story about the Egyptian diplomat.

"So anyway, this diplomat, Mr. Hassan, had been missing for three days. And reports were starting to come in from down in Accomack County about this shiny black Lincoln with diplomatic plates, parked in a ..."

Pepper looked at the baby. Newly freed from the high chair, she had been making eyes at Pepper all evening. Now she toddled his way. She had eaten with her hands and it showed. The kid moved pretty fast, actually. Pepper looked at the goo down the front of her shirt, and stuck between her fingers, and his breath came short and his palms—he wiped them on his pants—and leaned away from the oncoming baby, bumping into the boy next to him. "Oh. Excuse me," said Pepper.

Then somebody with a wet rag snatched the baby away.

Oh! There is a God!

Then Mrs. Runyon set little plates of something quivering and yellow, from its crumb crust to its creamy top, in front of each diner. Pepper breathed in the scent of lemon.

"Anyway," he continued, "Mr. Hassan had actually been up in Canada all that time. But his teenaged son …"

Mrs. Feldsted, down at the other end of the table, smiled and nodded and took a bite of her dessert.

"So did the son go to jail?" asked the boy next to Pepper. By the time Pepper answered him and looked back at Mrs. Feldsted, he saw her leaning over to Mrs. Runyon and he thought he heard her whisper, "…don't know many non-Mormons. They can be fascinating!"

* * *

Latham listened to the diplomat story. He relaxed. He and Ada had argued all week about Erval and Ruthalin and Joe Pepper. But maybe all you had to do was break bread with a man to understand him. Maybe it was possible to be friends without The Thing standing there in the way. You know, the Thing about religion, and "fantastical founding stories." It could elbow itself in there and make a man like Pepper think, *There's really nothing offensive about you except that you believe this Thing, for which I will always doubt your intelligence.*

Well, there was that crack back in Erval's garage. "I don't suppose I'm gonna get served any alcohol today, am I?"

Erval had only smiled.

"Ruthalin can whip up a mean powdered milk," Latham had

told Pepper. "For you, maybe that counts as an exotic drink."

Yes, Latham really could relax now, gently poking at the last crumbs of his dessert as the room rested in a small lull of silence, a lull that felt like goodwill glowing all around.

"Well!" said Erval, rubbing his hands together. "How about a little singing?"

The teenaged children's eyes widened.

Beside him, Ada began to cough. Her eyes watered. Maybe it was just the lemon in the dessert. If that stuff went down the wrong pipe, ay-yii!

"Heidi, what can you sing for Mr. Pepper?" Erval asked. "Huh? Are you my big girl? Can you help Daddy if he sings? Huh? Come on, help Daddy. 'The wheels on the bus go round and round.'" Erval churned his arms like locomotive cranks.

Heidi, three years old, lightly freckled, silky-haired, perfect little row of baby teeth, caught the spirit of things, cranking her arms too. "Round and round, round and round," Heidi and Erval sang together.

Latham looked over at Ada. No, she wasn't crying from the lemon. She was crying for real.

Latham tried to catch Erval's eye, but Erval pulled Heidi onto his lap, bounced her on his knee. "'The people on the bus go up and down." Erval rose from his chair and plopped back down. "Up and down … All through the town." *See? Dinner with the Feldsteds includes wholesome sing-alongs, cute children. Therefore …*

Ruthalin smiled, bouncing up and down halfheartedly in her chair.

Latham saw his daughters slip out of the room with Erval's teenagers.

And the look on Pepper's face as he looked from one end of the room to the other? *Like hell I'm gonna sing, "The horn on the bus goes … "*

* * *

Erval bounced his young daughter. And somewhere between the verse where the wipers on the bus go swish and the one where the signals on the bus go blink, Erval's wiring tripped. His circuits sparked. He thought, *Wait a minute! What am I doing with Joe Pepper in my house? Making friends with Them has never worked before. All it ever did was hurt! All those remarks about my virility—*

"*Wow, ten kids?!*"

"*You know what causes that, don't you?*"

—about wives—

"*Where do you hide the extra ones?*

--I'm tired of 'em! I'd rather be by myself, hammering things in my garage.

But—

Erval had a duty. His duty was to Share the Message.

Well, that was something different, then. Duty didn't care if you'd been burned seventy times seven. Duty demanded that he open himself up and warn his neighbor.

Even so, he began to sweat. And shake.

Maybe it's my conscience telling me: Erval, my boy, this isn't the time or the place.

Oh, no, no. No self-respecting, on-the-job conscience would ever say that.

He sweat more.

There's no terrible feeling here except my wilting courage. I'm a worthless, unprofitable servant! When Joe Pepper leaves my house, the chance will be gone—lost!—thanks to my spineless, faithless weakness.

He sang the last "All through the town!" and slipped Heidi off his knee. "I think it's time for a spiritual thought. Duane, bring me the book."

Erval saw Latham glaring at him.

Ho, ho! Latham has no courage either! Well, shame on him! "Duane, open up to Jacob, Chapter 12. Read that verse there," Erval pointed.

The boy read.

"Now, maybe we could have a song. How 'bout 'Servants of the King'?"

Across the room, Ada buried her face in Latham's shoulder.

Erval began:

Let us vow not to retreat as
we're marching to the field.
Let us flash the mighty sword
and wear the faithful shield!

* * *

Latham could not stop watching Pepper, who stared, open-mouthed, his interested, observant self battling with something far more elemental. Reporters in distant jungles probably looked like Pepper did right now:

Wow, I'm doing a story on cannibals!

Whoa—they're cannibals! Isn't there supposed to be a cauldron somewhere?

Hey! Why is the cauldron sitting right behind me?!

A few other voices sang along weakly, so weakly that if they had been in church right then, the chorister would have stopped them in the middle of the verse. "Brothers and sisters, are we all asleep today? Now, how are we supposed to sing this song? It tells us right here, in the upper corner, just under where it says '116 beats per minute.' See? 'With conviction.' Now, let me hear it.'"

But they weren't in church.

Oh well, Erval sang loudly enough all by himself to make the room echo painfully:

Scattering the foe we go and

as we march we sing,
We are servants of the King!

When the verse died away, Erval beamed triumphantly at Pepper.
Latham, his elbows resting on his knees, gripped his bowed head.
Glorious silence reigned except for some truck jake-braking out
on the bypass, beyond Erval's trees.

Latham looked up at Pepper again.

And the reporter let out a long, cleansing breath. Then he
pumped his fist into the air.

"Go team?" he said.

* * *

In the hospital parking lot, Slick got out of Pepper's car. "That's
your third cigarette since we left the office," said Slick. "I thought
you quit."

Pepper shrugged him off.

"No, really. When did this start up again?"

Pepper opened the trunk. "I don't know. Tuesday, maybe." He
pulled Slick's camera case free of where it had wedged between the
spare tire and a dirty parka. Then he led Slick to the door under the
shelter sign.

"When do we see the mayor?" Slick asked.

"He'll meet us out at the farm."

Down in the shelter, Erval and Bernie carried boxes up the steps.
Erval stopped to smile for Slick.

"No, just go on with what you're doing," said Slick. "That's what
we want pictures of. Can I go back in that room there? Wow, look at
this stuff."

Erval loaded boxes on a dolly and pushed them out into the sunshine, remembering his posture as Slick snapped away. Slick stopped
to jot things in a little notebook. Erval saw people looking down

through the second- and third-floor windows. A deliveryman at the kitchen docks squinted at them as he tapped his clipboard against his thigh.

"Could you turn this way, just a little?" said Slick as Erval loaded boxes onto the hospital truck.

When they were finally loaded, Erval glanced up at the people in the windows. He climbed into the truck. He put the key in the ignition. The truck roared to life. He nodded to Bernie, over in the passenger seat. He stuck his hand out the window and waved a fol-low-me to Pepper's car. Then he pulled out on to the avenue.

He checked his rearview mirror often, to see if Pepper and Slick made it through all the turns and lights. When he finally maneu-vered onto Ocean Highway, he opened the throttle and sped along, passing the newer churches and office buildings going up at the edge of town.

And a fine town it was. Erval bounced along, sitting high in the truck. He gripped the big steering wheel masterfully. He was sur-prised how at-home he felt, at the beauty of the fields, the angle of the sun, the familiarity of the crossroads. How could he and Ruthalin have treated this place as some sort of exile all these years? Why did they talk so much about going back to a place where they could attend more of the family picnics, where they could talk poli-tics and nobody would raise their eyebrows in shocked silence at their views?

Why, if they left Boxford, he would miss it all. He would miss the Main Street plaza, the signs along the highways offer-ing fresh oysters, and the Ocean City boardwalk, where he held Ruthalin's hand and bought her an ice cream cone, where they sat on a bench and watched the crowds stroll by, sand clinging to everybody's ankles.

He would miss the house, and the patio where he had cooked hamburgers for the Runyons and the Keatings and the Jaspers. He would miss the Runyons, who had the good grace to tolerate the utter confusion of having the Feldsteds around. The Runyons had never complained about the grass torn up by an especially vigorous football game, nor the bed frame that broke when Feldsted kids jumped on it, nor the barbecue meat that dropped into the Runyons' carpet.

He would miss the hospital. On nights when the storms blew through town and made the lights flicker, Erval donned his galoshes and headed for work. The night-shift nurses looked relieved when he walked through the door. Here was the man who knew just what to do, how the generators were holding up, how to direct the skeleton crew of maintenance guys.

Well, there was nothing to miss because Erval was happy to stay right here in Boxford. He had made his place here.

However, he shut off the sentimental thoughts, lest a tear slip down his cheek and make Bernie nervous.

His route today led him past the Crayton Poultry Plant. Wasn't it amazing that his pig farmer lived practically in Crayton's back yard? Erval felt like driving two laps around the parking lot, honking. And he would do it, too, if only he could be sure that Barco's office was there on the east side, and that the man would look out his window, his spade-shaped beard hanging agape.

Oh well, let's not gloat.

Erval turned up Zion Church Road, bypassing the chemical tanks and loading docks of the Crayton operations, passing farm lanes and forest patches, until he reached the little clearing that belonged to Corky Ferran. He turned in and rolled to a stop.

By the time Joe Pepper parked his car on the packed dirt, Corky had appeared in the open doorway of a shed. His spindly little wife stood on the house porch, wiping her hands on a towel. And when the mayor arrived, her work worn hands reached up and patted down her poodle cut.

As the wheelbarrow rolled closer to the pen, and the party of men rounded the corner of the shed, the Ferran pigs strained against the narrow posts. They seemed to know that something important was happening. They snorted and jostled for the best position at the trough.

Erval scooped the bucket into the wheelbarrow. He handed it to Mayor George. "Aim for that chute there," he instructed.

The mayor lifted the bucket. "Slick, you gonna want a picture of this?"

"Yep." The photographer rushed forward, putting the camera up to his eye. "Mr. Feldsted, can you hold the wheelbarrow up a little bit? Just so the crackers show. Whoa! Not that far, I guess. OK, Mr. Mayor, hold the bucket—yeah, like that. OK, look up, Mr. Feldsted. Over here. Turn just a little bit this way. All right now, can I get a smile? Come on, now. Am I gonna have to tell a joke? What did the hit man say when he opened the violin case?" He looked up from his camera. "He said, 'Who put the violin in here!' There we go. That's more like it! Hold it right there."

Erval gave it his best. This wouldn't look like those fake shots, would it? The ones where the mayor hands over the check to the winner of the speech contest and the photographer tries to make it look as if he just *happened* to catch the mayor and the winner at the very instant the check changed hands? *No, it will probably look just like that,* Erval thought, sadly.

The photographer clicked four times. Erval blinked. He looked down at the pigs. "Well?" Erval blinked again. "Are we ready?"

They'd better be. The pigs strained at the fence. A hungry pig was a noisy pig, even a dangerous pig. But really, was there anything more satisfying than critters who loved you because you showed up with the bucket?

The mayor poured.

Pepper took up a spot at the end of the trough. The photographer stood on an upturned coffee can and leaned over the fence. Bernie gripped a fence post and chewed his gum as he watched. The mayor kept smiling, ready for more pictures, if needed. The smallest pig dashed from butt to butt, looking for an opening.

Erval set down the wheelbarrow and peered in. The pigs rooted in the crackers. Their heads bobbed up. They turned away, waddling off to the corners of the pen as the smallest one finally found a spot. He sniffed. Then he uttered a small, curt snort and ran to catch up with the others.

All the men stared at the untouched crackers.

"Well," said the mayor. "I'll be damned." He watched the pigs, who didn't care if he was mayor or not.

"Can you give me some other quote?" said Pepper. "We're a family newspaper, after all."

The mayor laughed. It started somewhere near where his tie widened out. It spread upward, making his shoulders shake, his head waggle, his eyes water.

It was catching. Even Erval joined in, though he didn't really feel all that jolly. No, all he could think about was this town—*this mighty nice town*—where only a month ago, he was a hospital engineer that nobody knew. Why couldn't he just go back to being that?

"No, Pepper." The mayor wiped his wet cheeks and fought down the laugh spasms. "No other quotes."

Pepper put away his notebook. The photographer looked over his camera, shining a spot he found on the lens. Then he undid the buckles on his case.

* * *

As the last pink clouds glowed in the western sky, Latham found the truck in the hospital parking lot. He could see Erval leaning over the broad steering wheel, staring out at the measly shrubbery that marked off one section of the lot from the next.

Latham knocked at the window.

Erval started, raising himself off the wheel. He rolled down the window.

Distant motors rumbled over on the boulevard. Somebody opened a back door at the hospital. Latham heard dishes clanking inside the building, the squeal of a dumpster lid opening. "Well?" he said to Erval.

Erval's head flopped against the back window of the cab. "When did pigs change?"

By the time Latham went around and climbed into the passenger seat, Erval was on a roll. "Did I do something wrong?" he said. "Couldn't God have given me some kind of hint?" he said. "He used to be on my side. I'd be driving on long trips and He'd say 'Wake up, Erval, boy. Stay on your side of the yellow line.'"

Erval rubbed on one of his fingernails. "He was there when I was half knocked out at the dentist's and they had their pincers aimed at a tooth on the left side and the nurse suddenly said, 'Wait a minute, we're supposed to pull the one on the right side.' I mean, what's next? Is He gonna yank away the rose-colored screen He's always held up in front of Ruthalin's eyes and she'll look at me and say, 'You never are gonna tack down those baseboards in the kitchen, are you?' and that'll be it! She'll look at me forevermore as if she's sayin', 'I'm on to you, mister. You don't fool me one little bit!'"

Erval's window was still open. As more and more town lights turned on, the little breezes turned cooler.

Erval turned the keys. "I guess there's no place to go but the dump," he said over the rumble of the engine.

"Well, they won't be open now."

"Who cares? We'll leave 'em a present! Let not your alms be done before men and all that."

"Oh, yea and verily, and he that findeth thine alms traceth them back to you, buddy. Those boxes are pretty well labeled."

"Well, then find me a bridge to toss 'em over! Plenty of those around here!" Erval began to drive.

"So where are we going, really?" Latham asked.

"Well, *you* don't think I can go to the dump, so I don't know!"

Latham thought it best to be quiet. Until the third stoplight. "Why can't you just toss them in the hospital dumpsters?"

"You think you got all the answers, doncha?!"

"Gee, Erv, maybe that's your problem with God. He tries to get your attention. He tries to tell you, 'Erval, your shoes are untied,' and you snap at Him and say, 'You think you got ...'"

Erval made a rumbling sound in his chest. Latham imagined that's the kind of sound a bear would make if you woke up him too soon. Latham decided to shut up and look out the window. They passed the Arby's and the college campus and the Sand Hill Motel. "I'm surprised at you, Erval. All along, I thought you would take the crackers home. There isn't anybody who likes free stuff more than you do. You not only pick all the apples off the tree, but quite a few bruised ones off the ground. 'Hmm, these'll make fine applesauce.'"

Erval pulled over to the side of the road. He stared at Latham, the pink of the Sand Hill vacancy sign lighting his face. Then he cranked the steering wheel around in a U-turn and rumbled back up the boulevard in the direction they'd just come from.

"Where we going, Erval?"

Erval turned at the Arby's.

"Erval, we're going towards your house. Hey, Erval, I didn't mean it!"

"God's got my attention now," said Erval. "He's sayin', 'Some things are a blessing in disguise.'"

"Erval, I was saying things off the top of my head!"

But Erval drove on. At the end of his road, he backed into his driveway. He lifted up his garage door. He kicked a stepstool, a plastic bucket and some coiled rope to the corner. "Help me get these boxes in."

Latham lifted and carried, but he kept it laggardly. One stack, six boxes high, and then he'd brush off his hands and tell Erval, *Wish I could stay, but ...*

Oh. Wait. His car was back at the hospital.

The door into the house opened. Ruthalin looked out at them. "What's going on?"

"Have you fed the kids yet?" Erval asked.

"No."

"Well, then take the night off, Ruthie. Just call everybody around in ten minutes or so."

Later, inside the house, Erval lifted a brick of cheese, about the size of a railroad tie, out of the fridge. He gave Latham a butcher knife. "Cut this up."

"Erval, I don't think this is a good …"

Erval held up his hand. "Just. Cut."

Erval gathered jams—a little peach, a little raspberry—from the shelves in the laundry room. He unwrapped a new stick of butter. "Just for you," he told his daughter Heidi who watched, her chin level with the counter. "Aren't you a lucky girl? That's right. Jam. Anything you want. Some peanut butter? All righty, then." Erval reached into the cupboard for the peanut butter.

Latham stood against the fridge, his hands jammed into his pockets. He watched the family gather around for "Daddy's Special Dinner Night." He watched hungry children load up their plates, reaching across the table. He watched Erval's son Marc look on it all with the curled lip of skepticism.

"These crackers came from the shelter?" said Marc.

What was it like to be a son of Erval's? How many times had the boy been handed half an apple—*Nothin' wrong with it. I cut off all the bad parts*—or given a "new" bike—*Works great! Well, the chain slips a little, but we'll fix it up in no time.*

"That's right," said Erval. "From the shelter. But it's OK if we keep them."

"But weren't you looking for a pig farmer to take them?"

"Yep. All done though." Latham noticed that Erval wouldn't look at Marc. Erval just concentrated hard on the masterpiece of butter and jam coming together on his plate.

"And you're feeding us food meant for pigs?"

"Oh, don't get so excited! It was meant for humans. There's just some government foo-fah about it sitting too long on basements. That's all this is about."

Nobody else cared. Dinner was sugar! And cheese! And no vegetables!

"Well, won't the farmer want it all? Don't they keep big bins full of whatever they feed their animals?"

"Sure do," said Erval, his mouth full.

"Well?" Marc picked up a cracker and bit off the tiniest corner of it. "What happened out there? How much did he want?"

Erval's chewing slowed. His eyes darted around the table. He took a swig of powdered milk from his plastic cup and looked up at Latham. A bench scraped against the linoleum. A child sighed after a long drink. Impenetrable thoughts passed over Erval's face, like light and shadows across a moving car. Latham, palms upturned, shrugged at Erval. *Your secret's safe with me.*

That was the message he sent across the long table, across the spread of peach preserves and peanut butter and what-all, all the way over to Erval.

But that must not have been the message Erval got.

Nope. Honest Erv must have looked at Latham's face and seen, *If you lie, God will know it.* I'll *know it.* And so he said, in a meek and small voice, "The pigs didn't want them." Somewhere, a knife dropped to the floor.

"And you're feeding us stuff the pigs didn't want?!" Marc grabbed a few crackers from the center of the table, crushed them onto the oilcloth and stormed off the bench seat.

And like the last leaves on an autumn oak, the children blew away, one by one.

Ruthalin chewed with a studious frown. She dumped more jam on her crackers. She bit off another corner. She sighed and pushed her plate away. "I tried, Erval. I really did." Then she got up and left.

Erval watched her go. Then he lifted his chin and reached for more. He licked his fingers. He blended new combinations of jam. And he pretended his darndest that his best friend hadn't stood right there by the fridge and witnessed the whole mutiny.

Latham pushed away from the fridge. He sat himself in Ruthalin's chair, scooting it close to the table. He chose a cracker. He picked up a jam jar. He spread things around generously. He raised the cracker in the air, a toast to lost causes, and he looked at Erval.

Erval looked back, baffled.

Then the Golden Boy of Cardiff caught on. He raised a cracker in the air, too.

Follow Me, Boys

The station hall echoed with the rumble of waiting buses every time the door opened. The restroom door squeaked. A mother on the far row of chairs scolded her child—"Don't climb on that!"—as her bosoms threatened to spill out of her tank top.

April hoped Marc was too occupied with the leaves and carbons of his bus ticket to notice the difference between his own send-off and the one the family had given Kevin, just two years ago. Back then, Mom, Dad and nine Feldsted kids had spilled out of a van big enough for a reform school. Dad had cornered Kevin, man to man, and pulled out his wallet. Mom smiled through her tears and rubbed her hugely pregnant belly. When the bus chugged away, Kevin smiled out the window while they all waved wildly, shouting "Have fun at college!"

Now, as the station door swung shut behind them, the bus engine growled, spewing a cloud of fumes, its cargo doors opened up like bent insect legs.

April studied the bus driver, wondering if he was the kind that counted heads after a lunch stop, or if he just drove on with a shrug and a glance at his watch. She hesitated, then threw her arms around Marc's neck. "Dad would've come if he could," she told him.

"Yeah, sure." With one last mirthless smile, he was up the steps.

Then she could only watch his face through the window.

Seemed like she'd been seeing Marc that way all summer—from a distance.

That day in June, when she and Ginni Runyon sat outside the library, he'd been just a dark-haired dot across the river.

With only a few minutes left before Ginni had to go back to shelving books, the two girls had watched him guiding the lawn-mower over the bumps and hillocks of the hospital lawn. "I'm wondering if he's wearing the boots," said April.

"What boots?"

"Our neighbor, Mr. Golonka, died. And Mrs. Golonka brought over a pair of his boots. She thought maybe we could get some good use out of them."

"How awful!" A liver-smelling grimace marred Ginni's face. "What kind of boots are they? Cowboy boots? Rain boots?"

"No. Kind of square-toed. Zippers up the sides."

"What happened?"

"Well," said April, picking at the crusts left from Ginni's lunch, "all the princes of the realm had to try on the shoe, of course. Actually, just Dad, Marc and Tom."

"And?"

"They fit Marc."

"And he wore them?"

"No, he refused. But Dad thundered, 'They're perfectly good boots! The day I refuse to wear a pair of perfectly good boots ...'"

"By the way," April peered into a long Tupperware box at the end of the table, "there's like a dozen cookies in here. Are you plan-ning on inviting half the waterfront or something?"

"I wouldn't give me a hard time if I were you," said Ginni. "Not unless I wanted to be teased about those loose threads clinging to my shirt."

April looked down and flicked off a pink one. "Ah, the fate of someone whose mother sews for a living. Hey, aren't these the same cookies we had at your house Sunday night?"

"Fresh batch. Marc liked them, so I made more."

"Ginni, Ginni, what am I going to do to cure you of my brother?"

"You can try, but nothing's worked yet. Oh, and after your family left, my mom said she felt sorry for you, like you won't have any fun all summer, working for your mother like this."

"It's just the cooking and the errand-running. The LadyForm Bra Company is putting a lot of pressure on Mom. 'Ship us more or lose your job to Hong Kong.' So she's got to turn out enough bra bows to fill four or five boxes a week instead of the usual two or three. But, hey, I don't mind. Errands can be stretched, you know."

A sharp whistle pierced the air. The girls looked across the river. He waved at them.

"Well, well," said April, "there's my Irish twin."

Ginni raised an eyebrow. "Maybe it's his lunch break, too." She opened the Tupperware lid and began arranging the cookies in more perfect rows.

Marc's head appeared over the crest of the bridge. Nature gave him his mother's overbite, his dad's thick neck and square body. April, to her sorrow, had inherited the same square body, softened only by a smattering of freckles across her nose.

His hand dove into the cookies as soon he got to the table.

The day was a fine one, with a touch of breeze blowing in from the Atlantic, thirty miles away. It was the kind of noon in June that inspired the firemen across the street to pull the trucks out of the bay, hose them down, shine them up. The weather drew lunch-hour walkers to the brick path along the river, which was actually more like a lazy canal. Cars with windows down and bumpers declaring "Jimmy Carter. Not Just Peanuts" hurried over the bridge.

Then a pair of paramedics strode out the emergency room door, hopped into an ambulance, and pulled out of the driveway, siren whining. Well, for someone out there, it was not such a fine day.

"Remember when we used to go to the Dairy Queen just because we might see an ambulance going down the boulevard?" April asked.

"And as we watched it go," said Ginni, "you all made sure I remembered that your dad worked at the hospital. No, no, admit it, you wanted me to think he was the doctor that'd be on the scene, sewing on dismembered parts. Come on, admit it."

"OK, OK." Marc laughed. "So we didn't tell you he was just the plant engineer."

"Well, you could have told me that it was the engineer's job to stand there, handing the half-dead over to the nurses or something. I probably would've believed you."

"No, his job's a lot duller than that. About the only drama he gets is the irate phone call. 'The light bulb's out! The toilet's overflowing! Send somebody quick!' But I guess it's not a bad job for someone who hasn't got the courage or the imagination to do anything else."

"Marc!" April glared at him.

He just shrugged and took another cookie. "Gotta go, ladies," he laughed, and swung off the bench.

* * *

Erval Feldsted left the hospital at 5:30 every evening.

Marc sat beside him in the car. The boy smelled of good honest sweat, after a long day of mowing the hospital grounds, a job Erval had gotten for him the day after Marc's graduation. Now that they worked together, the father looked forward to talking shop as he negotiated the turns and stoplights of the route home.

The boy never said much. Dried twists of hair clung to his forehead. A stripe of skin, glowing white against his sunburned neck, peeked out from his t-shirt. He was tired, probably. But it was a good kind of tired, right?

Erval was always telling his kids that. That, and "Work makes things happen. Work brings rewards." Why, since Ruthalin had started sewing for the LadyForm Bra Company, the kids could have things like school pictures every year.

And Erval's own sweat equity had dotted the i's and crossed the t's on their house.

After turning by the meat-packing plant that blew out the smell of bacon for a half-mile radius, Erval motored down a curbless road, a strip of asphalt that wasn't sure whether it was city or country. Power-wash stalls gave way to simple frame houses, ending finally in stands of pine. His car pulled into the driveway at the end of the road, crunching over the pine cones and the gravel.

And there it was: his house.

Nobody thought he could pull it off. Brick, with four bedrooms (five, if you counted the pass-through room at the corner, where the three youngest boys bunked), and a kitchen big enough to seat all his ten children at dinner.

Some people had said, "Why not pick a dream that won't hurt so bad when you can't get it?" But he had gotten it. He had come out here after work, night after night, laying brick for the fireplace, debating window choices with Ruthalin. "Well, sure casements for the family room would be nice, but we don't have the budget for it."

And when it was done, he moved his family out of the aging white hulk they'd been living in, over in the broken-sidewalk part of town.

Now, he shifted the car into park. He reached for the door handle, only to face the black rubber gasket hanging from the door frame. Darn, but the thing was sagging again. The glue that held it in place always weakened in heat like this. He stuffed it into its channel again with no faith that it would stay there.

Marc, still silent, jumped from the car with more energy than you'd expect from somebody so exhausted. He dashed past this man, this creature that no eighteen-year-old ever wanted to become: hairy arms jutting out from his short-sleeved work shirt. A lone, thin tuft of hair holding its ground against the field of baldness on the top of his head. Shoulders drooping from the weight of the briefcase.

Erval frowned at the windows. He looked at the cracked and peeling paint. And those little moisture pockets that dewed up in the corners last winter—he shouldn't have gone with the cheaper models when he built this house. But it wasn't as if he had a big budget to work with, like at the hospital.

He walked past the couch in the garage. This was one of his "finds." It sat out in a wheat field one day as he drove by. He had slowed the van, all the kids moaning, "Dad, no! Please!"

But he had stopped anyway. "Looks to be in pretty good shape," he said, circling around, inspecting.

"Dad, don't! Remember the dryer?"

But he ignored their groans. "Help me load this thing in."

Now he shuffled through the gloomy garage and opened the door he had hung. He stepped onto the linoleum he had laid, where a few wisps of ever-present thread blew along the baseboards. He sniffed the air to see what might be cooking. Smelled like something with Campbell's Soup in it.

He put down his briefcase just as Heidi clumped by wearing a pair of boots, square-toed, with zippers up the side, much too big for her young feet. He pushed past Olivia, her nose planted in yet another summer-love library book. In the corner of the family room, his wife bent over her sewing machine. He leaned down for a kiss, his cheek brushing the heat-dampened curls at her neck. She handed him the latest aerogramme from Kevin, who was far away in Thailand, serving his mission.

When April finally called the family to dinner, Erval took his seat at the head of the long table. He turned to Marc for another try at the shop talk. "Watson giving you any trouble?"

"Nah." Marc freshly showered, his wet hair carefully combed, rolled up the sleeves of his white dress shirt.

"Keep an eye on him, if you could, for me. Kind of quiet-like, you know. Watson doesn't work any harder than he has to. Seems likes he's always off flirting with the x-ray techs or taking another smoke break."

"I saw him smoking at the Chevron station," said Tom.

Erval looked down the long table, past the two milk jugs, past the many small hands grasping at the bread plate, at his wife. "See what kind of fellows I have to put up with? I'd fire him, but it's not easy these days."

"That's what I mean," said Tom. "Maybe you won't have to fire him. Maybe he'll just sort of," he snickered, "fire himself."

A smile twitched at the corner of Erval's mouth, but he fought it off.

The doorbell rang.

Marc stood up. He wiped away the milk on his lip and grabbed the tie that hung on the back of the chair.

And Russ Buckman stood in the Feldsted family kitchen.

"Home teaching tonight?" asked Erval. Marc had been paired up for assigned visits with Russ, an exercise in older guys showing the younger ones how it was done.

Marc mumbled good-bye and followed Russ out the door.

Russ Buckman was a slip-on shoes kind of guy. He jingled coins in his pocket. He snapped his gum. He entered a room, scanned the action with his beady brown eyes and rubbed the beard shadow on his chin. He planted his hands on his hips and demanded, without saying a word, *When do we get started?*

You could always tell when Marc had been out with Russ. For the next day or two, parts and pieces of Russ spilled out of Marc like socks out of a laundry basket. Drive past a roadhouse and Marc told you, "Russ says they have the best oysters this side of Baltimore." Let Mom and Dad dress up for the annual hospital dinner at Ocean City's Queen Ann Hotel and it was, "Russ says they do a mean Beef Wellington."

Clearly this was a guy that got around, and in style, too, because

"Russ ordered his Thunderbird straight from the factory. It came with a blue roof and he sent it back because he'd ordered *white*."

In a house where couches that "looked to be in pretty good shape" just got adopted off the roadside, such tales were met with stunned silence. Who was this guy? Son of a brain surgeon? Spoiled by summer camps, stereos and ski vacations?

Not according to Marc. "Russ had a childhood about like Al Broadnax."

"Who's Al Broadnax?"

"You know, the head of the American Winners Institute. Russ is reading a book about him. Russ says Al reminds him of himself and the way he scrambled around as a kid, collecting bottles, mowing lawns. And now Al's a rich man. Owns a huge ranch in Colorado, raises horses. He and his sons go golfing in Scotland every year. Russ'll loan me the book when he's done."

"So I take it that Russ wants to be just like Al."

"Something like that." Russ had plans, big plans, Marc said. "Russ always says, 'Too many people are content with splashing around in a plastic, kiddie-pool kind of life when they could have the whole tile-terraced, palm-tree version." Russ wasn't going to stick forever with traveling the roads of three states, selling vent hoods to all the Denny's and Arby's and the Joe's Bar and Grills along the way. Not that it was a shame to do that. No, not at all. Unless you were satisfied to keep doing it year after year.

Marc could hardly wait to get his hands on the Broadnax book. Until then, Russ kept him busy with something else.

* * *

The voice coming from Marc's room had the fervor of a preacher, warmed up just enough for the sweat marks to break through his suit coat. "You KNOW it—in your mind and your heart—that you WANT what I've been talking about." How had someone gotten into the house? And why did he have to make it so hard for April to read her Ann Landers?

April peered into Marc's room. Nobody strange or new in there. Just Tom on the top bunk, and Marc on the bottom, bathed in a cone of light shining down from his headboard lamp, and Mom's tape player on his belly.

Back in her own room, she could still hear the voice's fire and cajolery through the closet wall. She heard Tom: "Some of us are trying to sleep in here!"

It was the time of night when Mom turned out the last kitchen light and Dad locked all the doors. In the bathroom, toothpaste foam escaped April's mouth as the voice, now moved to the living room, shouted about someone "willing to be paid just enough, JUST ENOUGH, to keep him an eyelash above BROKE."

April peeked around the corner. Marc switched the tape off as their dad walked into the room. "Whatcha got there?" Erval asked, his thumbs in his belt as he looked down at his son on the floor.

"Just a speech."

"Carter? Ford? Not that Jerry Brown guy, I hope."

"No, Dad."

Erval sat on the couch. "I didn't know you were interested in politics." The father propped one leg over the other and settled in, draping his arm along the back of the couch. Finally, a moment when they could understand each other, man-to-man. His face lit up like a talk show guest's. *Tell us how your new mousetrap works, Mr. Boopquist. Why certainly, I'd be glad to.*

But Marc just lay there, his hands caged around that tape player, his lips tightly closed.

April didn't want to watch this anymore. She ducked back into the bathroom and spat toothpaste noisily into the running water. She sat on the edge of the tub, cradling her head in her hands, hoping the silence out in the living room had broken. But when she listened, it was still there, as hard as her bones against the white porcelain.

Suddenly her father stood in the bathroom doorway. He examined the wallpaper, which was peeling rather severely. Then he went upstairs.

Things didn't used to be this way.

Whatever happened to the days when Marc trailed around in the back yard, following Dad as the spinning blades of the lawnmower spat out grass? And when Dad went to the hardware store, who walked right behind him, admiring the same flashlights and extension ladders and screw-in doorstops that Dad admired? Who was it that got in the car first when Mom said, "Anybody want to visit Daddy at work?"

His basement office at Tidewater General was just two doors down from the morgue. The office never failed to enthrall his children, who were allowed to visit in small, manageable platoons. Behind the door labeled "Plant Engineer," men in coveralls met urgent demands, hauling ladders away to check the burny smell just reported in the pediatric wing. Sometimes Dad handed out fifteen cents for them to spend at the vending machines down the hall.

Dad himself worked in an inner sanctum, the beam of his desk lamp shining down on a set of plans just in from the architect. Even April liked to be there, sitting across from him at his desk, coloring a picture, imagining Tidewater General's own version of Joe Gannon somewhere upstairs, valiantly saving the life of some beautiful but reluctant woman that refused surgery on her brain tumor.

Later, at lunch, white-coated doctors, Important Men, walked out of the cafeteria with Dad. They followed him past the elevator, lingered with him outside his office door, discussing the expansion plans up on the fourth floor.

Marc and April would look up at their dad and the doctor, both men talking with their hands. The children watched the passing cast of characters, who all nodded to their father. Women in scrubs. Men in overalls.

A fellow suited up in the best wool, his hair FBI trim, clicked down the hall in his shined shoes. The bulky briefcase at the end of his arm was embossed with the letters, UPJOHN. He looked deep in thought, pondering the mission ahead of him. Then he brightened as Dad and the doctor parted ways.

"Heyyy, Dr. Herbert. I've got tickets to the Orioles and Tigers. Could you use some?"

The doctor held up a dismissive hand as he returned to work through the construction zone shortcut.

Marc's lips parted. What luck! When had he ever been in the right place at the right time like this? His eyes watched as if the man had just dropped from parted clouds.

The man's good shoes clicked nearer. Dad seemed unaware of his approach. But any second how, the man would tap Dad on the shoulder and offer those tickets. He probably gave them away to Important Men at the hospital, and Dad was Important, no doubt about that.

But when he caught up, he walked on by with the briefest of nods.

Marc couldn't say he'd never been to a baseball game. Three summers ago, Dad had taken them to see the Brandywine Blackbirds.

They had earned their way there, spending six dawns cleaning up the cigarette butts, straw wrappers and caramel corn at the county fair.

Erval Feldsted had a warm spot for schemes like this. No reason in the world why his children should feel bad that other dads took their kids to baseball games. If the Feldsted children wanted to go, there was always a way. He'd find them a work project. Then, because of what they'd done to earn their place on those bleacher seats, the Feldsted children would appreciate the game more than any other child there. They'd learn for themselves that work is good for the soul, that work makes things happen!

Erval's excitement for the game never quite matched his fervor for the clean-up project. When he got off the phone with the fair chairman, he rubbed his hands together in a way that must have made his old calluses burn. "They said they'd be glad to have more help!" When he herded all his children age 8 and over into the family van and took his place behind the trucker-sized wheel, he broke into a rapturous "Heidy ho! And away we go!"

Wounded tomato slices that had fallen off sandwiches into the flattened grass; flies on a corncob; toilet bowls clogged with swollen tissue—none of it bothered him. None of it bothered him because he was saving his family from his own unintended mistakes. Sure he was the farmboy that made good, but now, here he was, off the farm, with a bunch of children that couldn't possibly learn those farmboy lessons. It wasn't enough to tell them tales of that day at dawn, and him a thirteen-year-old boy with his eleven-year-old brother, gripping their shovels like Moses' and Aaron's staves as their father pointed down the line of leaning fence posts and sagging barbed wire. It was not enough to tell them how their dad handed them their lunch bags, waved good-bye and drove the wagon off in a cloud of dust, not returning until the sun dipped behind the distant Utah buttes.

No, there was nothing in the telling that made the children understand. But maybe they'd figure it out, steeped in the rubbish of the county fair.

* * *

"That's not enough! Your neighbor probably wants it too! But he's AFRAID of success! Just the fact that you're HERE TONIGHT shows something. That shows you're NOT LIKE your neighbor. You're not WILLING to be just barely better than BROKE!" The man on the tape was, no doubt, mopping his forehead with his white hanky now.

April wandered into the living room and slid onto the couch. She thought Marc might turn the tape off again, but he didn't. "… You're not SATISFIED. You know there's something MORE…"

"What is all this?" she asked.

Marc held up a finger and walked into his dark bedroom.

"… want it BAD enough. You have to BELIEVE…"

He returned with a brochure. April opened the glossy pages and studied the bottles and the tubes in the pictures.

"Russ sells this stuff," Marc said, "and he's going to get me started with it. It's all from the moyocuni plant. See, here's the CuniShield. That's from the sap. Just a drop on your pulse points repels insects."

And with the voice on the tape winding up for the altar call, April flipped through pages of ointments and lotions and cosmetics—CuniSoft—even household paints, all derived from the lush, white-flowered plant pictured on the front cover.

Actually, it was less like selling, said Marc, and more like just using all the stuff, and showing others how to use it, too. When they learned to use it, and introduced it to other people, money began flowing back your way. If you did it right, if you did it the way Russ explained, money came in every month. Buckets full of it. "I mean, all it takes is a couple hours a day. Give up two or three TV shows a day and do this instead. And there you are. You can quit your job, and the cash is still rolling in. I mean, only an idiot would have a job. Right? Only an idiot would carry a briefcase and trip all over himself trying to be somewhere at 8 o'clock every morning."

And the speaker ended in a shower of applause that still rang in her head as she laid it on her pillow that night.

* * *

April pushed the doors open and stepped from the cool of the Larkin Building into the hot July noon. Having just handed the telephone company its money—"Hurry, it's too late to mail it," said her mother as she dropped the check into April's hand—she blinked at the bleached-out light of day and jay-walked to the shady side of the street, where she'd parked the family van.

She started the motor, pulled at her shirt where it stuck to her ribs, and glanced up the street at the time and temperature displayed on the Shoreline State Bank. 12:30. Maybe Ginni was on her lunch break now.

April found her at the usual table. Ginni looked up from a magazine.

"Is that the latest *Seventeen*?" April said.

"Nope. Back issue. The only kind they'll let you take out."

April scooted on to the bench and looked at a page portraying a sad girl drawn in frayed pencil lines.

"I was just turning to page 287 to see if she took the bottle of pills or not."

"I see," said April.

Ginni arrived at the back page.

"Well?" April waited. She shouldn't care about the fate of the sad, pencil girl, but these stories—they sucked you in.

"Ooooh, look here!" Ginni pointed to the opposite page. "'Stop Dreaming About Becoming a Stewardess. You're Just Steps Away With This Handy Guide.' Oh, do you have a piece of paper? A pencil?"

"Ginni, why?"

"The uniforms. They look so crisp and cute. No, no, don't roll your eyes. I mean, remember the girl in *Airport*? That belted jumper she wore? And the snappy cuffs on the blouse?"

"She got blown up, for heaven's sake! Why would you want…"

"Yes, yes, but before that, she just looked so pretty and efficient, talking on the little speaker phone, with the accent and all."

"Are you going to send away for the accent too?"

Ginni shot her a that-will-do look. "I'm not sending away for anything just yet. I don't have the $3.95. But when I get it …"

They heard a sharp whistle from the river. They turned. Marc stood on the bridge, waving.

"Some people," he said, when his shadow fell over the table, "have the time to sit and read a magazine."

"Ginni's just planning how to spend her money."

"Except that I don't have that much," said Ginni. "So I have to plan really good."

"Oh. Well." He swung his legs over the opposite bench and sat. "Maybe I could help you out."

April looked at Ginni. If Marc had ever loaned anybody $3.95, it had been a secret up to now.

"*You* could help me?"

"Sure. And you could help me back, all in the same move."

Ginni raised a skeptical eyebrow.

"You could sell Moyocuni with me."

"Oh, no, no, no, no. Selling's not something I could ever do."

"I know how you feel. Really, I do. I didn't think I could sell anything either. But actually, you don't have to. You've got the product, see? Very good stuff, high quality, helps bug bites and all that. You get it and use it yourself. Then you tell other people about it and get them to try it. And it's so good, naturally they will want to use it all the time ..."

"That sounds like selling to me," said April.

"No, it's not, because you're just using a product and getting others to do the same. And you train those people to find others to use it. Then, as they move the product, whatever money they make, you get a cut because you found them, trained them, and sponsored them. And the people they found and trained—your people get a cut, you get a cut. The possibilities are unlimited."

Ginni gripped the magazine, fingering the corners of the pages. She studied his face, which was frozen like a TV pitchman's, testifying about toothpaste that *really* whitened. "I just don't think I could do all that," she said.

"Believe me, I know how you feel. I felt the same way. But when you think about all that money coming in, you know, and what you could do with it, well, why wouldn't you try something like this if it could buy you your dreams? What are your dreams, anyway? What do you want?"

Ginni froze. No way was she going to say out loud what she really wanted.

"Do you want a red Firebird?"

She looked surprised.

"A Corvette? A cute little Volkswagen? Ice-blue maybe?"

Now she looked as if she needed to sneeze.

"No? You're not into cars? How about beachfront property? A 70-foot yacht? What? What is it? A couple snowmobiles? A private jet?"

"I don't want any of those things."

"Well, you must want something."

"I do. I want this." She held out the open magazine.

He read the fine-print ad. "'Stop Dreaming About Becoming a Stewardess'? You want to be a stewardess?"

"I want to get the book. It'll explain how."

"Why do you want to be one?"

"It's a neat job. You get to travel."

He absorbed this information. "Tell you what. If you'll sign on and help me sell Moyocuni, if you'll work real hard at it, you can travel all you want. You won't need to get a job to do it."

"It's not just the travel," said April. "She wants to wear the uniforms, you know."

His brows knit together. He looked as lost as a boyfriend at a baby shower. "So? Buy a bunch of uniforms!" He shook his head. "You know, if you work for the airlines, you're their slave. Sure, you get to travel, but only where they say and when they say. You probably don't get to see much of Paris or whatever, because you're only there long enough to rest up for the next flight." He shrugged. "But it's up to you. With Moyocuni, nobody tells you what to do. You can take it as far as you want."

And April knew Ginni would say yes. Ginni would do anything for Marc, anything to prove that she wanted what he believed worth wanting.

* * *

Ginni looked happiest when sitting across the picnic table from Marc, studying brochures, learning the party line.

"No, with that kind of person, you don't play up the financial security angle," he told her. "You say, 'You can make friends doing this.' That's what gets 'em."

She looked less happy on the day he said, "Now, let's make a list of people for you to approach." She struggled over the blank page, strangely forgetting every person she had ever met.

"How about your parents?" he said. "That's a natural."

Ginni screwed up her face. The price of love was so high. "Can't we try somebody else?"

"What? You don't think your dad would like to dump his professor job and cruise around the world or something?"

She chewed on the end of her pencil, then brightened. "Maybe it will get him out of his sweater vests and into one of those cool Ascot-tie things." She wrote "Latham and Ada Runyon" across the top of the page.

"You might try the Laid-Off-In-Your-50s approach," Marc told her. "That works great on guys your dad's age."

When the phone rang in the Feldsted kitchen that night, April knew it was Ginni. April heard her voice wailing into Marc's ear.

"Wait!" he told her. "Don't do anything! Tell you what. Meet me at the Dairy Queen."

April followed him out the door and into the car. When they arrived, Russ was already there, patting Ginni's hand as she cried into a pile of red and white napkins.

"He said, 'What's this? You're selling something for school? In the summer? Too bad it's not Girl Scout cookies, har, har. I never turn away Girl Scout cookies, har, har.'" She sniffled. "And then when I told him the price, he goes, 'Twelve-fifty! What—are there little flecks of gold or something in the lotion, har, har, har.' And then, when I suggested how he could quit his job," she shuddered into another napkin, "he said, 'But I *like* my job. And don't give me that crap about guys getting laid off in their 50s! I have *Ten-yure*, young lady! Or don't you even know what that means?' Oh!" she moaned. "I told you I could never do this."

Marc slipped into the booth and put his arm around Ginni. He looked at Russ. Any ideas here?

"Now, Ginni," Russ began, patting her hand. "It is Ginni, right? See here, there are no problems in this life. Just opportunities. And do you want to be stuck working at the library all your life? It is the library, right? The library controls your time. They control your money. What does that mean? That's right, they control your life. Are you gonna just shrug your shoulders and accept that?

"And you," he pointed at Marc. "What have I told you, a million times already? That's right. You can make excuses, you can make money, but you can't make both. And no wonder we're not making what we ought to. We can't have this negative stuff all the time."

And as Marc took his chewing out like a man, Ginni, still shuddering a little, leaned into the arm he laid across the back of the seat. She was enjoying that part way too much.

* * *

Marc became the church button-holer. He cornered Dan Keating by the church drinking fountain. Dan, fresh off the plane from a two-year mission to Guatemala, needed money for school, and fast. Why not see what Moyocuni can do for you, Dan?

Then he went brow to brow with Sister Tarasco. His parents had whispered about the Tarascos for years, about how they were in the bishop's office at least twice a month, pointing fingers at one another for various unspecified marital problems. But finally, they were calling it quits. So Sister Tarasco couldn't just stay home anymore, ignoring her housework. Sure, she could sling mashed potatoes at her children's school lunchroom. But why settle for that when she could act like a kept woman, Moyocuni-style?

Not everybody could be cornered. When men opened the restroom door and saw Marc at the urinals, they backed out. *We can hold it just fine, thanks.*

April was not sure Marc noticed the shunning. He was too full of taped speeches that goaded him to "BELIEVE!"

* * *

The box sat on the kitchen table. Children climbed over it all afternoon. They asked their mother to open it. She looked up from her sewing machine. "It has Marc's name on it. We'll have to wait until he gets home."

When he walked in that evening, his shirt clinging to his chest in the usual wet spots, he moved the box to the floor to make way for a supper of hamburger pot pie, two pans worth. Then they would not let him delay any longer. He cut the box open with a knife.

Lifting away the flaps, they saw the rows of yellow plastic bottles inside. Ruthalin, the most curious of all, reached inside.

Like a good salesman, Marc let her rub the lotion over her hand, smell it, read the label. "So how much is a bottle?"

"Twelve-fifty."

"What! But the high-dollar stuff down at Rite-Aid is only $2.89."

"But Mom, the Moyocuni is a rare plant. Harvesting it and getting it all the way here from Venezuela and extracting the various parts, well, who would bother it if it didn't do all the neat things it does?"

"I just don't see ..." she shook her head. "I just don't see how you're going to make money selling ... It's outlandish!"

"It's not so much the selling where I make my money. Mostly I sign up other people to sell under me, and they sign up others. Then, any product that they move, I get a cut."

Erval narrowed his eyes. "Yeah, but first it has to be a good product at a good price."

"Look, Dad, this is the wave of the future. Making a living by producing things is on its way out. The world is changing. People don't want to be chained to desks from nine to five anymore. Don't tell me you wouldn't want that for yourself, Dad. You know how you're always complaining that there's never enough time for the window project or whatever."

Erval's frown lightened a bit. He looked over the yellow bottles like a lawyer considering his next line of attack. "Are you saying this all comes from just a few hours of work a week?"

"Actually, it's a lot more than that at first. But pretty soon, your organization grows. You have money coming in from your downline. And at that point, your time is all your own."

"That's some pretty fancy claims there, son. How well have you looked into this?"

Ruthalin stopped smelling her hand. She put the bottle back on the table.

Marc sighed. "I know what I'm doing, Dad."

Erval put up his hands. "Fine. But it seems to me this is a mighty brave new world we're talking about here. I just don't see how nobody has to go to work. Didja ever think that some fellow has to come in and punch a time clock, to fill all the little yellow bottles with the overpriced Muna-Guna here? ..."

"Moyocuni, Dad."

"...Or maybe a chemist has to show up to extract the sap from the plant. And I'm thinking there's got to be a secretary somewhere, keeping track of the shipments."

"Well, Dad, maybe there are people that still want to do that sort of thing."

"No, son, it's not a matter of 'want to.' It's a matter of 'that's how the world works.' People still have to do the things that need …"

"Look, Dad, I know what I'm doing. I know the program, and I know it only comes through for you if you are willing to put in a lot of hard work …"

"Wait a minute. I thought your Moya-Goya was promising you a life of leisure here …"

"… and I sure am meeting a lot of people who aren't willing to do what it takes." Marc plopped bottles back into the box, as if to protect them.

"Say, son, you weren't thinking of signing your old dad on to sell little yellow bottles, because …"

"No, I sure wasn't, because I don't think you want to stop being poor."

"We're not poor, son," said Erval.

"Marc!" Ruthalin put on the look she always wore when a base-ball came through the window. "You shouldn't talk that way about your father! If you could just hear what your aunts and uncles say about him. They're amazed at what he's been able to pull off …"

"It doesn't take much to amaze some people, does it?"

"… He's gotten an educated job. He's been able to build a house big enough for all of us."

"On which he cut corners all over the place! Yeah, that's the part the aunts and uncles don't see, living all the way out there in Oregon and Utah. They don't see that, maybe if he hadn't chosen the cheap-est windows, he wouldn't have to come home from work every night and lose his whole evening cutting wood to replace the rotting sills. Maybe if he'd chosen a carpet pad thicker than a graham cracker, he wouldn't have to dream up work projects to raise money for a bet-ter one! I mean, who else do you know that drags their kids out to the fairgrounds to pick up cigarette butts and fry baskets and— and scumbags out behind the cattle barn—"

"There is nothing dishonorable about picking up litter," cried Erval. "And you kids got a baseball game out of that."

"With not enough money to buy a hot dog!"

"Do you know how much a hot dog costs, son?"

"And we thought it wouldn't hurt our children to learn how to work," Ruthalin bristled.

"That's right, son. It's how we solved problems in my day, and it was a tough time then, believe you me."

"What problems does it solve?" Marc cried. "You're barely keeping up."

"And what's so bad about it? Lots of people can't even boast of that."

"Don't tell me how it is for lots of people! Do you think I can't see it for myself? Do you think I don't choke on the two-percent milk every time we eat at the Runyons' 'cause it's so much richer than the powdered stuff Mom mixes up? Do you think we don't notice that they have lots more boxes under their Christmas tree? And some of 'em are as big as furniture! Meanwhile, back at our house, Heidi gets bike streamers made from a bread bag. And she's thrilled! Just like she's thrilled to play dress-up in Mr. Golonka's boots. Do you think we don't notice that lots of people out there aren't asked to wear a dead guy's boots? People think we'd be glad to have 'em! People know the Feldsteds will take stuff nobody else wants!"

"It didn't hurt me, son, and it won't hurt you!" Erval's voice rang from the walls to the ceiling beams to the linoleum. "And the day I'm too proud to wear a perfectly good pair of boots is the day that I ..."

"Look here, Dad!" Marc pointed his finger into his father's face. "I can't honor you or whatever by reliving *your* times, *your* problems." He closed up the box flaps, swishing with contempt. "You got answers for everything, doncha Dad? But mostly you got answers for problems that aren't around anymore." He picked up his box and left the room.

* * *

April sat on her bed. Looking across the room, she wondered: How could Olivia sleep through the arguing and shouting? Through Marc kicking and throwing things next door? How could Tom sleep through it?

The door opened and Marc looked in. "I need paper."

She scrounged through a pile next to her bed and came up with a few sheets.

"Not the lined stuff," he said. "This is a grown-up message and I don't want some school-boy piece of paper!"

"I'll look around."

When she returned from the kitchen drawer where Mom stored paper and envelopes, he had already retrieved the typewriter from her closet.

"They're talking out there about you. They're saying they don't think they've done enough for you and maybe they need to do something special before you leave."

"Oh boy. I can't wait."

"What are you writing?"

"My resignation. I'm sick of mowing lawns."

"But you can't quit! You need the money for school."

"Yeah, you're right. I can't quit, not yet. But if I wait until I can, I'll lose my nerve. Then I'll be like *him*: timid." He rolled a piece of paper in. "I wanna see this letter every morning and evening until then." He pounded furiously on the keys. "So what do you think two people like that mean by 'something special'?"

"They're talking about a camping trip."

"Camping!" he snorted. "It figures."

* * *

Two days before Marc's departure for college, Captain Erval

banged around in the garage, directing children up the ladder into the attic to retrieve the tents and the lanterns, Ruthalin's cot, and especially the giant Styrofoam cooler, big as a hope chest. He'd gotten it from the hospital, where it was used to transport organs, severed limbs and other gore.

He dispatched Marc to the Gas-N-Go for bags of ice. When Marc returned, Erval loaded gear onto the little trailer he'd made from salvaged wood, while April stood in the doorway, holding the phone. "For you, Marc."

She went back to her sandwich- and cookie-packing. But she could hear him—"Hey! How's it goin'?"—until he stretched the phone's long cord far around the corner, into the living room.

He re-appeared at the door to the garage, holding the receiver against his thigh. "Where we going, Dad?"

"Sheephouse Neck. Same as last time. We'll be by the river."

Marc carried the phone away again.

"Who called?" April asked, when he came through the kitchen again.

He shrugged. "Did you pack your swimsuit?"

"Why? Come back here! Why do I need my swimsuit?"

"Ya never know."

April had invited Ginni.

When Ginni arrived, they packed the whole family into the maxi-van. Soon, they were on their way, with the little trailer wiggling along behind. Erval drove along the gently curving roads, past mailboxes at the end of lanes, past bushes that blew in the van's wake, past the long, low buildings of a chicken farm. The forest closed in, then cleared away for yet another chicken farm.

Once inside the state park, they spread over three camp sites, pitched their tents, tied their garbage bag to a white ash tree, all while a whistling Erval fanned the campfire to life.

Later, full of hot dogs and marshmallows, Marc fell asleep to the hum of cicadas. He slapped at another mosquito against his bicep and regretted having a father who hated crowds, distrusted oceans, and therefore never took them camping in the sea-breezy air of Nassowango Island.

In the morning, haze hung over the trees and smoke wafted from beneath the griddle where Erval, whistling again, flipped pancakes. Ruthalin yawned, and measured a heaped spoonful of Tang into a pitcher of water.

Erval was eager to try the Foggy Bottom Trail this morning. "But have another pancake, Duane. It's a long time 'til lunch. Derek, you stop fussing with your brother," he shook his spatula, "or you won't be hiking with us!"

As soon as he put the griddle over the fire to burn off the pancake bits, and as soon as Ruthalin released kids from wiping the oilcloth clean and putting away the egg cartons, and as soon as he lined up his troops and checked their feet on suspicion that someone would try to march into the woods wearing their drugstore thongs— he clapped the fishing hat over his balding head and led off into the woods.

Soon enough, children complained that they would never find camp again, at least not in time for lunch. So Erval sang, in a voice that startled the birds into silence, his wood-tramping theme song, something from his favorite Fred McMurray movie:

> *Follow me, boys!*
> *Follow me!*
> *When you think you're really beat,*
> *That's the time to lift your feet.*

Marc brought up the rear. He even sang along, sort of.

> *Swallow me, boys,*
> *Swallow me!*
> *Worms and bugs are great to eat,*
> *Mashed to bits by stinky feet.*

Tom giggled at the words until, as the lead hikers' footsteps echoed across a plank bridge, Heidi began to cry and point at the water below. A pine cone—her hike souvenir—swirled slowly in the river's lazy flow.

"I'll get it!" Tom jumped off the path. Kneeling on the muddy banks, he reached across the water, his fingers closing, dipping, missing.

The sun rose higher. Marc looked at his watch. He pulled his shirt away from his neck. If he wasn't back in camp by 11:00… What were they doing out here, a bunch of sweaty hikers, holding their breath on a plank bridge, and Heidi bawling like the world would end, and Tom wading, stumpy-legged in the water, reaching into the webby world under the bridge? "Can't you get another pine cone?" Marc said. "It's not like they're hard to find out here."

Tom waded back to the bank, empty-handed. He scanned the forest floor. He found a nice, craggy forked branch. Then he returned to the river. He caught the pine cone with his branch, and swept it to shore.

Heidi quit sniffling and they were on their way again. They trudged through spots of shade and sunlight. They slapped bugs attracted by their sweat. Erval promised that, sure thing, they'd rent some fishing poles and even a couple canoes after lunch, and find a shady spot on the river and … Marc looked on at his little brothers' excitement with a cold pity, until finally, *finally*, they found their tents in the clearing again, catching Ruthalin in the act of bagging a dirty diaper.

Marc lifted an overturned bowl on the picnic table and tore off a piece of leftover pancake. He laid on the bench in the gappy shade, still swatting bugs. Then he heard the motor idling out on the camp road.

* * *

April looked up from the rock she still had not coaxed out of her shoe. She saw a shiny Dodge truck turn into the campsite, and Russ Buckman behind the glare of the windshield. How did he know the Feldsteds were here? And behind the truck, a boat hung halfway out into the camp road.

The bass tones of the motor trembled under the trees as Russ greeted her father through the open window. His wife Danae, in all her Ivory-Soap loveliness, with a long braid down her back today, smiled from her side of the cab. And their three boys leaned over from the back seat.

"How's it goin'?" Russ, ever the salesman, acted like Erval's nearest and dearest friend. "I was wondering if we could borrow your son for a little while."

Erval's eyes wandered over to the boat. Russ stepped out of the truck and stood dwarfed beneath the boat's bow, his arms folded, his head tucked back on his neck in a pride-of-ownership swagger. *Yep, new toy. Gonna try it out today.* Erval walked along as Russ ran his hand down the red stripe on the starboard side.

Russ had even christened her already: *Cuni-Babe*, written in fine, swirly script above the stripe.

Erval circled the boat, politely asking about the fuel specs and the trailer hitch, not terribly interested in the answers. But it bought him time to debate with himself. *Do I let him go? Or am I still the Dad around here? Am I still the one in charge?*

He might have saved himself the trouble, for when he and Russ finished their lap around the boat, Marc hoisted a duffle bag into the truck bed and brushed off his hands.

"Ready to go, buddy?" Russ asked.

"Sure enough."

Small brothers clung to Marc's t-shirt. "Can we go too?"

Heidi pled with Erval, "What about me, Daddy?"

Erval looked over the babbling defection before him. He frowned and opened his mouth. Nothing came out.

"Wellll," Russ looked at Danae, "I don't know about today. Maybe … How old are you?" He clapped Tom on the shoulder.

"Sixteen."

"Tell you what. We'll take anybody sixteen or over today, and then we'll pick another day to take the rest of you."

April wiggled her heel into her now-rockless shoe. She caught her breath. He might as well have invited her to step onto the mountain slopes of a calendar picture, the idea was so exotic and delicious. No wonder Marc warned that one never knew when one might need a swimsuit. She had heeded the warning, annoyed as she was with all his crypto-mystery.

She climbed into the truck bed. Ginni, Marc and Tom were already settled against its hard metal ribs. They grinned at their amazing luck. They laughed loud and joked with Danae and refused to look at anyone but each other, because if their eyes wandered just three inches to the left, there would be all those disappointed faces staring back at them, and Dad, too, standing there with his thumbs in his belt, his shoulders hunched, his eyes squinting against a sudden patch of mid-day sun that shone down on his bewildered head.

Maybe Dad would forgive this. Maybe he would understand that any kid would want to feel speed and spray and sun-dappled water. And if he couldn't give it to them, he should let them go with somebody who could.

The wind plastered April's hair across her face as they sped past forests and chicken farms again. They turned onto a side road. They passed through a village where miniature lighthouses and wishing wells adorned the lawns of porchy old homes, where ivy girdled the shady trees. Beyond the village, the trees gave way to marsh grasses. Then the road disappeared into the glittery waters of Nassowango Bay.

Russ turned the truck on the broad apron of asphalt. April hoisted herself out of the truck bed and stood with Ginni under a lonely-looking streetlight. Out in the lapping waters, a fortress of broken pilings guarded the approach to a forlorn old crabbing shack.

Far out into the water stood Nassowango Island, a faint purple streak on the horizon.

Russ, grinning in his Ray-Bans, backed the *Cuni-Babe* down the landing, between two piers, directed by Marc and Tom. Danae, on the pier, snapped her sons into life jackets.

Then they were off.

The afternoon wore itself away as they bounced along ahead of the boat's churning wake. April knelt on the back bench, elbows on the stern, bathing in the spray. She lent a hand to dripping skiers as they climbed up the ladder. All of them but Danae were bumbling novices, but April cheered when Tom managed both feet on one ski, if only for a moment. She gasped when a sharp and thrilling turn of the boat swung Marc across the wake, where he nearly collided with one of those crab-shack pilings. As for her own turn in the water, she mostly remembered Ginni, over on the other ski rope, screaming her amusement-park scream.

Russ idled the boat out on the bobbing waters and Danae produced cheese sandwiches and Orange Crush. She ducked into the cuddy cabin to change her toddler's diaper. When she emerged again, she smoothed out a blue cotton hat. "The sun's getting to you, young lady," Danae said, and she settled the hat on Ginni's head.

Ginni looked out from under the floppy brim. "Do I look like an old-lady gardener now?"

"With all the lime green and magenta in that beach towel," said April, "you look like a color-blind old lady gardener. You know, you don't have to stay wrapped in your towel like that."

"I do too. My legs are white and horrible."

April sighed. "We're all friends around here. Nobody cares."

Ginni raised her chin and tucked the towel more firmly around her waist. Then she stood to watch as they reeled Jeremy Buckman out into the water. He wanted to try the one-ski trick himself.

April turned her face up to the sun and played a mental slide show of the day. She saw Marc, his wet hair separated into curls;

Tom offering a corner of his sandwich to the youngest Buckman; Ginni who, with one hand on her hat and the other gripping her towel knot, smiled into the breeze. She also saw her father, slouched and unreadable, looking up at Russ's truck as it drove away, but she blinked the image away and looked out over the rippled bay.

When the rope played out and the *Cuni-Babe* jerked into motion, the knot in Ginni's towel loosened. All that lime green and magenta fell away. She scrambled to catch it. Her hands fussed and tucked.

Meanwhile, the wind lifted the brim of her blue hat and carried it away to the water. Ginni stood, surprised, patting her head.

Marc tugged on Russ's Hawaiian shirt. It was his wife's hat, after all.

Russ cut the motor and looked back.

"I'll get it," said Tom, and he dove over the side of the boat.

Whale-humping through the sparkling waters, he followed the patch of blue. It floated away as if it had envied every other creature on the bay today and wanted to show that it, too, knew how to skim the waves.

When Tom returned, he perched on the swim ladder, rubbing water out of his eyes. He grinned, all Boy-Scouty and helpful, in spite of the way Jeremy pushed past him on the ladder, which made the hat leap into the water again.

"Aaaghgh!" Tom jumped after it.

All hands on deck untangled lines, handing Jeremy his, stowing the others. When Russ was satisfied, he turned the key and put his hands on the throttle of the now-humming boat.

April rested in her seat. The purr of the accelerating boat made her drowsy. Marc, up in the spotter's seat, rested back on his elbows…

Then April felt the bump.

She looked at Marc. Had he felt it too? He ran a languid hand through his hair, then turned to look at her. Reading the disquiet in her eyes, he sat up. "Where's Tom?"

She tried to remember the bump. Was it a scrape? A mere tap? Maybe just a little rock of the boat? No, there was a definite catch-and-release to it.

"Russ, cut the motor!" Marc shouted.

April didn't think that Russ heard.

"I said," he gave Russ a streetfight shove, "cut the motor!"

April looked over the edge. As Marc jumped in the water, a blue hat floated in the dying wake. She sank against the wall of the boat. She summoned up Tom's face, the grinning, dripping one of just a minute ago. It seemed terribly important to hold on to that face.

But the face that rose from the water was pale and stunned. Tom's eyes darted from the sound of Marc's shouts to Danae shooing the children up to the cockpit. Flaglets of blood swirled in the water around his emerging body until his leg appeared.

Then, April only heard Ginni, vomiting over the side of the boat.

* * *

April gathered the blanket tighter around her shoulders. Some blue-haired volunteer had handed it to her. She looked now in the mirror at her own curls— dried, finally, and mussed from dozing against the wall out in the waiting room.

She opened the bathroom door. Down the hallway, past the nurses' station, a nurse stepped in on her parents. They rose.

They'd been waiting, watching doorways, rising like this for hours. First, it was the doctor, talking in hushed and authoritative tones, saying things like *Four units ... Mid-shaft, like this*, as his hands sliced across the meaty part of his own calf.

Completely severed?

Fortunately not but, and whatever the doctor said next made Ruthalin's hand fly to her mouth. April didn't need to hear it. She had seen the tangled meat and protruding bone herself. She had watched the blood soak through Ginni's precious towel while waiting eons for the Coast Guard boat.

Save the leg?

The doctor had crossed hairy arms over his scrubs.

How do you deliver bad news? How do you drop barbells without cracking the floor?

We can try. He's gone upstairs. You can wait there.

And now, here they were. Every time April had nodded off, then awakened to the jolly sounds of TV-land from the softly humming set in the corner, the world felt as normal as dust motes and lawnmower noise. She could almost believe Tom sat up in bed right now, laughing and happy, the little brother she had always known. But now, the canned laughter and Pepsi jingles had given way to the national anthem.

And that nurse stood there. She held out the clipboard and pen to Dad.

A clipboard could mean lots of things. Surely not death. More units of blood, maybe. Or transfer to another hospital. April stood at the corner of the station, where two nurses chattered about perms for men. *It doesn't mean they tried and couldn't save it.*

He did not reach for the clipboard.

He did not look at his wife's stricken face.

The chatter died away. The two nurses looked at the waiting room, at April, at each other. The tall one with the coarse hair smiled, sympathy with a professional polish. News travels fast in a hospital, April guessed. *That was Erv Feldsted's kid they brought in this afternoon. Nice guy, Erv. Tough, tough break.*

And Erval Feldsted lifted the pen away from the clipboard and handed it back to the nurse.

April turned for the elevator. Inside, she pressed the button she knew best, B for basement.

The doors opened. They revealed, behind the gleam of vending machine glass, Pay-Days and Snickers, hard-puck bear claws, greenish tuna sandwiches. She leaned her forehead on the glass, trying to decide. But she knew none of it would help.

She wondered where to go next. To the right, the night lights of the silent cafeteria glowed out into the hallway. To the left, she knew every bend and doorknob and nameplate.

She turned left.

Just beyond the last corner, she found Marc, on the floor outside Dad's office. His elbows rested on his drawn-up knees. His feet were a cold, waxy white, slipped into Russ's sandals.

He looked up, troubled and whisker-shadowed. He slid his back up the door, struggling to his feet.

She held out the blanket to him.

He took it, his fingers fumbling with the edges.

She lost patience and gathered him into her arms. He clung to her, the blanket rumpled between them. She would have let go, but a cry—deep and strange and lonely—rose up out of him, and then another. And another. And another, echoing down the hallway outside his father's office.

* * *

The bus engine hummed, emitting a steady chug of fumes, its cargo doors opened up like bent insect legs. She hesitated, then threw her arms around Marc's neck. "Dad would've come if he could," she told him.

"Yeah, sure."

With one last mirthless smile, he was up the steps. His face appeared in the window.

She stood, pinned to the oily, gum-dotted sidewalk, seeing this thing through until the bus creaked away from the gate and rolled toward Mill St. It waited there, its turn signal blinking like a bored zoo lion at high noon. Then, moving into a break in the traffic, it wheezed down the street.

April got into the car, alone.

FLIRTING LESSONS

The brisk November air hit Ginni Runyon as she descended the steps of the Greyhound bus. Ahead, a light on the St. Louis station wall shone over a collection of weather-beaten picnic tables. A billboard loomed over the alley: "If You've Got the Time, We've Got the Beer."

The coolness out here, at 2:30 in the morning, was unexpected and rude. As it drifted up the sleeves and down the collar of her pea coat, she missed the drowsy warmth of her seat. Shoving one hand into a coat pocket and, with the other, adjusting the backpack on her shoulder, she moved along with her fellow passengers, all of them scowling and blinking as the newly awakened do.

When she boarded the first bus a day and a half ago, a note of aversion had latched on to her trip, like an ant crawling into a pant leg. It rode westward with her across the country. It bothered her faintly when she found herself at less than arm's length from people whose hair hung like ripped cloth and whose teeth were a gallery of stains and gaps. She ignored it, lest it spoil the breezy sense of adventure she had expected. But she felt it again when her coat jostled against another passenger or touched a mysterious stain on the bus seat (and she brush-brush-brushed off the coat) or when she stepped over a dried stain of vomit.

And then, there were the moments when Ginni'd pull her little folding brush out of her backpack, only to glance up and find some runaway type watching her unfold it. "It's like these people resent us," Ginni whispered to April Feldsted and Shelly Galvin, the two girls she traveled with. "I can hear her thinking, 'Sure don't get no cute things like that, 'less I shoplift 'em.'"

April just smiled and shook her head. "Got to curb that wild imagination, Ginni."

But, no, Ginni didn't think she suffered from wild imagination at all. When she slid another half dozen Chicken in a Biskit crackers into her mouth, she looked up and caught the queen-sized black girl in the seat ahead watching her. The curl of the girl's mouth definitely told her that the girl wished there were a little justice in this world, a little something that would make the tall and slender ones (like Ginni) get fat like anybody else who eats whole boxes of snacks.

And now, in the night air of St. Louis, she looked ahead for April Feldsted and followed the line of travelers into the station.

Ginni expected the place would be deserted at this time of the morning. But she was wrong. She cut through the jumbled line of passengers and suitcases queued up for Memphis, and then another line bound for Dallas.

Across the cavernous waiting room, April found seats over by the snack bar. She wadded up her puffy parka, probably intending to sleep more. The oldest daughter of ten kids, April could sleep anywhere, draped over anything. It was a family trait, just as much as her overbite and that light dusting of freckles over her nose.

Ginni caught up and sat down, settling her backpack on her lap. "Where's Shelly?" she asked.

They looked back at the doorway, where the flow of incoming people had slowed to a trickle.

"With *him*. I think he took a smoke break. Did you see them out by the picnic tables?"

Ginni shook her head. "How long is she going to play bus boyfriend with him?"

"About another hour, I guess. I heard him say his bus to California leaves at 4 o'clock."

"We wouldn't have these problems if she hadn't come along."

"Well," said April, opening the flap of her overstuffed, crocheted bag, "you know they weren't going to let us leave town without her."

Ginni looked into the face of the man across from her. Hunched in a sweatjacket, hidden behind a beard that crawled up his cheeks in uneven lines, he looked like the last drugs he'd taken were wearing off badly.

Maybe this man was what Ginni's parents imagined when she told them, "April and I are planning a road trip."

She and April had conceived their adventure over cafeteria trays of half-eaten sloppy joes and untouched canned peaches. "Every senior is supposed to get a college visit, right? Well, I just got my license. You've got yours. We can read a map. No problem!"

But when Ginni presented the plan to her parents that night, her mother's face froze in the same aghast look as the time Ginni told Mr. Haffner where the family hid the spare house key.

"Driving cross-country from Boxford to Provo all by yourselves?! Two high school girls alone?!"

And before Ginni could think of what to try next, her mother was on the phone with the Feldsteds. Ginni listened from the stairs. She heard phrases like "Where do they come up with these things?" and "Well, I was hoping you'd see it that way."

When her mother hung up, her father said, "That's all we need. Some trucker in Nebraska discovering two wide-eyed, unchaperoned girls."

"And I can't forget," said Ada Runyon, "how the Pokusas' daughter died, setting out for Atlanta on three hours sleep and rolling across the median not two hours into the trip. That's exactly what these girls would do, stay up half the night, watching movies in some motel room, expecting they could …"

So the whole trip was off.

Then the phone rang. Mrs. Runyon had picked it up. "Hello… What?… I don't know," she said. "That's seems kind of extreme, sending the girls all that way… You mean you haven't heard from Marc at all?… Oh, now he wouldn't blame himself for Tom's accident, would he? … Well, failing *two* classes.… I see your point. Something's not right.… Oh, I agree. No driving, uh-uh.… And there's the Galvins' daughter, Teresa. The girls could stay with her."

So the trip was on again, only it was by bus instead of a car. And because the girls would land in the clutches of Teresa Galvin, it seemed rude not to include Teresa's little sister, Shelly.

Or it seemed that way to the mothers.

But then, the mothers only knew the Shelly of the Sunday School class. The Shelly of the Friday night movie line, the one who yakked on and on about being on the phone last night with all two hundred of her closest friends, was as hard to bear as sitting on a middle seat, right there on the hump. That kind of aggravation might be tolerable for a quick ride to Dairy Queen, but a three-day road trip was a whole 'nother story.

Then again, spend a week with Shelly and maybe her easy-flirt skills might rub off on Ginni. It might be worth it after all.

At any rate, Shelly boarded the bus with Ginni and April on an unseasonably balmy Friday night in November. They stretched out, three across the long back seat. By Norfolk, they had eaten the Chicken in a Biskit crackers Ginni had packed along. By Richmond, they had told each other the kind of tales that made them lean in and listen close. "Yeah," said April, "nobody saw Marc off when he left. Just me. I think Mom and Dad were sleeping off a night at the hospital, but none of us know what Marc thinks." By Washington, sitting halfway up the aisle on a new bus, they had succumbed to the rocking rhythms of the ride. It lulled them to sleep, jerked them awake, then lulled them back again.

And now, in St. Louis, in the wee hours of Sunday morning, sleepy Ginni understood the dazed look on all the other faces in this cavernous room.

She gazed up at the ceiling. From the looks of things, baroque-era painters and carvers had once been busy in here. Since then, from the looks of things, bus passengers had been just as busy scuffing up the balusters, the columns, the moldings.

April pointed beyond the line to Dallas at *him*. He came through the door, tucking a pack of Camels into his shirt pocket. He followed behind Shelly. Dressed in military camouflage, he scanned the room, his boyish face a mix of wariness and wonder at tall buildings and crowds.

He'd boarded in Dayton, his eyes sweeping back and forth, looking for an empty seat. He skipped the one by the man who jerked in his sleep. Then, when he reached the grandma with the peacock-studded purse in her lap, he glanced at Shelly in the seat behind, at Ginni and April across the aisle. He must have decided that sitting by grandma would do. He had thrown his duffel bag into the overhead and settled in.

His name was Danny. Three days from now, he told them, he'd be back at the base, suffering under the thumb of his sergeant. But for now it was, "Piece of gum, anyone?" and "You all aren't sisters, are you?" and "Utah? Well, don't let those Mormons get ya. Oh. So you all are Mormons."

And it was Shelly, petting a strand of her stick-straight brown hair, sitting on the arm of April's seat, saying, "So, do you have to wear your uniform when you travel?" and "Have you been in any wars?" and "So what kind of town is Elderberry, Ohio?" Holding court there on the seat arm, Shelly didn't care how many passengers up and down the aisle could hear her switched-on friendliness.

In Indianapolis, when the grandma with the peacock bag got off, Shelly moved in beside him.

And somewhere in the cornfields beyond, Ginni woke up hard

against the cold window and looked across the aisle. There was Shelly, sleeping with her head on the shoulder of Danny, her Marine.

She poked April awake and pointed.

April looked, sighed and shook her head.

"What about Will back at home?" said Ginni.

"What about him?" April wadded her coat into a pillow and went back to sleep.

* * *

Teresa Galvin drove down the street, the darkness punctuated by the glare of a streetlight every half block or so. The maple donut in her hand hampered her steering a little as she moved through the jumbled Provo neighborhood filled with little shot-gun houses and boxy apartment buildings. Her sooty-white house was the second one from the corner, the porch light still on. Carlene was no doubt in bed by now, but her other roommate, Nancy, liked her late nights on the weekend.

And it was late. Teresa was pretty sure it was past midnight by the time she exited through the automatic door at Smith's Supermarket. She wasn't one of those Mormons who slipped in for a loaf of bread on her way home from Sunday School. Or, at least, she hadn't for a couple years now.

But she was the kind of Mormon who dashed in as the sands of Saturday night thinned out and slipped through fast. Tossing sugared cereals and peanut butter into her basket, (Crunchy or creamy? Who knew? No time to read the labels at this late hour) she escaped with her receipt just as the clock over the door ticked right up to the line. Which didn't really feel like a line at all. The parking lot, lit by its greenish lights and freshened by a breeze that crawled down her neck, didn't look or feel any different on her way out of the store than it did on her way in.

But at least the chore was done. Which was good, since this

was her last chance to shop before she dashed out of the house on Monday morning, reporting for duty at the kitchen of the Canyon Manor Senior Home.

Now she turned on to her side street and parked beside the crumbling curb.

She shoved the last hunk of doughnut into her mouth. She checked the rear-view mirror, her liquid-blue eyes looking back at her. She wiped a spot of frosting from the corner of her mouth and flicked down a strand of her bowl-cut hair. Not that she'd want to be caught fussing with her hair, since she'd figured out, by now, that she was not the kind of person anybody would want to look at. There really was nothing sadder than some homely dumpling at the dance, dressed in a flouncy dress that made it plain to all the world that she'd made an effort, even stood in front of the mirror telling herself, *Yes. This will change my luck.*

A little basic effort was OK. Teresa didn't want to look like some drooler who needed a nurse to wipe her chin. But beyond that, what was the point? So what if this town was a magnet for thousands of young Mormons looking to meet up? It hadn't done a thing for her.

Hoisting two sacks from the passenger seat, she got out, kicking the car door shut with her knee. The crepe soles of her shoes crunched through the gravel in the alley. Under a disc of light from a streetlamp, she opened a creaking gate. At the side door, she pointed her key toward the lock. It would not reach, not with her arm around the heavy, crackling grocery sack.

She knocked with her knee instead. Then she stared at the window, waiting.

To look through it was to see a wavy, dizzy world. Yes, the house needed work, though it wasn't as if it hadn't been worked on already. This college town was full of landlords, old duffers who constantly hammered on their own basements or some house across town. *Let's tuck a bedroom upstairs under the eaves. How about another one behind the kitchen? Here's an unused corner. Let's make an extra bathroom.*

The more they hammered, the more renters they could stuff in, be they students, or single girls like herself who, aging faster than spotted bananas, weren't ready to leave Provo yet.

From inside, a set of fingernails richly polished in burgundy swiped the flowery curtain aside. A face with well-drawn eyebrows peered out, then opened the door.

"Thanks, Nancy." Teresa stepped inside the kitchen. Her sacks rustled and clunked as she dropped them on the table.

"Garrett dropped off another sleeping bag," said Nancy, scratching above her eye with one of those perfect nails, careful not to disturb the eyebrow or the smoky shadow. Nancy obviously spent some time on herself. It was as if she looked in the mirror every day and said, *Yes, I am pretty, so pretty that nobody notices the extra two hundred pounds below this face.*

"Oh. Good. I guess we have enough now."

Carlene, Teresa's other roommate, wandered in from the back of the house, awake for some reason. Teresa had never known anybody but her mom to wear a girdle, and she never would know that Carlene wore one, except that Carlene walked around the house in it all the time. Stacking albums into the stereo, answering the phone, checking the fridge for another diet Dr. Pepper—whatever called Carlene out of her room, she evidently considered herself sufficiently decent as long as she was dressed in her power panels and her cross-your-heart bra.

This time, she came out just to be sociable. She sat at the kitchen table. It was so small that, when they sat together, all their knees knocked together under it.

Teresa dug through the bags. "I hope these girls eat all the Fruity Pebbles I bought them. I sure don't want to finish them up."

"Aren't they a little old for cereal like that?" Carlene leaned in, as if to peer into the bags.

"I really don't know what to think." Teresa was glad the bags were tall. Carlene couldn't see in (though Teresa could see the thinning spot on the top of Carlene's head all too well). Teresa didn't want anybody looking inside the sacks. She had bought herself a second donut too and, while this household had an unspoken but stiffly upheld rule about "my cupboard" and "my treats," Teresa always feared that until her donuts actually made it into her cupboard, they were prairie dogs on the open plain, likely to be snatched by any hawk flying by.

"All I can see," she said, digging further, "is my little sister walking down the streets of Provo, giggling with her junior-high friends, all of them convinced that 'We're passing for college girls, oh yes we are!'"

"But they're not in junior high anymore," said Nancy. She sat at the table, holding a stack of Grasshopper cookies, from *her* cupboard. "When was the last time you even saw your sister?"

Teresa thought of the picture sitting on her dresser, of that ridiculous swoop in Shelly's hair. Innocently, she carried the "empty" grocery sack up the steep, shallow steps to her bedroom and returned with the picture. "Maybe even before this." She sat at the table.

And there she was: Shelly, the eighth-grader with a strained smile, her bangs carefully draped into a barrette. By the time the photographer snapped the picture, a tired strand had broken away from the swoop. But since Shelly couldn't see it, she probably thought she looked as smart as the last time she had checked in the mirror.

"And how are we going to entertain these girls for a week?" Carlene asked.

"Did you know," said Teresa, "that she called me and hinted that maybe we could throw a party for her. 'You know,'" Teresa mimicked her sister's young breathiness, "'introduce me to some boys.' I had to tell her, 'You do realize, don't you, that we don't mix with the young peachy-faced ones?'"

"But we have Brent in our ward," said Nancy.

"Right," said Teresa. "The drugs really did a number on him."

"But they say he's off them now," said Carlene. "And I hear his hallucinations have calmed down a bunch."

"OK, then." Nancy split her cookie. "How about Garrett?"

"Who wears a toupee," said Carlene.

"Then how about Earl?"

"Nothing wrong with him," said Carlene.

Teresa flicked chocolate cookie crumbs across the tablecloth. "Except that he's always wind-burned from going off into the wilderness for weeks on end." She propped her chin in her hand, wanting to be in bed but too tired to go there. "It's like she expects us to crash some Frisbee game up on campus. She thinks we can just recruit some ... some *children* and bring them back to our little old white house here. Promise them brownies and some out-of-town girls."

"Well, that sounds risqué," said Carlene.

"Actually, there's lots about Shelly that's risqué. You're about to meet the make-out queen of Boxford County."

Nancy and Carlene raised their eyebrows.

"Oh, yes!" said Teresa. "My mom tells one hand-wringing story after another. 'I caught her lying on the living room couch with that ... that yay-hoo she brought home, the TV off when it was supposed to be *on*, the lights off when they were supposed to be *on*.'"

They all studied the junior-high Shelly in the family picture.

"Hmm, she really doesn't look like the kind that would ruin those nice boys up on campus," said Nancy.

And with renewed anticipation for the Monday-afternoon arrival of the Make-Out Queen of Boxford County, the girls of the little old white house counted up the borrowed sleeping bags one more time, then went to bed.

* * *

Shelly walked through the St. Louis Greyhound station as if she had started the trip with Danny instead of with her friends.

Ginni waved her over. But Shelly just clung to her blanket and walked past the arcade games, past the short-order grill and the universal symbols by the restroom doors. Danny followed her, carrying his duffle and her suitcase.

When they arrived at the Coke machines, Danny parked the luggage by the nearest wall. They stood before the machine, holding hands, like newlyweds deciding between the Whirlpool washer and the Maytag. She pointed to a button. He dug in his pocket, dropped in the coins and presented her with a cold can of Mountain Dew. She snuggled down on the floor next to his duffle, looking up at him one last sweety-glanced time before he paid a visit to the ticket agent.

"We aren't invisible, are we?" Ginni asked April.

"Come on. We've seen this before. Remember how she was with Mike Truitt?"

"Yes," said Ginni, "but we're far from home. I should think she'd want the comfort of a familiar face."

"By now, this guy is a familiar face. She's slept with her head on his shoulder, after all."

"How can she stand it? I mean, none of us have showered for—what?—two days now? I'm afraid for *you* to be within six inches of *me*."

The ticket agent stapled together ticket parts and handed them to Danny. He returned to his duffle bag. As he took over the luggage watch, Shelly strolled their way.

She stood before them, drinking deep from her Mountain Dew. "Danny just changed his ticket. He was supposed to get on the 3:55 to Los Angeles. But he's gonna ride a little longer with me." She drank again, her face a study in satisfied wonder. *These things just happen to me. I can't help it! I'm a guy magnet.*

It couldn't be her looks. Her brown hair fell past a face with a nose too round and eyes too small. If they cast Shelly in a movie, it would never be as the tiny blonde whom the hero lifted down from the wagon bed. No, more likely she'd play the lead girl's best friend, from the hopelessly ethnic family whose grocer father wiped his hands on his apron and offered the girls a cabbage roll when they stopped by the store after school.

But even if Shelly was not quite pretty, she had the most interesting secrets to share in the back seat of the bus.

What inspired all the secret-telling was a couple early in the trip, way back in Richmond. The girl wept when the loudspeaker crackled to life and announced the bus for "Williamsburg, Hampton, New Bern, Charleston and points south." After some severely schmoopy kisses and some whispered I-love-yous, he climbed aboard. She disappeared into the Richmond night.

"What do you suppose their story was?" Ginni had asked as she dropped coins into the vending machine.

"They looked younger than us, even," said April, wiping the dew from a can of root beer.

"I can't imagine saying, 'I love you' to anybody," said Ginni, breaking open her PayDay bar.

"I'm sure you imagine it all the time, saying it to my brother."

"No, I want Marc to say it to me. I can't imagine choking the words out myself."

"I've said it." Shelly popped an M&M.

They huddled around her. Really? To who?

"I've said it lots of times."

And even though April narrowed her eyes—*If you've said it lots of times, then how can you mean it?*—they slurped up every word of this story.

Shelly confessed she'd been kissed, too. Well, they knew that, but when was the first time?

"With Mike Truitt. My mom took me over to do homework. We were watching TV. I think it was *Six-Million-Dollar Man* …"

"You think?" said April. "You don't know?"

Shelly smiled a smile full of secrets. "Not that I was paying much attention to the show! My mom," she rolled her eyes, "my mom says I need to go talk to the bishop." Which was what hormone-addled

Mormons had to do if they went too far beyond kissing.

In any case, bishop probably knew what Shelly Galvin was up to. Nobody could forget the day at Brandywine State Park when one of the stake people tapped him on the shoulder. "We've got a couple kids in a van with Boxford County plates."

"Well, I shouldn't think so," said Bishop Keating. "All our youth are weeding flower beds. That's what we brought them here to do."

"You might want to check. Somebody saw these two making out to beat the band."

And when he found the van—his van—and opened the doors, Mike Truitt emerged. Shelly followed, her t-shirt askew, her lips chapped, her eyes cast down at the state park gravel but her mouth fighting back a small, proud smile.

Now Shelly stood at the arcade games, toying with the joystick as her Marine wrapped around her from behind, shoving his hands into her sweatshirt pockets.

They watched as Danny whispered in Shelly's ear, as she playfully slapped him away.

Then the happy couple left the Tail Gunner game, gazed unhungrily at the vending machine full of off-brand chips, then wandered back to where his duffle leaned against her suitcase and blankie.

The night wore on. Passengers lined up for the 3:55 bus to Springfield, Tulsa, Albuquerque and so on, the one Danny was supposed to be on. Instead, he sat in the seat next to the wall and stroked the down on Shelly's cheek as she dozed against him.

April and Ginni looked at each other.

"Blecchh!" said April.

"Double blecchh."

"I could've predicted this. I didn't see it coming, but I should've. I should've seen, when he got on the bus ..."

"How does she do it?"

"... that he was just like Will and Mike and all the others, only buttoned up into a uniform, and that she would end up in his lap, somehow. Ginni, wipe that look off your face. That is *not* a 'double blecchh' look."

"Well, aren't you just a tiny bit jealous?"

"Huh! Are you saying you wish it was you over there getting pawed by Danny?"

"No, not him! Just … you know."

"Oh, right. You'd like to play that little scene with my brother."

"Gosh," Ginni looked around, "do you have to tell the whole world?"

"But jealous? Of Shelly?" April screwed up her face. "What's she got? This guy? And Will?"

* * *

Will first appeared at a church dance. He spoke in an unknown tongue. "Yeah, I'll be using a Holley 850 dual pumper. I got the Eldebrock Hi-Rise manifold already."

Ginni had followed the sound of this brassy voice down the hallway and around the corner until she found its source perched on the edge of an overstuffed chair in the foyer. A pair of lambchop sideburns clung to his pink skin. His wiry body looked like it might launch skyward at any minute as he continued his story: "But I still need a four-foot stroker crank and a full dry sump set-up."

Alan Mulryan, sitting in the opposite chair, looked like he understood this tongue.

Shelly, her legs crossed, her sandaled foot swinging, looked like it didn't matter if she understood or not. What mattered, Ginni was sure, were the half dozen boys draped over the couch arms and slouched against the sofa skirts, flipping each other with neckties. They were all here because of *her*.

What mattered were the people that walked by, and saw everyone here because of *her*.

What mattered was Will, showing off because of *her*. "… I

decided to go to a 4.88 gear but the car launches really hard, then pulls to the left...."

Oh, you could tell that life was good for her when she held court! Well, mostly. One of the younger boys threw a shoe past Shelly's head, and Ginni saw the flash of annoyance that crossed Shelly's face. It might have been fun to see her lose her cool, but Shelly was too smooth for that.

She just sighed. "I'm thirsty."

The news rippled through the foyer. Alan Mulryan stood up. "What do you want? A Sprite?"

"Oh, could you?" Shelly looked up into his eyes.

Alan bolted away, followed by all the lemmings.

Will watched them go. "Kinda pesky, aren't they?"

Shelly smiled at Will. "I feel like walking."

So they strolled.

They acted like two lovers standing on a bridge over the Seine, intoxicated by the spring blossoms and the lights shining on the water. But no, this was not Paris. It was a church hallway, with cook-out announcements on the bulletin board and a framed painting of Jesus by a fishing boat and a drinking fountain with a reef of lime deposit growing in the bowl.

The next time Ginni saw them, the dance was over. Just as everybody put on their coats, Shelly and Will appeared, all hand-holdy, as if they'd been steadies for months. "Let's stop at Friendly's on the way home," Shelly suggested to the group.

"Can we?" she asked the chaperones.

Will followed them there in his mufflerless car. It wasn't the one that launched really hard, but it was a manly car all the same. And when the group scooted into a big round booth at Friendly's, he scooted beside Shelly. He looked at her as if she were the prized 4.88 gear he'd been looking for all his life.

When the hamburgers came, he bit into a bun that stretched from sideburn to sideburn. He dipped his fries into a lake of ketchup. When the lake ran dry, he opened the bottle. He was just about to turn it upside down and spank out more when his eyes narrowed. His lips parted.

He peeled away a ketchup booger dried to the neck of the bottle. And then he ate it.

Ginni saw April push her plate away.

Shelly smiled as if she were still holding court.

And Ginni wondered: how hard was it, really, to attract lint?

* * *

Shelly picked up bits of his aftershave, clinging to his collar. She had caught that scent back in the Dayton station, when the driver gave them 15 minutes.

There Danny was, sticking his neck out to look ahead at the line, his slouchy duffel at his feet. There she was, passing by, intent on the bathroom and the vending machines.

She smelled it full-on now. She opened her eyes. He lay asleep, the shadow of down darkening his upper lip. She looked beyond, where Ginni stared into space, gripping the collar of her coat against her neck. April slept, looking exactly like a child who had learned to zonk out anywhere in the station wagon. A mom kept calling: "Jayden, don't run." "Jayden, get off the floor!" Wayworn passengers sat surrounded by their luggage.

She had caught the scent again when he got on the bus. He had searched the seats, the way they all do, looking for an empty one. He saw her. He wanted to sit with her. She knew it. But the only space was beside that grandmother.

So he sat there.

She saw him pull out the Juicy Fruit. She knew he would offer her a stick.

But he offered it to the grandma.

Suddenly, Shelly was less sure of everything. And she had been sure of herself since little Gary Adams, the newest boy in the sixth grade, followed her onto the skating party bus. Afterward, he bought her a Coke float and clung by her side until she ditched him and spent the rest of the party skating doubles with Alan Mulryan.

She didn't know what she did. But whatever it was, it worked. Whatever it was, it made her get along better with boys than girls. Girls resented her and shut her out. Boys showed off for her. They let her join them when they shot baskets or threw rocks in the river or swam. Their voices on the other end of the phone were thrilling. Their shadows, when they drew near waiting for a chance to talk to her, were empowering. She felt like she made the planets move.

But when Danny offered gum to April, Shelly's life passed before her eyes. What had she done wrong? April was boring. Nobody had *ever* passed up Shelly to strike up a conversation with that kind of girl.

Then he offered some to Ginni. Why Ginni? Tall, gangly, thought she was special. Craned her neck, looked around with superior eyes at Shelly's house, no doubt noticing the chipped paint on the porch swing, and the tilted floor by the stairs.

So when was the last time Shelly had felt that move-the-planets feeling? And could it have been The Last Time For All Time? Was she losing her touch?

No! This couldn't be!

So she sat on the arm of April's seat. "Elderberry, Ohio? What kind of place is that? Really? No, I've never been anywhere near Ohio, except for—. Are we still in Ohio? We just crossed into Indiana?—Yeah, so, I've never been near Ohio except for a few minutes ago. Nooo, I don't think you're all farmers. When did I say that? So, are you? No? A garbage man? Oh, your dad is a garbage man. No, I never went near them. I was always scared of them. They tossed things into that big truck and pulled the lever. Once you've seen the truck chew up an entire couch … No, I'm fine, thanks. This stick of gum's still good. Well, OK then. I'll save it for later. So, tell me …"

And he'd been telling her ever since.

And then he changed his ticket, just to be with her a little longer.

Did she still have it? Yes! Yes, she did, she told herself as she dozed against him and his duffel bag. *Yes, she did,* as they called the bus for Kansas City and Denver and she stood in line beside him, smelling the scent of boy and menthol and clean shirt that he gave off. Yes, she did, as they woke up to billboards high on the Missouri hills and bare trees in the Kansas ravines and dark settling over lonely acres of corn stubble, as they snuggled to the tales of his first joint and his high school's worst cafeteria dish and things moms say and what the Pacific Ocean looks like.

When the bus rocked, she drifted off to sleep, picturing him in Quonset huts, just like the ones she'd seen on TV. And she pictured his letters in the mailbox beside that chipped porch swing at home, and his handwriting—*When you come out here, we'll* ... She pictured folding things into her suitcase as April and Ginni sat on the bed, silent with awe that she was going to join him in California and what would her new life be like? Ruffled kitchen curtains? Bicycling on the boardwalk? Reaching for rice on the grocery store shelf while Danny put Spaghettios in the cart? Watching the street from their second-floor balcony while Danny wrapped his arms around her from behind?

She woke to the night-lit bank buildings of Denver. She held his hand as they walked into the station, letting go only to stock up on M&Ms and Mountain Dew.

On the next bus, they sat far, far behind Ginni and April. When the driver switched off the lights and the Mexicans across the aisle fell asleep, they commenced a quiet and juicy kissing.

* * *

The first thing Ginni heard when she stepped off the bus was the throat-clearings of a truck jake-breaking its way toward the freeway ramp. The morning sunlight slid across the roof of its trailer as the rig eased off the Interstate and turned in here at the West Winds Truck Stop.

If the driver had any problem at all, he could get it fixed here. Giant signs claimed that the West Winds sold truck fuel, truck repair, truck tires, truck washings and, no doubt, truck-sized lunches of coffee and chicken-fried steak. Offering it all at the West Winds kept the trucker at a safe remove from Dixie Junction, Utah, a town nestled against the rhino-rump mountains somewhere across the freeway.

The West Winds also received Greyhound buses, transferring drifters from route to route, making little Dixie Junction an important place in the Greyhound world, all out of proportion to its significance in the rest of the world.

Ginni spotted April up ahead, opening the door plastered with Newport cigarette posters.

Inside, Ginni pushed past the wall hung with cough drops, batteries and condoms. She caught up with April in the two-seater bathroom. "So," said Ginni, studying her image in the mirror, "this is the face I'm wearing into a town full of college boys?"

"All I know is, there better be three showers at Teresa's house," said April from behind the stall door, "or there'll be a serious fight about who goes first."

"Please don't remind me about Teresa."

"Why? What's the matter?"

"My stomach does these little clenches when I think about her. It did it when our parents added her to the trip."

"Why would your stomach do that?" April left the stall and turned on the sink water.

"If you tell her you've got the worst cramps of your life, she gives you that make-me-care look."

"Yeah." April dried her hands. "I wouldn't want to be a woolly worm in Teresa's path."

Ginni took one last hopeless swipe at her now-oily hair and gave up. Leaving the restroom, she walked out into fluorescent brightness. Across the store, Danny and Shelly walked so closely down the aisles that their ears nearly fitted together like chairs meant to hook in a row. They reached for things that Ginni could not see. Ginni turned away. She studied a display of personalized key rings. Geraldine, Gina, Glenda, Gloria. Nope. So far as the key-ring maker was concerned, she didn't exist.

"We'd better eat," said April, pointing toward the menu board over the grill.

"Meet you there in a minute."

Ginni squeezed past a trucker reaching for a box of Vivarin. She searched the shelves for her Chicken in a Biskit. A packet of trail mix caught her eye and after she looked it over and put it back on its hook, she turned to find Shelly at the end of the aisle, her fingers with their bitten nails plucking an assortment of sugar-glazed and crème-filled goods off the shelves.

"Well," said Ginni. She felt her face flush. Wanting sugar was so embarrassing.

But Shelly acted terribly absorbed. The apple pie or the cherry? Such a big decision!

Ginni stood there, quite sure that she was as visible as the cans of Pringles and bags of marshmallows all around them. Ice clattered from a dispenser into someone's cup. A man asked for Marlboro menthols, "two please." The till rung, and the cashier quietly prompted a trainee, "No, you can just hit the cancel. Like this."

She turned and walked away.

She stopped again at the key rings. They swayed and clicked as she searched them once more. She heard Danny's voice and turned to look. He and Shelly spread their goodies, all packaged up in shiny plastic, before that trainee cashier. Shelly stood as if her body simply wouldn't turn a few degrees to the right, say, in the direction of the key rings.

Nope, there was no Ginni here.

Ginni walked toward the sizzle of the grill. "I hate moments like these," she whispered as she slid on to the lunch counter stool next to April.

"Moments like what?" April mounted a stool.

"Like when you see somebody you know in a store and you *know* they don't want you to acknowledge them."

April looked back at the register. Shelly was already gone. "My mom says that's how people act when they're doing something they don't want you to see."

"What aren't we supposed to see? That she's living on Hostess Pies?"

"And to think," said April as she stared up at the menu board, "that she chose empty nutrition over the chance to eat all this wholesome … 'Chicken Koop Buster'? Any guesses what that is?"

* * *

The next bus out of Dixie Junction idled beyond the diesel pumps. The sandy-haired driver looked like he'd eaten his share of Chicken Koop Busters. As he handed back what remained of her ticket, Ginni followed April up the steps.

She shouldn't have taken so long to finish her grilled cheese sandwich. Every other passenger, it seemed, had escaped the West Winds before she and April did. Now the people sat secure in their seats, staring back at her.

Ginni finally found a place a couple rows behind April. She settled against the rough upholstery. She watched the billboards of Dixie Junction give way to a landscape of scratchy bush, thirsty dirt and loneliness.

There wasn't much to look at inside the bus, either. Disheveled, puffy-eyed people. Which reminded her that she looked pretty ruined herself. And Provo was hardly two hours away. And she had loaned Shelly her little mirror. Ginni got up to retrieve it.

She gripped the seats to steady herself against the sway of the bus. She passed unshaven cheeks, sleeping mouths drooping open, another probable runaway working her way through a package of powdered donuts.

Which might be what Danny and Shelly were doing right now. At least Ginni hoped so. *Please don't let them be making out.*

She arrived at the back of the bus. She looked at the bathroom door, at the last few seats before her.

She saw only a Mexican boy with a wisp of a mustache, and a pockmarked man who looked away from her.

She walked the aisle again. How had she missed Shelly's stick-straight brown hair? But there was no Shelly. There were only the unwashed masses, stirring, looking up at her as her eyes darted from seat to seat. There was only, outside the windows, white lines and gravelly road shoulders. And there was *no Shelly.*

Ginni walked forward, her hips bumping the seats. She tapped April's shoulder. "She's not back there."

April blinked awake. She fingered the edges of her parka, draped over her like a blanket.

"Shelly's gone. Danny's gone."

"That can't be." April wiped the corners of her mouth. "Did you check the bathroom?"

"How can I …? No. I'm telling you. They aren't there!"

April stood up, dropping her parka into the seat. She followed Ginni back. Fellow passengers, roused by the way the girls bustled down the aisle, watched their progress.

Ginni was right. No Shelly.

* * *

"You left our friend behind," April told the driver.

"She wants to ride my bus, she shows up before I buckle my seat belt."

"But she's a long way from home …"

"Miss," the driver looked up in the mirror, "we're all a long way from home."

"You can't do this!"

"Was that the girl with the soldier boy?" asked a grandma in the front seat.

"Was Danny supposed to be on this bus with us?" Ginni asked April. "Wasn't he supposed to change again somewhere?"

"Look, mister, we can't just show up without her!" April said. "What's she gonna do?"

"Behind the white line! You wanna ride my bus, you stand behind the white line!"

"Her soldier boy'll help her," a grandma patted April's arm as the girls walked away from the white line.

"I'll bet he will!" sniggered a man with a three-tooth grin.

Ginni blinked back tears. "We're in *trouble*."

And there was nothing to do but watch the ghastly desert and the occasional striped butte and lonely billboard go by. There was nothing to do but think about how Teresa Galvin would take news like this.

* * *

Teresa parked next to a skeletal tree. A light dandruff of snow floated down from the gray sky, with little flakes resting in the grooves of her windshield wipers. She glanced at the car clock. 2:05. Ten minutes until bus time.

She opened the sack over in the passenger seat and took out the long maple donut. She would have gotten the chocolate one, too. But the guy standing behind her, waiting his turn at the donut case, had given her such a look—*packing some pounds in those pants, aren't you?*—that she left the chocolate one, perfectly glazed, fresh and spongy, behind.

Since she had last visited the bus station, someone had painted a blue stripe around on the place. There it was, stretching like a belt across the concrete blocks, making the squat little building look like a laundromat.

She mowed through her donut much too fast. A vast disappointment settled over her as she shoved the last bite into her mouth.

Then she stepped out of the car, pulling her gray wool jacket a little tighter. She walked across the patching veins in the parking lot.

The station door squealed as she pulled it open. A jaundiced light shone over the world inside—the off-brand chips in the vending machine, the fiberglass chairs bolted to the floor. And beyond the rack of route brochures? Why, it was the man who had stood behind her at the donut case. She had been in such a hurry to disappear back then that she had failed to notice his Greyhound-issue tie. But here he was, sitting behind the counter, frowning over the carbon smudges on his thick fingers, rubbing at them with his hanky.

Teresa slipped back outside. Let him have his lonely old station. She wasn't going to sit there in those orange chairs, subjecting herself to more Looks—oh no! She got the looks even when she was nowhere near a donut. And they said, *Came here to find a nice clean-cut Mormon boy, did you? Couldn't find him, could you? Now you're sitting around waiting for a message from God about what to do with yourself, aren't you?*

Come to think of it, Mr. Smudged Fingertips in there could stand to lay off the donuts himself. Had a belly that added up to too much chassis for his axle, he did.

A pay phone hung on a front corner of the building. Teresa leaned against its boxy frame. She shivered against the cold steel.

She really needed to get out of this town.

* * *

Ginni woke up to a building of granite and pediments passing by outside the bus window. It looked governmental and important.

"Welcome to downtown Provo," said April.

Now Ginni nodded toward a boy and a girl framed in one of the store windows, sipping from white mugs. "Well, goodbye to all that," she said.

"All what?"

"That's the kind of thing I was hoping to do when I got here. But I'm sure that once we're in Teresa's hands, she's going to be on the phone to our parents and we're going to be grounded royally …"

"Well, really, Ginni, what can they do to us?"

"I'm thinking I'll be sleeping on a cot next to the washer in the basement, that's what."

"No, I mean what can they do to us all the way out here? How can you ground somebody when you can't even touch them?"

Ginni considered this as the bus turned onto a back street. As if to seal her mood, everything outside the windows now was boxy, mud-colored and bleak. "They can send us to Teresa. All you have to do to ground somebody is make them miserable, which is what we are about to be."

And as the bus pulled up to the ugliest little station of the entire trip, there stood Teresa Galvin. Ginni's gut stirred. She remembered a prison guard in a late-night movie, a woman who made the inmates scrub the walls with their toothbrushes. And this was how Teresa looked *before* she knew about Shelly.

She nudged April. "Let's just stay on the bus. Maybe it goes to Montana or something."

"Huh?" April screwed up her face. She stood and put on her parka.

Then the bus driver looked up into his mirror before he squeezed out of his seat. Was he staring right at Ginni?

She stood up. Like cattle parading down the chute, she followed April. Passing the driver's levers and window stickers and precious white line, she stepped down into Provo.

She pulled the collar of her pea coat tighter and locked eyes with Teresa. Was now the time to tell, as Teresa glanced at the bus steps, watching and waiting for one more girl to appear?

Ginni decided to look at the bus steps, too. *Why not pretend just a few seconds more?*

"Teresa," said April, "she won't be getting off."

Teresa's eyebrows lifted. "She decided not to come after all?"

"Oh, she came. But, she ... well, she was with us up until Dixie Junction."

"What happened there?"

More snow dandruff floated down through the air.

"I don't know," April said.

Teresa's face clouded over. "You don't know?"

Ginni wondered if they still had a place to sleep tonight.

"I asked the bus driver to go back for her. But," April threw up her hands, "it's his bus, and he makes sure you don't forget it."

"Did the bus leave her behind? Or did she disappear before the bus left?"

April shook her head slowly. "I just ... don't know."

* * *

Teresa opened the door of the station. The man in the Greyhound-issue tie leaned over his counter, his ear cocked at a small woman who pointed toward the restroom. She pushed up beside the lady. "Sorry, ma'am. This can't wait— I need you to call the Dixie Junction station now!" she told the station guy.

His mouth hung open.

"I mean it. Now! We've lost a 17-year-old girl, about my height, straight brown hair."

"Would you like to fill out a fo–?"

"Look, mister, maybe all you're used to are your typical Monday afternoon problems like—" Teresa turned to the lady, "like whatever your problem is. What *is* your problem? Are they out of toilet paper in there? Did a nasty drunk expose himself to you? Well, I'm sorry, but this is more urgent than all that." She turned back to the attendant, who had seen the light and dialed up Dixie Junction.

"Sorry," he said, when he hung up. "Nobody like that there."

"Well, did they look *everywhere?*"

"Miss…"

"Behind the station? In the dumpsters?… "

"Miss…"

"I mean, I really need to know—Is she a body in a ravine somewhere, or just a girl stranded at a lonely station?"

"Dixie Junction wasn't all that lonely," said Ginni. "It had loads of truckers and everythi…"

April flashed Ginni a look. *Shut up! Now!*

"What?" said Teresa. "What about truckers?"

"Nothing," said April, her eyebrows shot up like *It's the honest truth!*

"Well, anyway," said Ginni, "the last time we saw her, she was with her Marine."

"*Marine?*" said Teresa. "Oh, this is getting better all the time!"

She could not absorb it all, something about a boy from Ohio headed for California, and Shelly sleeping on his shoulder. She turned to the Greyhound guy. "Is there a bus to California out of Dixie Junction?"

He flipped through his tables and schedules.

"When did it leave?" she asked. "Where did it go?"

He looked up. "10:25. Las Vegas, Barstow, Victorville…"

"Las Vegas?" Teresa closed her eyes, gripping her head. "No. She didn't."

"What?" She heard April say. "What about Las Vegas?"

"Haven't you heard?" said Ginni. "Elvis wedding chapels? Quickie marriages?"

"For movie stars, yeah. But ordinary people?"

"This is not ordinary." Teresa opened her eyes. "This is rash, this is stupid, this is… just like Shelly." She turned back to the attendant. "How do I find out where she got off?"

He shrugged. "We aren't running a kindergarten field trip here."

Teresa tightened her jaw, glared at him one last time, then walked away.

* * *

Ginni watched out the car window as Teresa drove into a neighborhood of narrow, brooding houses. They passed dinky porches cluttered with tricycles and stacks of loose bricks. After Teresa parked, she led them down an alley and unlocked a side door. Then she stepped into her kitchen. "Here it is. The other girls will be home in a while."

Ginni lifted her suitcase over the threshold. She looked around at the dull yellow walls and the chipped white cupboards, at the dish drainer and the plastic tumblers. She imagined the 1920s housewife who first lived here, sealing little jars of canned jam with wax and wiping her hands on her apron.

April sat at the kitchen table. So did Ginni, overcome with defeat. What was supposed to be a half week of smiling at the boys in the student union had gone all wrong. So even though Teresa asked them if they wanted a glass of milk, Ginni wasn't about to say yes because, judging by the way Teresa tossed keys on the counter and slapped cupboard doors shut, Ginni didn't want to be resented any *further.*

Teresa led them to the living room couches, where they would sleep. She pointed April to one bathroom, then led Ginni to the other one upstairs.

When Ginni left that tight little corner bathroom a half hour later, combing through her wet hair, she found a heavy girl stepping through the kitchen door. Her scrubs looked like they'd been stuffed with pillows.

"Whew!" she said. "And they said it would be snowing by now. I don't believe them." She plunked down her roomy purse, adjusted the waist of her scrubs and examined April and Ginni before her.

"Bet it felt good to wash off all that bus grime." She reached into a cupboard and pulled out a stack of cookies. "So," she held out cookies to the new girls, "didn't we say we were going to order Chinese?"

"Nancy, please. Give it a rest, huh?" said Teresa.

Nancy looked around the room. "Well, we're still taking them to Heaps of Pizza tomorrow, aren't we? We've talked it about it for weeks. You're gonna like ... wait a minute. Where's the other girl? Aren't there supposed to be three of you?"

Teresa explained all about Shelly and Dixie Junction and how her parents had sounded on the phone just now.

Nancy the nurse gave an appropriately stunned gasp.

So did Carlene, when she came in from her long social-worker day.

So did Garrett from next door, when he stopped in to ask if they had Reddi-Whip.

By the time all of Garrett's roommates showed up, the phone rang.

"Shhhh!" said Carlene.

Teresa took a deep breath. "Hello? Oh, hi. You heard, huh?" She put her hand over the mouthpiece, mouthed some name, pointing across the alley. "No," she spoke into the phone, "we've been waiting to hear. I don't know."

And the phone kept ringing.

"I can't have them calling all the time," Teresa complained. "They're tying up the line, in case Shelly *does* call."

So Carlene said to tell people to stop calling. A couple of the guys left to knock on doors around the block, which silenced the phone—but brought twelve more people through the door. Ginni and April sat among them, useless or accused—who knew which?— on a couch covered by an itchy Indian blanket. Well, probably not accused, because all those people offered them Fig Newtons and ice cream and some raw cookie dough one girl hadn't had a chance to bake yet. And here came Garrett, with Reddi-Whip from the supermarket down the street, and his store-bought pumpkin pie.

"Shouldn't we help or something?" Ginni whispered as Nancy passed her the bowl of cookie dough.

"I don't think so," Nancy whispered back. "You'll notice that Carlene has seized the floor here. These chances don't come along for her every day." She bit off half a spoonful. "Well, they do down at the agency. Down there, every day, she takes her cases under her wing and says, 'Are you taking your lithium?' Or, 'You can't say yes to your sister-in-law! That's how you ended up in jail the last time.' But none of us ever see her in action, do we?"

Ginni watched Carlene, over at the table, asking police-show questions like, "She's not eighteen, is she? Because if she is, she's free to go."

"Trust me," Nancy muttered as she licked her spoon clean, "Carlene is having the time of her life."

Through a murky window, Ginni saw night advancing. The thought of Shelly just taking off like that—and they were pretty sure she had gone on her own will, weren't they?

Weren't they?

Well, no, they weren't, not when Carlene called April and Ginni in to the kitchen for questioning. "Did he seem dangerous?"

"Well, ..." said April, "how can you tell? I mean, really."

"Aren't Marines trained to kill?" said Ginni.

The room erupted. "Ginni!" "Don't even!" "Yeah, the enemy, but ..."

"But what if all that training takes them kind of close to the edge," Ginni said, "and they tip right off it right after they meet a girl on a bus and ..."

"Ginni, please!" said Teresa.

Ginni shrank under Teresa's scowl.

Carlene held up her hand. "We aren't even going to think about that. Now, did you see her luggage still in the station?"

No, they didn't see it anywhere. Of course she took her luggage. It had everything she needed. And you just don't take off for parts unknown without everything you need. Or do you? Ginni wondered. Don't you count carefully? *Seven pairs of underwear, $40 for lunches. Yes, yes, that's right. No, no, let me count again.* And to just … go! Without counting again, without knowing if what was stuffed into your pockets and folded in with your pajamas and your shampoo was enough for whatever lay ahead, well, … it was …

It was perversely intriguing, that's what it was. This was bound to turn out interesting. Not that Ginni would say so out loud, but whatever happened next would … well, yes, they all cared about Shelly and didn't want her tied up in a room somewhere but, just in case she already was, Ginni wanted to know: Did she struggle? Did she scream? Did she try to escape?

By now, they were out of ice cream. But they still had chocolate syrup. Ginni held out the spoon they gave her and somebody poured it full, straight from the can. She ate it while the quiver of *what's next* snaked through the room.

"I don't think we should wait to call the police," Carlene told them all.

One of the guys read the police station's phone number off a fridge magnet, kindly provided by some local funeral home.

"No, you want the police in Dixie Junction."

"What do you mean, you can't remember what she was wearing?" Teresa demanded of Ginni. "She wore it for three days, didn't she?" She got up from the table, the picture of exasperation, and headed for the stairs.

Carlene followed.

April watched them go. "Obviously, she needs comforting." She looked at Ginni.

"You do it," said Ginni.

April started for the stairs.

But Nancy held up her hand. "Remember: Carlene *owns* the job," she whispered.

And since Carlene was doing the only thing that needed doing, the rest of them watched one of the guys balance his spoon on his nose. Then, they all wanted to know how he did it. So he showed them and they all tried. Nancy gave a little cry of joy when she got her spoon balanced, but she quickly clapped her hand over mouth. After all, they were gathered here over very grave circumstances.

Then the phone rang.

Twelve spoons dropped into twelve laps. Ginni heard footsteps from the stairs—did the room always shake when Carlene walked through it?

"Hello? April? Yeah, she's here."

It was Marc. He wanted to come right away when he heard.

* * *

Ginni settled into the backseat of Nancy's car. A shopping bag full of yarn—the sheeny, white kind, perfect for baby booties—crowded her feet. Across the seat, a jumble of holey tennis shoes, liquid laundry detergent and an empty M&Ms bag, the big party-bowl size, littered the upholstery.

"So what kind of nurse are you?" April asked up in the front seat.

"I work in dialysis," said Nancy. "We had a guy today who kept trying to pull out his chest catheter. They get old and forgetful, tired of coming in and sitting there for four hours week after week. It gets sad."

Nancy's eyebrows lifted as she checked traffic before a turn. Her fingernails rested just so on the steering wheel. "The thing you have to watch out for," she went on to April, who nodded with interest, "is the bruising. If you don't get the needle in just right, their arm just blows up, full of blood."

Ginni wished it would stop, all this talk of a sad job that filled a sad life. She looked out the window. She wanted to be one of those girls on the sidewalk in their belted coats. They were girls with bright prospects, girls somebody would want. And if Ginni did not figure out some way to break out of her same old self, she too would end up in a car like this, describing her daily routine to some young girl whose careful smile hid what she really thought: *How do you go on, day after day?*

Now Nancy's car approached a cluster of towers. "Here's where Marc lives," she said.

And Ginni walked into his building.

A dozen college boys sat in the commons room. They looked up from the tangle of boxy orange and red couches.

Ginni edged away from Nancy.

"We are being looked over," April whispered.

"Shelly would know what to do right about now."

"Right. Sit down by biggest misfit in the room, chat him up, have his arm around her in ten minutes."

"Yeah, but how does she figure out what to chat about?" said Ginni. "Or how to *make it happen?*" Ginni stole a glance at the boys. Most had textbooks open in their laps. One spun a basketball on his finger.

"Just walk up and start blathering about anything. Go ahead and try it."

She stood, paralyzed, blinking towards the night-blackened windows far across the room. She could feel them turning back to their books.

Then Marc stepped out of the elevator. "Any news?"

"Nothing yet," said Ginni, as she threw her arms around him.

Over Marc's shoulder, she saw April's jaw drop. Ginni pulled away, shocked at herself.

But in the car, he sat with her in the back seat as they told him all.

"He got on in Ohio," said Ginni.

"We didn't suspect a thing back there in Dixie Junction. I mean, how could we?" said April.

"And Teresa kept saying, 'I need to know! Is she a body in a ravine somewhere?'"

Marc slipped his arm around Ginni. She settled into the crook of it, the Friend in Shock. "And the guy at the Greyhound station, he was really kind of callous about it all. Don't you think so, April?"

April turned halfway around in her front seat. Ginni could see her eyes sweeping over the scene—Marc's arm, Ginni resting against it. April rolled her eyes and faced front again.

* * *

Back at the house, Ginni resumed her spot on the Indian-blanket couch.

Marc sat beside her.

Until Nancy reached for the Sugar Pops in the kitchen cupboard. "Anybody hungry? Marc, how about you?" she called from the kitchen.

Then he was gone.

So Ginni went for Sugar Pops, too. She joined Teresa, Carlene and the rest of them as they sat, waiting, waiting, waiting, around the silent phone at the center of the little kitchen table. They doodled on junk mail. They arranged and re-arranged the spoons. They tried to stay hyper-vigilant, for that was the one thing they could do for Shelly. Wasn't that so?

But the creeping mists of fatigue settled in. People stood up, yawned and announced that they really had to be going, "but you'll let us know as soon as you hear anything, won't you?"

Garrett and company offered Marc their lumpy couch.

"Might as well," Marc said. "No doubt they've locked up the dorm by now."

* * *

When Shelly awoke and looked out the bus window, a sad land-scape of bent, squat trees passed by.

It was a rustling among the passengers that woke her. Shelly didn't know how they all knew it, but every time, when they were still miles from Washington or Indianapolis or Las Vegas, people stood up, reached for their bags in the overhead, threw on their coats. Then, twenty minutes later, Washington or Indianapolis or Las Vegas suddenly rose on the horizon.

Maybe it was a certain billboard, or farm, or rock that clued them off.

And they had been riding by a lot of rocks lately. Rocks like ships' prows. Rocks like arches. Rocks like walls, hugging in close to the bus.

Danny stirred beside her.

She caught a quick breath. This was like coasting downhill on a bike, only more grown-up. *Look at me! Look at him! Look at me with a man, not a boy!*

She had laid against the utter hardness of his shoulder all through the trip and listened to his stories.

"It's called the Crucible," he had said of the final challenge of boot camp, while they rode through counties full of scrub and brush. And rocks. "We'd hike six miles. We'd start at 2:30 in the morning, and it was, like, so cold my fingers felt like they were being sliced off by a cheese grater."

"Oooh," she said. "But it's only six miles, at least."

"Oh, that's just the first part. It went on for a couple more days. And don't forget, we were carrying guns and ammo cans and the rest."

"Oh, my!"

"Not to mention that one of the heavier guys kept getting mys-teriously hit by a 'sniper.' And since Marines never leave casualties behind, guess who kept getting the duty of carrying him out?"

She had looked up at him then, suddenly sure that she could never again tolerate the stories Boxford boys told. *Yeah, I raced him down Bear Swamp Road!* Or, *I'll just get on at Crayton's. They're hiring right now.* Yep, last week, Will was The Bomb, the Big Man, the pinnacle. Now, suddenly, he was just a poor guy stuck in Boxford County, the born-there-lived-there-died-there kind.

And she was here, flying down that hill. The real high began when she had said yes to Danny back in Dixie Junction. She had been leaning against an outdoor wall back at the West Winds, pinned there by Danny, his warm breath on her face. "Why don't you just come on to California with me?" he whined softly.

They were half-hidden in this little spot, shielded by stacks of truck tires, *Buy 3, Get One Free!* She looked out to where two men with overhanging bellies conferred, a red truck hood gaping open high above their heads.

"Beach-ezzz," Danny said. "Palm treeeees. You know you want to."

She laughed. "Danny, we have beaches a half hour from Boxford. It's not like I've never seen a lot of sand." She laughed again at the mock pout on his face. "Why don't you come to Provo with me?"

"Oh, you don't understand. I'm expected back Tuesday at noon. And they don't take kindly to 12:01. Once you sign on the line, they own you."

And he pinned her to the wall again.

She had closed her eyes. She could taste his last cigarette there on his probing tongue. And there against the wall, breathing in the spruce and smoke and sweat that was all of him, she said yes, she'd go on to California.

And then they had rushed inside and bought fried pies and Milk Duds, as if *that* would cure the hunger that had been building, building, building out by that brick wall.

And now they were far down the road, stirring awake like the other passengers. When Danny opened his eyes, he held out his hand. She gave him the Budweiser she had kept hidden for him in her blanket.

He had bought the six-pack in Las Vegas, finishing one bottle, stashing the rest in his duffel bag. "Do you want one?" he had asked her there, as they stood on the oily parking lot of a 7-11.

"Uh-uh," she had told him, holding her blanket, adopting a pose familiar to every Mormon girl and boy: *I don't do that.* And as she watched him tip his head back and pour it in his mouth, she had suddenly remembered a dark-paneled basement room where she *had* done it once upon a time.

She remembered that she had clipped her bangs back that night in tiny barrettes—very junior high—and worn a citrus-bright shirt that skimmed above her bare midriff. She had grasped the can. She knew its aroma, had smelled it at baseball games and parades yet never known that smell was *beer.* She had taken a sip. And smiled coolly, even though she wanted to spew it out of her mouth, all over the cheap couch, all over her friends standing there bouncing to the beat of the music, every one of them with a can in their hand.

But so what? That night was like an old sneaker in the back of a closet now. Who would find it, or even want it?

So she, in her Mormon Girl pose, had strolled beside Danny down Fremont Street in Las Vegas. They made their way past parking decks and towering martini glasses that would shine in neon later that night.

Back at the Las Vegas station, Danny had dug two bottles out of his bag. "Here," he said. "Hide these in that blanket for me. That way, I'll have something handy." He winked. "In case I get thirsty on the bus."

And now they were here, wherever here was, blinking awake against the setting sun as it shone through the bus windshield. And Danny wanted that last beer.

"I'm sorry it's warm," she told him.

But he drank it in stealthy swigs, keeping an eye on the driver.

"Fifteen minutes!" the driver barked, and they jostled their way into the aisle with all the other riders who wanted to make the most of fifteen fast-moving minutes.

Just as at every other stop, Danny pulled his duffle bag down from the overhead and carried it with him. Some stuff was safe to leave behind, like a blanket with a nearly-finished beer hidden in its folds. A bag was not.

They stepped down into the town. It was a way-too-familiar routine by now, all of them released from this tin can for a few minutes of freedom, grabbing something to deaden the boredom before stuffing themselves back into the can again.

She waited beside a pay phone while Danny hoisted his bag onto his shoulder.

Behind the bus, across a courtyard, the Golden Arches beckoned.

They walked in. Within minutes, Shelly held a chocolate shake, her lips locked around the straw. Another week on a bus and she would no longer fit into her size four jeans.

Back outside, as dusk settled over the town, Danny stuck a Marlboro in his mouth and flicked his lighter. And flicked. And flicked. He shook the lighter, peering at it through the gathering darkness. Tossing it to the ground, he dashed into the station.

Shelly followed him, her cheeks hollowed in as she sucked hard at the milkshake. He searched racks near the ticket counter. If only he had wanted playing cards, or post cards, or a Snickers bar .... "Damn! Whoever heard of a bus station without lighters?"

He stalked out into the gathering night. She minced after him, her hand damp from the dewy cup. She could see him searching the faces of this backlot, searching for anybody with a light as he turned that cigarette in his fingers. "Danny, where are you going?" She ran to catch up. "What are you doing?"

He passed the front windows of the McDonald's and stood at the lip of a highway, looking up and down at the traffic.

The town had a shorn feeling. It was the same swath of asphalt they had seen in every other town, the same noise and exhaust fumes, the same neon signs, offering tires and gas and pancakes. Yet it was bare and empty and open. Far up the road, a few palm trees stuck up like feather dusters. Across the highway, a half dozen starter trees stood at perfect intervals in front of this burg's version of a mall.

A semi, the last of a small parade of traffic, rolled past, its mud flaps flaring. He reached for her hand and they ran across the road, landing at a 76 station. Dodging the cars pulled up to the gas pumps, he went inside. And there, beside the cash register—plenty of lighters. He dropped his duffel, chose a green one and dug out his wallet.

She caught up as he stood in line. She took his arm, leaning against him with a delicious air of possession. She smiled at the Oriental man behind the counter, who looked as if he wished the customers would drop dead. Failing to get him on her side, she looked away and saw Danny's open wallet. The picture of a brown-eyed girl smiled out at her.

"Who's that?"

"Hey, what the—!"

She took the wallet and pranced away from him and out the door, studying the girl's blonde hair, the dimples under her cheeks, the tiny necklace dangling at her throat. Shelly could hear Danny behind her—"Give it here!" She stepped off the little curb beyond the door, digging the photo out of its little plastic sleeve. Turning it over, she read "love, Marianne" in a juvenile, left-leaning cursive. She turned, waving the photo—"Who's Marianne?" just as he bore down on her and grabbed it back.

Little muscles in his jaw pulsed out and in as he stuffed the picture and the wallet in his pocket and took out his new lighter.

"Who's Marianne?" she asked again.

"Ancient history, that's who." He lit up.

"Is she here in California? Because—"

Because Shelly's picture of "going to California with Danny"—
and she never even knew that she had a picture—was crumbling
like a sand castle right now. The part about stowing her suitcase in
the spare bedroom at his house? Going, going. And the part about
his mother toasting frozen waffles for them the next morning?
Also going. As well as the part about a day, or maybe two days, at
Disneyland.

What? Did he think she was going to live with him in some
cheap apartment? *I don't do that!* Well, sure, she had pictured meeting him at the basement couch, as soon as his mother's house got
dark and quiet, where they would do plenty, then hurry back to
their own rooms before the inevitable parent radar kicked in and the
mom came out of her room, tying the belt on her bathrobe and calling out, *Danny? Did you hear a sound? I thought I heard something.*

Nope. Gone. All gone.

And in its place, Shelly saw only the cheap apartment. With a
Marianne in it. Because—had she forgotten this?—his mom would
be back in Elderberry, Ohio.

He walked in long strides, past the customers at the self-help
pumps, scrubbing the bugs off their windshields. She struggled to
keep up, finally meeting him at the curb before the highway.

"Is she here in California?" she asked again.

"No, she's back in Ohio. Now, come on! We gotta get back to
the bus. "

They waited for a rusty blue pickup to get out of their way, then
scrambled across all four lanes, his smoke wafting back at her.

And they walked around the corner of McDonald's and
looked ahead.

The bus had gone.

* * *

"But it has my suitcase! How do I get my shampoo? And my

jeans? I bought them special for this trip!"

The Greyhound lady's black face was hard, like a schoolteacher's. *Too late! Too bad!* And her forehead was shiny. Shelly wanted to take a Kleenex and wipe it off.

"And my blanket is still on the bus!"

The lady cocked her head. *You think you got problems, White Girl?*

Shelly stalked away, looking for the door out of this bad dream. She sat on a wooden bench. Everything here looked real enough— the sickly yellow lights in the ceiling, the mop bucket with its squeezy jaws over by the restroom doors, the old ticket stubs blown into the corners. But now was the moment she wanted to wake up and find that the smooth table top of her life was not up-ending itself, spilling her blanket and hairbrush and footie socks and Boxford High and the bedroom of her house on Vine Street into a maw of unfathomable depths, never to be seen again.

Danny would fix this problem. Look at him, over there by the Greyhound lady, nodding as she unfolded timetables and pointed at speckles on the page and said things like "9:55 ... 7:10 ... 10:18 ..."

Or maybe not. He made the problem, after all. He *needed* that stupid lighter, couldn't do without it.

How many times in Greyhound-world could you change your mind, darting here and there? Shelly opened the zipper on her denim purse. The ticket inside no longer looked like the crisp and official document it had been when Danny handed to her back in Dixie Junction. It looked desperately used, like everything else beside it—the hairbrush choked with brown tangles; the pictures, bent at the edges; the hair ties, too loose now to hold a ponytail; the Kotex, which had picked up a tad bit of triple-berry blush from one of the three potted lip glosses that stirred around in there day after day; the dimes and pennies, sunken to the very bottom, one gummed up with something green, and she didn't want to pick at it and see what it was.

In the end, the accordioned ticket had brought her to Mars. Yes, Mars. Sure, this town had gas stations and easy burgers and a mall, if you could call it that. But beyond the neon lights, it was a big, lonely rock out there. And it was one thing to land on Mars with a uniformed man and quite another to land there without a clean pair of panties to your name.

She picked the dime out of the bottom of her purse. She stood up. She walked past Danny and the Greyhound lady. "You can blah-blah-blah take care of that blah-blah-blah when you get to Temecula blah-blah," the lady told him.

And Shelly stepped out into the night.

She faced the phone booth, its door half-sprung open. Oh, she could guess what her mom would say when she dropped the dime in and dialed the house on Vine Street: *Shelly,* (a long pause here, a heavy sigh) *think! For once in your life …*

Then her mom would call Teresa. It would be Teresa who delivered the lectures, as if keeping boys in line was some easy discipline, like remembering to answer the phone in a low and pleasant voice. But what did it matter how you answered the phone if nobody ever called? What was being good if nobody ever invited you to be bad?

She shoved the dime back in her purse. There had to be some other way out of this.

She sank onto the bench against the station wall. And she kept sinking, lying down until her head rested against the paint scars on the probably-gray slats. How long since she had given in to gravity? Wasn't this how bums slept? No, she was not a bum. Things were not that bad yet. She just couldn't think, that's all. Couldn't think anything except how she smelled of skipped gym showers, of how the hair on her head was matted like it got during winter school breaks, the kind where no one was in town and she had nothing better to do than slump in front of the TV.

"Hey!"

Her eyes blinked open. Danny stood before her.

"Don't you know bus stations are dangerous?" he said.

She pushed herself up slowly.

He sat beside her on the bench. "You're probably all right if you stay inside the building, though. 'Cause you never know what shady characters you might meet outside those doors." He hooked his chin over her shoulder. "And *I'm* a shady character."

"Don't, Danny." She pushed away. "Gosh, I'd give anything for a shower right now."

They listened to the whine of traffic.

"Maybe you just need a real meal," he said.

She looked at his face there in the dark. Why so chipper, and on short snatches of sleep, no less? She breathed in, expecting the yeasty smell from one of the last beers in his duffle. And when would he have managed to drink it?

He got up from the bench. Buzzed or not, he was the only one with any idea of what to do next.

She got up and followed him.

* * *

Evie don't much like Mondays. Give her a Friday night anytime. Oh, she may go back to her trailer complaining about her feet and sit there on the couch 'til 2 in the morning, too tired to put her plate in the sink. But she'd rather be darting like a roadrunner and juggling plates right and left and just plain confused with orders than sitting there asking herself, *Evie, do you want refill the napkin dispensers or wash the salt shakers tonight?*

Mondays, they just draggggg. See here—she can tell. Look at her, smoking another one, and it ain't even six o'clock yet and she come on at four. But she's got more time on her hands than suits her and there's only so many napkins to refill, you know?

So far tonight she's had Shorty and Ardean Maxwell, it being Monday and all, come for their usual, which is a hot turkey sandwich for him and the chef's salad with extra Roquefort for Ardean. But that's it. So far. She could just cry sometimes, with how slow it gets.

'Course she knows she'd cry worse if she was up the road waiting tables at Leedy's. They can't keep help more'n three weeks up there. Mr. Leedy's gonna have to lock up the doors for good one of these days soon, on account of Mrs. Leedy sticking her nose into what all, sending the girls home in tears and making the cooks consider using them sharp knives on something other'n onions 'n celery.

No, she knows she got it better at the Calico Grill. It's an easygoing kinda place. Mr. V. knows she been waiting tables since before he could feed hisself, so he don't bother her none. Oh, he and his girlfriend stop in for dinner every night and when he's done, he stirs the gravy in the steam table and counts a couple a things in the walk-in, then he goes away and leaves the crew pretty much alone. And Evie does mean alone, at least on Mondays, when she's the only girl there. And Marshall runs the grill *and* the dishwasher. That's how slow it is.

It is so slow, she could go out and smoke by the dumpster, but it's too late now 'cause the door squeaks open and she's got customers after all. They settle in at table four by the front window.

The guy, a Marine, shoves his duffle bag far into to the booth, where it sits there like there's three people instead of two.

As for the girl, she's been sleepin' on her left side 'cause that's where her hair has been pressed flat and shoved high. And Evie thinks, *We got us another runaway.* They see plenty of 'em at the Calico Grill. That's what you get when you put your coffee shop this close to the Greyhound depot.

Now Evie may be a small woman, but she can handle 'em. Marshall'll tell anybody that she's gotten her fair share to maybe turn around and go home. Though Evie lets him take care of them dopers that come in and pass out at the lunch counter. He can clean up their puke. She ain't touchin' it.

Evie grabs a couple menus.

By the time she gets to table four, the guy in the camo is playing with the salt and pepper shakers and the girl looks like she wishes he'd quit moving everything around like his own toy platoon. And as

Evie fills a couple water glasses and heads their way again, she hears, "If she's such ancient history, why is her picture *still* in your wallet?"

"Drop it, OK?" The Marine pushes the salt and pepper back toward the window and smiles up at Evie. "Couple cheeseburgers," he says. "Coke for you?" he asks the girl.

Evie walks away, writing on her pad. "Anyway, what are you so worried about?" she hears him say.

And while their cheeseburgers sizzle back on Marshall's grill, Evie wipes down the lunch counter. And that Marine boy passes his wallet across the table and the girl looks hard, probably at that picture they been talking about. And Evie can tell the girl's believing every last word of whatever story he's telling. Evie'd bet her Friday night tips that she could tell the whole story herself, she's heard it more times than she's heard herself cough. *She don't understand me. She can't handle me. She's crazy.*

Now if Evie was him, she'd be working less hard on that story and keeping a good eye on the wallet.

"Up!" says Marshall, and Evie drops her rag in the bucket. The cheeseburgers sit in the window, the buns gleamy with grease. Marshall yanks the ticket. Evie grabs the plates, her fingers flinching at the hot spots. She hurries away to table four. It may be the only time she gets to hurry all night long. She wishes it were at least a Thursday, and she was really knocking it out, getting that feeling she gets when she's gotta remember to check with the cook for table eight's chicken fried steak, and set up a new party at table fourteen and see if table one's ready to order yet and clean up the high chair and everything on the floor at the corner booth. G'almighty, she won't lie, but she hates to see somebody bringing a baby in here. Oh, law, what they leave behind!

Evie swoops in, landing the plates before the Marine and his girl.

"You're sure you don't want any?" he looks at the girl, waving the pie menu. "Lemon meringue? Apple?"

Evie reaches for the pad in her pocket.

The girl shakes her head.

Evie smiles and nods. She ain't gonna push it and tell them that she's got a weakness for banana cream herself, even though she can't finish a whole slice.

And she thinks she's gonna have to get to those salt shakers after all. She gets herself a bin. She can hear the faint pad-pad-pad of her shoes as she goes from table to table. She can hear the whine of traffic beyond the front windows. She can hear the clink of the collected shakers as they ride with her from table to table, sliding around in the bin. And she can hear them talking.

"All I really want right now is that shower," says the girl.

"We can get a room," he says. "There's time, before the next bus."

Evie don't wanna know the rest. She just keeps herself busy over at table six and wishes she can't hear him say, "Yep. Travelodge. Right behind this place."

Uh-huh. Does he think that girl don't know the difference between renting a room at the Travelodge and renting one at the Moose Lodge?

"I said, a shower. And that's all."

Evie thinks it's time to drop the check at table four.

"Everthing OK here, young lady?" she says. "Anything else I can get for you?" Evie sees he's left a wad of money there on the table. He's already at the edge of his booth seat, eager to get out of the Calico Grill.

* * *

When the house was finally dark, Ginni lay in her sleeping bag on the couch. A dim beam of light shone somewhere back in the kitchen. A toilet seat banged shut. Voices mumbled in a distant hall. A kitchen chair scraped the floor.

In the dimness and the quiet, Ginni thought about how she'd take the news, if indeed Something Terrible happened. She thought about how many seconds, exactly, that she would look stunned. Then, how many seconds of shedding a tear. She thought about calling her own mother and telling her, and how there would be just a little catch in her voice.

Then Ginni thought about Shelly's funeral, and how she and April would stand together at the grave's edge, and all the other mourners would look at them because they were The Last to See Her Alive.

"You asleep?" she whispered to April, just inches away on the floor.

April stirred. "I *was.*"

Ginni watched the glow of a car's lights passing by outside, just beyond the living room curtains. "Do you think people will blame us?" she whispered.

"What!?" April raised up on her elbow.

"If something terrible happens."

"Quit thinking like that!" April whispered fiercely.

"I can't help it!" Ginni whispered back.

"And what could we do anyway? Stay awake all night, watching her on the bus? Jump across the aisle and pry her head off his shoulder?"

"Yes," said Ginni. "What could we do?"

"Now will you stop all this and go to sleep?"

Ginni laid her head back down. She thought about looking up in class, and seeing a plainclothes officer at the door, calling her out. He'd want a description of Danny. He'd ask questions just like Carlene asked. And her classmates would watch her as she returned to the room after talking to the officer.

"August," said April.

Ginni looked down at her. "What about August?"

"If she gets pregnant, she'll have the baby in August."

"April!"

"Well, I worry about her. You know how she's always saying 'I really need to talk to the bishop'? You know how she told us, on the bus, back by Richmond, that she's done 'everything but'?"

"Well, why doesn't she get herself into the bishop's office?"

"I don't know." April shrugged. "She's real sure that she can always stop just before 'but.' But one of these days, she's going to slip right past it. And there she'll be—one of the girls that doesn't fit into her desk anymore."

Ginni laid back. She inhaled the mustiness of her sleeping bag, felt its worn, campy fabric. "Better pregnant than dead, I guess."

"Ginni! ..."

"Well, she always picks the dangerous ones. Remember the curly-haired guy who used to sit in the back of choir? And she bragged that he had just shown her his switchblade?"

"Oh, him. Did he drop out or something? I haven't seen him for ages."

Ginni studied the shadows across the ceiling. Just thinking of the people in Shelly's orbit felt like walking into a dirty gas station bathroom.

"No, I don't think it's the danger," April went on. "Her switch-blade friend was just another case of her going on and on about her enviable life. What she doesn't get while she's sitting there telling all, and petting at her little bitten-off fingernails and complaining that she couldn't get to her algebra because she was on the phone with seventeen different boys last night, is that none of us envy this life of hers. I mean, I'm not anybody's definition of popular or anything, but I can sure tell the difference between the cheerleader kind of popularity and this K-Mart version."

Ginni watched a light beam from a car outside travel across the wall. The house creaked. Shelly would have been comfortable here. This house, with its scarred wooden door and its dimly lit rooms, was not much different than what Shelly might see out her bedroom window back on Vine Street in Boxford.

What's it like to grow up on Vine Street anyway? What's it like to come to school from that side of town and watch the girls who leave every day in their convertibles and take over all the best tables at Sal's Pizza for an hour, then cruise on home to Riverside Drive, and throw parties on their parents' boats, and get talked about on Monday mornings for how much vodka they can put away?

What's it like to sit on a porch where the concrete at the corner of the top step is broken, and watch the moms in hairnets come home from their shifts at the Crayton Poultry Plant? Do you sit there on the step, pent up like a shaken Coke, waiting to bust out?

Here I am, world!

What's it like to discover that you, too, can make the boys come around, just as much as those girls in the convertibles can? OK, they're not the boys in the golf shirts. They're the drop-outs who come to the school dances and lean against their rumbling muscle cars out there in the parking lot. But really, what's the difference? When you're lying there in the dark, doing everything but, who cares what kind of shirt he just dropped on the floor?

Then again, why would you be anywhere in the dark with boys who own switchblades, who give off fumes of threat just like those rumbling car engines?

Ginni rolled over and looked at April in the darkness. "So where do you think she is right now?"

April shook her head.

"I'm thinking," said Ginni, "somewhere in the desert, about five miles off the road. I'm thinking blood trickling in the dirt, and ..." She sat up. "Aren't there snakes in the desert?"

"You know, you really need to buy a leash and clip it on to that imagination of yours."

Ginni lay back, chastened, frowning.

"I'm trying," said April, "to picture the new Shelly, the one after this."

"Assuming there is an after. Assuming there is no baby in August."

April sighed with irritation. "OK. Fine. But this new Shelly would sit in the lunchroom with us, *not* scanning the room with her eyes and deciding who she's going to drape herself around next, you know?" April sat up, hugging her knees. "This would be a wiser Shelly, a pickier Shelly." She ran her hand over the last rolled-up sleeping bag, the one Shelly was supposed to sleep in. "Maybe she just needs to find one good guy who will cure her urge to hunt."

Ginni could hear April settling back in, breathing deeply.

"Well," said Ginni, "my money's on the policeman that cuts the duct tape off her wrists."

* * *

Shelly tested the water. It had gotten hot pretty quick. She unwrapped the little bar of motel soap and plucked a bleach-scented washcloth off the chrome rack. She unzipped her jeans and let them fall to the floor.

She could hear the TV as she checked the water one more time.

It seemed silly to make him wait out on the balcony. That's what she had told him to do, back when they sat in a booth at the Calico Grill and he kept insisting that a room at the Travelodge would solve all her problems.

Oh really? Because one of her problems was that she had nothing right now, nothing but gum wrappers and that hairy brush and whatever else was stuffed in her little denim purse. Even her lunch money ran low. She'd chinked too much of it into vending machines, figuring that Teresa would give her more for the trip home.

"And how much is a room?" she had asked.

"I'll pay."

"Oh really? And you'll give me the key? And wait outside?"

He had held his hand up, scout's honor. Or something. She never really knew what that Scout hand-thingy was.

But once they stood at the door of room 208, she couldn't make herself tell him to stay outside.

Anyway, bathroom doors have locks, for goodness sakes. It couldn't be any worse than babysitting, where you parked the kid in front of the cartoons and slipped away for a quick rinse.

The water shot over her, strong and hot. A last whiff of her bus-trip self, steeped in diesel fumes and cigarette smoke and scratchy, promiscuous seat fabric, rose up in the steam and ran off in suds down her arms. The shampoo—how long since she had smelled anything sweet?—dripped past her closed eyes. She flicked water off her face and opened her eyes.

A faint shadow moved somewhere beyond the white curtain. "Danny?" She held her breath. The water drummed around her. She wiped away the shampoo suds that ran down her face and peeked out of the curtain.

There was no Danny, just a steamy mirror and her clothes, deflated, on the floor.

She closed the curtain. She pressed it down, down, down against the wall, sealing herself off and—had there been a click of the door a minute ago? She braced her arms against the shower walls, waiting. She listened for the TV.

She could hear nothing but the hot water, spraying.

She sealed the other end of the curtain and dug into the soapiness of her hair.

When she turned the water off, she stepped out onto the weak little mat. She wrapped herself in a towel and bent down, picking through her clothes.

T-shirt? Gamey, but not a total ruin. And, like, what else did she have?

Panties? She tossed them into the garbage and adjusted her towel.

The bathroom door opened. "Danny?"

He walked in.

"Danny! You said you'd wait out there." She could smell the

beer breath as he pulled her to him. She could hear Sister Keating's voice—*Let your dance partner lead*—now, of all times.

She saw the cheap bedspreads out in the room.

"You look so pretty," he said.

Oh really? With her wet brown hair plastered to her head?

He turned her around and pushed her out of the bathroom.

"Danny," she looked for a towel bar, a doorknob, an anything to hold on to. "I don't do that." His push was like wind, the kind that captures storm doors and pins them backward against the clapboards. "Danny, I *don't do that!*" And she caught one last glimpse of herself in the clearing mirror.

* * *

Evie leans against the counter and stares at all those salt shakers. She feels for the pack of Salems in her pocket. Monday nights are gonna kill her of lung cancer, she figures.

She sees Marshall as she walks past the order-up window. He leans against the big steel sink, eating the eggs with hot sauce he has just fixed himself.

Pushing through the kitchen door, she walks past the celery crates and greasy old potato chip boxes. She steps out by the dumpsters and flicks her Bic. Blowing smoke rings into the night air, she looks over at the office window at the Travelodge, where the night manager swivels in his chair, staring at Monday night football on the lobby TV.

Evie blinks at a wedge of light breaking open on the blacktop. Looking up to the second floor, she sees a girlish shape standing in a doorway across the balcony, looking around as if her pet dog has escaped. Then the door shuts.

When Evie finishes her Salem, she stamps it out good. Marshall's playing the radio in the back of the kitchen, with some sports announcer going nuts over a throw to end all throws. She heads for the screen door back to the kitchen. It's all great until her nursey shoes slide on something and she finds the earth isn't underneath her feet anymore. Just as she figures how much a broken bone and six weeks off of work will mess up her life to no end, her elbow knocks hard against the back wall and her feet find the blacktop again and she grabs her throbbing elbow. She says all the words that used to get her kicked out of class grades six through ten (when she quit school) and she kicks the stucco wall which not only whacked her elbow a good one but scraped off a hank of skin. She looks down at the dark pavement.

Lettuce. Them outer leaves Marshall wrenches off before he hacks the iceberg stuff into salad.

She rubs her elbow some more and practices the piece of her mind she's gonna give him after she turns off his radio with a click that means *no more ball games 'til I forget this*, and then she sees a girl walk across the parking lot with a denim purse hanging from her shoulder. She looks back at the balcony which is just a row of dark doors now, every one of them closed.

Evie leans against the back wall of the Calico Grill. She lights up another cigarette and watches the girl walk out to the highway. She's pretty sure it's the girl from table four. She wonders what happened to the Marine. He give her that old line about going to the corner for some cigarettes? And what's she gonna do out there on the highway? Walk up and down, gettin' honked at by every trucker b'tween here and Victorville? She don't look like the type that makes money the old-fashioned way.

Then again, maybe she is. You never know.

Then again, maybe she ain't, but she will be 'bout a half hour from now.

Evie rubs her elbow again and strains for one last look, even though it don't do no good to think about girls like that once they're out the door. They blow in to town, they blow right back out and nobody can save 'em all.

And anyway, Evie belongs to Mr. V, from when she come on at four 'til when she turns off the neon sign and counts the till at twelve or so, and she can't go 'round following lost girls. So she stamps out the cigarette and walks in through the kitchen.

"Marshall, can you make me a BLT, or are you too swamped back here by the ten o'clock rush?"

Marshall, leaning against the butcher block, rubs his nose on the sleeve of his t-shirt and blinks like he'd rather not, like he was just thinking of going out and smoking by the dumpsters himself, but why argue over a plain old BLT?

After she pours herself a cup of coffee and sets it on the crew table and stirs in the Sweet 'n Low, and after the BLT appears in the order-up window and she eats it as slow as possible, she figures she can't get out of doing the salt and pepper shakers no more.

So she stands behind the lunch counter up to her elbows in poured-out salt and chrome lids and boredom and car lights passing out there beyond the windows and thoughts about her husband Hal and whether he and his truck made it all the way to Pensacola, or whether he broke down in Texas like he did last time. And then the door of the Calico Grill squeals open and there's that girl again.

She comes in, sits at the lunch counter. She looks down at that denim purse in her lap. Evie can't hardly hear what she's saying. "What's that, honey?"

"I said, what time do you close?"

"Midnight."

The girl nods. She don't order nothing. This is the kind you send right back to the bus station. Well, Evie'll give her five more minutes. Evie don't give people no trouble, not unless they give it to her first.

She sees this kind a thing all the time—somebody sitting alone, trying to act like it don't bother them none, like somebody'll be along in a minute and nobody should feel sorry for 'em. As if Evie can't tell what's going on when they check their wristwatch and read the kiddie games on the flipside of the placemat for the fifth time and look out the window as if whatever's out there deserves to be on a postcard or something.

But really, what's the story on that Marine?

Evie grabs the coffee pot and starts pouring. "Honey, do you need help of some kind?"

The girl stares into the coffee.

"Did that boy hurt you?"

And the girl looks at Evie like *You're crazy* and Evie says, "'Cause I could call the cops if you want me to..."

"No!" The girl pushes the coffee away. "We're just traveling together." She swivels back and forth on her counter stool, trying to smile at Evie. "He changed his ticket to be with me. Back in St. Louis." And she flips her hair behind her shoulders, looking all special like she's Priscilla and he's Elvis.

And Evie hates to break it to her that she's been had, so she just asks, "Where ya from?" and "Where ya goin' to?" and the answer's so screwed up, Evie decides she'd just as soon get back to the salt shakers. But on the way there, she passes the pie case and gets an urge for banana cream. She gets out a couple little plates.

And Evie serves up pie.

And the girl traces little fork patterns into the cream on top, which makes Evie a little bit mad 'cause she's out $1.65 for a piece of pie that might not get eaten, not to mention that cup a coffee there. And then the girl says, "I think he got lost. He might not be used to towns like this. He's only from a little place called Elderberry, Ohio."

And a car honks out on the highway and Marshall, back in the back, bangs a pan against the sink.

"Well. Then God help the U.S. Marine Corps," says Evie, but the girl don't crack a smile. So Evie pours some coffee for herself. She stands there at the lunch counter, feeling the steam rise up to her chin. "So, ya think he's too lost to find his way over to the bus station?"

The girl looks down at that pie. She eats a little bit a that whipped cream, but don't say nothin' else.

Oh, yeah, Evie's thought of takin' girls like this home with her and dustin' 'em off and sendin' 'em back to wherever they belong. 'Course, nobody does that, not if they hope to die of natural causes. But this one's got the same look that Evie used to see on her twin brother, Eddie. He was the kind of boy that was slow to catch on. Thought the sons of grocers and insurance salesmen that said Hi to him were really his friends. Laughed along when their buddy-like smacks on his back nearly knocked him over. But when they chanted things like, "Eddie, Eddie, under the bleachers, tried to kiss the history teachers," she would find him later under some tree, his lip trembling, his eyes blank like he had no idea what to try next.

'Course if she lets that girl sit here all night, she can't go out and have another smoke.

She rubs her sore elbow. She looks up at the clock.

* * *

Ginni heard the phone ring.

Her eyes opened slowly, pierced by the light beam from the kitchen. Someone answered.

Sleep pulled her back.

Wait a minute. A phone could mean …

Ginni raised up on her elbows, fully awake now. She shook April's arm.

Ginni heard Teresa's voice. "Well, how did she get there? … Can you put her on the phone? … Oh, I guess. Yeah, let her sleep."

Ginni shuffled into the kitchen, squinting against the light.

"Yeah, I'd better," said Teresa. "I don't know." Teresa put her hand over the mouthpiece. "Nancy, how long does it take to get to Barstow?"

Nancy unfolded a tattered road map. She measured with her fingers.

Teresa spoke into the phone again. "That's eight hours. I can't start a drive like that right now."

"That was Evie," she told the gathered, puffy-eyed girls as she hung up. "She's a waitress at some place called 'The Calico Cafe.'" She held up her hand against a flurry of questions. "Not now. I'm beat." She looked at Ginni and April. "You wanna go to Barstow tomorrow?"

* * *

She slept a sleep of deadness.

She had ridden home on the ripped seat of Evie's finned car — down the highway a couple blocks, around the back of the mall and into the lanes of the Desert Villa Mobile Home Park. The whole place sat smack up against a wall built to block out the truck noise that roared down the freeway beyond. Not that the wall worked as intended.

Shelly had followed Evie up the steps to her trailer, stubbing her sneakers against a fat and jagged rock that counted, she supposed, as porch decoration.

Once inside, Evie had opened a bedroom door and pointed to the bed covered only by sheets gone a hard-water gray. She handed Shelly a pilled blanket and then left her alone. And the last thing Shelly remembered was that she really ought to take her shoes off, but for the effort required to reach that far …

She must have dreamt of cheeseburgers and malts and diner tables and parking lots for when she awoke to a cloudy sort of light coming from the window, she continuing chewing on a question that had jeered at her all night long: How could she have believed that story of his, "Got to check up at the front office. I'll just be five minutes and we'll be on our way"?

It was not so much that he left her. What bothered her was that someone *knew* he left her.

And now, here she was, in that someone's trailer house, on a bed that wasn't quite civilized, in a room with a bare fish tank, big as a desk, over by the closet, and a blue-toned picture of Jesus on the wall, the most yearbook-like portrait she had ever seen of him.

And she really didn't want to look at a picture of Jesus right now.

Although she wasn't sure what happened back at the Travelodge counted, it had all gone so fast. It was just bam! and roll off and light up and disappear into the bathroom.

It all felt kind of … normal.

All except for the strange musk that followed her like campfire smoke with every move she made. It was still on her now.

She scooted off the bed. A snag on her thumbnail caught on the sheets, just as it had all night long. She opened the bedroom door. A window in the narrow hallway looked out on the back side of the mall, on doors that said "Hickory Farms" and "Hobbyland."

Evie was still sleeping off her shift, apparently.

Shelly shut herself in the bathroom and clicked the lock. She squinted at herself in the mirror, and felt that snagged nail against her jeans.

Evie have anything for this? She opened a drawer and dug through the bobby pins, the rattail comb, the can of Aqua-Net. The next drawer was a jumble of painfully prickly rollers, some gauze that wouldn't stay in its mangled box, an old tube of white lipstick. White? Really?

She checked the medicine cabinet and found rusty clippers there.

She ran water in the bathtub, good and hot. She sat into it, scalding half of herself pink.

A screen door somewhere out there slammed. Shelly sat up, the bathwater slapping against her. A car idled, probably easing itself over one the Desert Villa's wicked speed bumps. She listened, waiting for its low rumble to go away. When did her stomach muscles clench up so? Why did every wall feel thin, every door weak?

And how *had* Danny managed to break into the bathroom?

If he had been the murdering type … She plunged deeper into

the water, until her hair floated, until air bubbles escaped from her ears and the water rushed in, sealing out every noise but the inner-space hum in her head that told her she was alive.

Alive! So there!

She rose up out of the water. She pulled the plug and stood up and dried herself with a yellow floral towel on the rack, dropping it on the floor when she was done. Take that, Evie, and your greasy dive and your poking into Shelly Galvin's business, and your hinting around, *Is there anybody ah could call fer yew?* and *Did that boy hurt yew?* as if it *had* been rape.

No, there is nobody you can call for Shelly Galvin, especially when you might tell a story of *He left her behind* and *She just sat there, not knowin' whut to do.*

You know, not every boy on a bus was a psychopath and not every time a friendly girl said hello and how're you doing and what kind of place is Elderberry, Ohio, was she cuddling up to a cobra. Just maybe Shelly Galvin knew what she was doing and, OK, so Danny disappeared, but he had deadlines, you know? The U.S. Marine Corps didn't take kindly to their men running in late. But you all wouldn't know that because none of you ever talked to him, did you? None of you spent hours and hours getting to know him, finding out about the tricks he'd taught his pet Labrador back in Elderberry, and none of you knew that, every birthday, he asked for short ribs and corn on the cob and baked beans for dinner. None of you knew that because none of you paid him any mind. None of you talk to anybody you don't already know. And now you're giving Shelly Galvin a hard time because she puts herself out there, and it makes people follow her around and buy her cokes and risk the wrath of their sergeants, changing around bus tickets and all.

And she slipped back into her shirt and jeans (Last time! Once this was over, they were garbage!) and walked out to the kitchen to find the phone.

Only there wasn't one.

Not on the wall. Not on the breakfast counter. Not on the end table over by that couch.

There was a skillet sitting on the range, ready at any moment to fry up an egg or two. There was a dish of butter; Evie was, apparently, one of those people who didn't believe it ought to go in the fridge. There was a waning loaf of off-brand bread.

Shelly undid the twist tie and helped herself to a couple slices. She sat at the breakfast counter, pulling off the top crusts, thinking.

She saw Evie's purse, slouching against an empty coffee can.

She only took a twenty. To take it all would be really low, but to take just enough ... to stick it in her denim purse, along with the six weeks' worth of saved wages from her ice cream-scooping job at the Boxford Mall, wages meant to buy herself a souvenir hooded sweatshirt from the BYU Bookstore ...

See? No more hooded sweatshirt! Shelly herself was giving up something longed-for because this was, after all, an emergency.

And she twisted the knob of the front door of the trailer and pulled on it carefully, just in case it was one of those doors that made sucking sounds when it opened, and she stepped out in to the jumbled lanes of the Desert Villa Mobile Home Park.

Which way had they come in the night before, or early this morning, whenever it was?

She walked past black metal front steps, hard-packed dirt yards, plastic flowers in pots and duct-taped windows. Around a bend in the lane, she found a little red brick building. Inside, behind a few racks of candy, a man sat in the shadows, his arms folded, his face wily as though he considered himself the eye on the street around here.

This couldn't be the way Evie drove in last night. Shelly turned back, passing a laundry shack and a woman in a housecoat, shaking a rug.

Around the bend again, she saw Evie, a small figure sitting against the railing at her door, blowing smoke rings. She stubbed out the Salem and grasped the forward railing, leaning in Shelly's direction. It came across like royalty summoning a subject.

Shelly could only walk forward.

"Out for a li'l stroll?" Evie asked.

It didn't sound like a nicety. *How are you this morning? Did you sleep well?* No, it was more like *Nice of you to get up this morning* when you shuffled out of the bedroom at noon and saw a cold plate of toast waiting for you. Shelly didn't trust herself to say anything until she could read Evie's mind. What did the woman know? Was this the moment to 'fess up and hand over the twenty? Or should she just hide it in a couch cushion when she had the chance? Or just … use it? In an emergency, of course.

"'Cause I'd appreciate it," Evie went on, "if, when you leave my house, you'd lock up the door."

Shelly looked her in the eye. It was all the contrition she could manage.

"So?" said Evie.

"I was thinking," said Shelly, "of catching the next bus."

"Yeah? Well," she shrugged, "have it your way. But you oughta know I already called your sister. She's on her way."

"But you don't have a phone."

Evie pointed at a phone booth up the lane.

"You know," said Shelly, "if I had wanted her called, I would've done it myself. Some people have dangerous relatives, you know, and people think they're so helpful, calling up these relatives and … And anyway, how did you know where to call?"

Evie shrugged again. "I snooped in your purse. But don't worry, I didn't take nothin'. I ain't that kind."

For Shelly, the difference between guilt and diarrhea cramps was a pretty fine line. Maybe Evie, standing there like that, was actually blocking her door. Or maybe she still didn't know about the twenty.

"If it's all the same to you," said Shelly, "I just want to take my chances with Greyhound."

Evie looked her up and down. Then, with a flourish, she swept her arm towards the road out of the Desert Villa Mobile Home Park.

Shelly walked out. She walked around the mall of Mars, right by the squirty little developer-planted trees. She crossed the street at McDonald's. The drive-up order box squawked at a blue station wagon, "Sausage Egg McMuffin, hash browns and a medium coffee. Is that everything? That'll be $3.71, please."

She walked into the bus station. She gathered up her return ticket to Boxford, her ice-cream scooping money and that twenty, hoping it was enough, but re-adding it in her head, just in case. Then she walked up to the counter. "When's the next bus headed towards Maryland?"

"Six o'clock tonight."

Shelly looked around at the wooden benches, the taped boxes passing as baggage, the sprinkling of passengers. They all ate breakfasts of Funyuns and vending-machine honey buns. They bided the slow hours, looking around at signs and doors and people they had already looked at a hundred times before.

By now, she was like the rest of them, shuffling and staring at nothing, worse than nursing home patients. Who in this sad little hall could remember what they were before … before they ended up here?

Shelly tried to remember: was the Happy Dragon restaurant back home next to the floral shop or after Pizza Hut?

Did her mom's housecoat have buttons or snaps?

Had she asked to go to Boxford? Or to Provo?

Did she sleep on her side or her back? When she used to sleep, that is. Back when she used to put off going to bed because she wanted to talk a few minutes on the phone with … with … um … Will. Yeah. Will was his name.

Boy, never again. She'd fall into bed before the sun faded from the sky. Every night. If she ever got back to Boxford. Or Provo, wherever it was she was going.

If she could wait until six o'clock, and then, of course, wait the day or three or whatever it was until she could lay flat out on her back, just let every muscle go slack and shut the curtain on her brain. If she could just wait that long. Then she'd feel better.

She looked at the people slumped in the benches, waiting.

And Shelly Galvin did not like to wait. If there was a way to feel better now, she was all for it.

She turned away from the ticket counter and walked out the door.

* * *

She sat on Evie's front step—not that she could remember how she got there. And the last thing she remembered, between the time Evie opened her door and when Shelly fell back on the bed was that she could still smell that musk on herself.

* * *

It was the best 532 miles ever.

Ginni no longer cared if Shelly messed up the whole trip by running away to Barstow. If Shelly hadn't done it, Ginni wouldn't have Marc all to herself here in this backseat. This was a moment she'd been waiting for since they stopped playing ambulance-to-the-rescue games way back in childhood.

Of course, everybody tread carefully around Marc. Back home in Boxford, there'd been an accident the day before he left, leaving Marc's younger brother with an amputated leg. Really, what was Marc to think when he left the next morning and his mom and dad stayed in bed, exhausted from a night of waiting up at the hospital? That they thought he caused the accident? That they were glad to have their black sheep out of their sight? Why else was he failing two classes, and never writing home? Ginni had expected to find him walking around Provo with a brickload of guilt like a hump on his back.

But he seemed fine today. Ginni shared her Chicken in a Biskit crackers with him. And they argued genially about which movies had been shot at those obelisk rocks over there in the desert.

He teased her. "You're ticklish, aren't you? Yes, you are. Look how you jumped, and I was still five inches away"

She teased him. While Teresa filled the tank, the rest of them went inside the gas station and tried on reading glasses at the little display near the cash register. "You look like your dad!" Ginni gasped.

"No way!" he said as he darted towards the tiny mirror and checked himself out.

"Yes, even with that tag over your nose. Doesn't he, April? Here, let's find you a pocket protector and you're all set for next Halloween."

He teased her when she put on lip gloss:

"Look at you, trying to look like a model."

"Am not!" She flushed.

"Yeah, ya are." He ducked as she threw the lip gloss at him. "You're doing that look. You know, the one where they try to look stuck-up and mad and sexy all at the same time."

Even if *that* mortified her (yes, she was doing The Look, practiced it every day), even if Teresa wouldn't tell them much about this Evie and even if she wouldn't stop at the red sand dunes to let them feel the sand—although she did stop in Dixie Junction, just out of curiosity, which was OK because Ginni had long run out of Chicken in a Biskit—still, this was better than anything Ginni could have imagined. The whole drive had that larky feel, like when the power goes out and there's nothing to do but play board games by candlelight. The entire ride convinced Ginni that she *could* flirt and that she would *never* end up like Teresa and Nancy and the rest of them.

And when Teresa announced, "Ladies and gentleman, we have arrived," Ginni awoke from a nap—nestled against Marc's shoulder—and blinked at the spindly gas station signs that appeared on the horizon.

* * *

Evie was a delicate thing, standing there, holding open the door of Trailer #18 at the Desert Villa Mobile Home Park, kicking some big desert rock out of their way. The reddish hair at the top of her head was all nesty and stuffed into bobby pins. The rest straggled to her shoulders.

She pointed toward a back bedroom. "She's sleeping again." She stepped out. "Oh, let me get those out of your way." She kicked aside a pair of dirt-crusted boots. "Hal musta worn the other ones when he left on his run."

"So she's OK?" asked Teresa.

Evie shrugged. "I'm sure she's shook up some, though she don't wanna let on." She shook a cigarette out of the pack and lit up. "I offered to call the cops, but these girls, they think they can handle anything."

"Cops?"

Evie looked at the kids. She nodded to them. Then she waved Teresa inside a little ways. Teresa breathed in the fry oil scent, the furniture long-steeped in smoke. "I heard 'em talking about a room at the Travelodge," Evie whispered. "An' I know they didn't go in there to watch no *Gunsmoke* re-runs. Leastways, he didn't. Then I think I saw her comin' out of that second-floor room, but he was gone. She said she thought he got hisself all turned around in a big town like Barstow." Evie eyed Teresa. *And she thinks we'll believe that one, don't she?* "So anyway, I brought her here and put her in the spare room. She's sleepin'. Or maybe she's sittin' in there admittin' to herself that he ain't really lost. I don't know."

"I'd better go find out," said Teresa.

She followed Evie past a bar stool of torn vinyl, past mugs stained with deep brown rings, past a folded-open TV schedule, with flower petals doodled in the margins. Evie pointed at a bedroom door down the hallway.

Teresa knocked. "Shelly, you in there?"

"I'm not dressed," said a muffled Shelly.

"No biggie. I've changed your diapers." Teresa jiggled the door handle. It was locked. "Shelly, open up! After what you've put me through in the last twenty-four hours ..."

"What *you've* gone through? What about me?"

Teresa frowned at the door. The battle to keep Shelly pure and virginal had always been safely remote. The broken curfews, the dubious alibis—they all showed up in Mom's letters. Like a skirt in the wind, no matter where you held Shelly down, she found some other way to blow free. It was all amusing enough to make Teresa rip open those letters from home, even *before* she fixed her usual double-sized mug of hot chocolate. She could just hear Mom and Dad lying awake at night, wondering what to try next.

But now, Shelly was here, on the other side of this cheap, probably hollow door. Teresa jiggled the handle again. "And what's this I hear about a Marine and a *motel room?*"

"I needed a shower."

"You what? While he was in the room? How stupid is ..." Teresa stared at the door. "Why didn't you just let him dangle you over the balcony, huh? Don't you know what can happen when ..."

"Teresa, when I want advice about boys," said Shelly, "I'll get it from somebody with *experience*. You know?"

Teresa looked down the hallway, where everyone in the kitchen pretended not to listen.

"And," Shelly went on, "that wouldn't be you, now, would it?"

"Shelly! Open this door!" Hot damn!—why weren't her parents smart enough to keep the family floozy at home? "Evie, you got a key or something?"

Teresa could hear Evie rummaging through a drawerful of clinking junk as Shelly went on in her muffled, taunting voice " … for turning twenty-six and never having anybody ask you for so much as a walk around the block."

Teresa gripped the door jamb. "Oh yeah?" The urge to put a hole through something surged through her. She could see herself aiming, punching, could feel how satisfying it would be. But she fought it down. "Well, at least I don't tag along with scum that," she lowered her voice—there were innocent youngsters out there in the kitchen—"that uses me, then loses me. I mean, where's your big Marine now, huh?"

"He wasn't that big," Ginni murmured out in the kitchen.

"They don't need to be," said Marc. "It's the scrawny ones you need to watch out for."

"Hmm," said Evie. "Come to think of it, I ain't seen that key for some time now."

"So," Teresa spoke to the door again, "why don't you quit hanging around where you're not wanted and come on back to Provo …"

"Like I said, you'd know all about not being wanted."

"Shelly!" Teresa slammed her elbow at the door, then glanced down the hall. "Ten minutes! Be outta there or … Gosh," she walked back to the kitchen. "I can't remember why I even care!"

"Let me try," said Marc. He walked down the hall and knocked on the door.

"It hasn't been ten minutes!"

"This is Marc."

"Oh."

Shelly opened the door.

* * *

That's how Ginni and April found them, hugging there in the

back bedroom. When Marc broke away, Shelly swiped her thumb over right cheek and her left, flicking away tears.

"I'm just starving, that's all. What I'd give for a little Taco Bell right now," she said.

"Well, why don't you ask Teresa to stop there?" he said.

"I would, but I'm not her favorite person right now, in case you hadn't noticed."

"Let me see what I can do." Marc left the room.

And the three girls sat on the bed together.

She was now an exotic creature, somebody who had been through the spin cycle of trouble. Ginni wanted to hear the tale, to live it. She wanted to feel the thrill of the running away, just without the dead thud of running aground; the warm solidity of that uniformed boy, as if it were next to *her*, but not the sharpness of his axe or knife or open palm, or whatever he might have used.

And what was this bit about a motel room? She sat with April, waiting for Shelly to reveal all.

"I'm just really worried about him," Shelly told them. "He just disappeared. Like that." She snapped her fingers.

Um, yes. From all indications, he dumped her. Shelly hadn't figured that out yet?

"Well," said April, "can we help you pack up or something?"

"The bus went on without us. My suitcase is somewhere in San-whatever-it-is by now."

What? "No clothes?" said Ginni. "No mascara? No clean socks?"

Shelly shook her head and waved her hand towards San-whatever-it-is. No! That was a misery Ginni did *not* want to live, not even vicariously. Shelly leaned back against the wall. "I'll be so glad to get out of here. This place is lonelier than the moon!" She yawned. "And I really, really need to talk to the bishop."

Ginni looked at April. April looked back, stricken. Oh, the burden of guilt! Oh, her imperiled soul!

But Shelly, picking strands out of her hairbrush, looked just like she did when she climbed out of the van with Mike Truitt. "I just really ought to talk to him."

Outside the bedroom, Evie and Teresa, their voices low and their heads together, broke it up as Shelly settled herself on a bar stool. "You don't have to whisper about me," she said. "I guess I'll have to see the bishop when I get home."

"Look, Shelly, we get it, OK?" said April. "You're the experienced woman now. You know stuff we don't know." She folded her puffy parka over her arm, opened the door and stepped out into the Barstow breeze, leaving Shelly to swivel on that bar stool.

There was nothing to do but go to the car.

Outside, Ginni looked across the car roof at April. "Why should I feel this bad? I'm not the one that did it. I'm not the one staring the jaws of hell in the face."

"Well, then stop," said April.

"Sure thing. Right away."

Ginni looked at the trailer next to Evie's. Its numbers peeled away at the corners. Somebody had planted red plastic flowers in the dirt, a bravely homey touch. Not to mention the "curtain" in the window, which anybody could see was a bandana.

She opened the car door, only to face a smashed cracker box on the floor, and bits of lint stuck to her pea coat.

Marc joined them. He looked back at Teresa and Shelly on Evie's step, saying their good-byes. "Oh, well, every family needs a screw-up." He grinned.

"Enough, Marc," said April. "Just because you think you're our family's …"

"You'd think," said Ginni, "there'd be some voice telling her to stop."

"A girl goes behind the door of some motel room," said Marc, "and what does she expect is gonna happen? Angels will rescue her?"

April frowned at him. "It's not all her fault."

"Riiight." He crawled into the backseat, tossing aside his blue sweatshirt and some beef jerky wrappers.

Ginni settled into her own seat. Soon they'd be out of this dismal place and she'd be back to sleeping on his shoulder.

Then Shelly appeared at the passenger side of the car.

She looked over the front seat and back, as if deciding between the bigger cookie, or the one with more chocolate chips.

She chose the back. She settled into the middle, bouncing in the seat a little, leaning into Ginni's space as she checked her image in the rearview mirror. She pulled her hairbrush from her purse. It made a rhythmic, carpet-scraping sound as she worked it through her scalp. Hairs floated through the air. Ginni flicked away the ones that landed on her lap, and the brushing went on and on.

"This hump hurts my butt," said Shelly.

So Marc offered to sit on the hump.

Teresa got in the car, plugging the key into the ignition.

"Any chance we could stop at Taco Bell?" said Marc.

But before they could leave the Desert Villa Mobile Home Park, Shelly opened her door. "Just a minute. Forgot something." She ran up Evie's steps and poked a piece of paper—or was it a dollar? Ginni couldn't tell—under that rock on the stoop.

Back in the car, Shelly spread her coat over her legs. Ginni wondered what she had stuffed under that rock. But when Shelly looked up and caught her staring, she glared back as if curiosity was the height of rudeness. Never mind that someone back in Provo worked an extra shift, to cover Teresa's absence, or that two girls came on a college visit and hadn't seen much of the college yet.

And as they pulled into the drive-through at Taco Bell, the sun disappeared, leaving an aura of purple and orange behind.

Soon, they rode away from the neon lights of Barstow, into the desert darkness. They rode away to the sound of the tires singing on the pavement, and the rattle of food wrappers, and Shelly shaking her cup.

"What is this? I think they gave me all ice. I'm still thirsty."

"Here." Marc offered his. "No, go ahead."

"Well, if you don't mind."

Suddenly, Marc's arm stretched along the back of the seat. His hand rested on Ginni's shoulder, warm and thick-fingered. She looked at him, his face lit by the dials up front, his arms spread like a gull at full wingspan.

She knew the other arm was around Shelly.

But he flashed her a look just like he had when, on the trip down, her head had fallen drowsily against the seat.

This look, this arm—it was the kind of thing that happened to girls when they grew up and got pretty.

She had watched Shelly and other girls to see how it was done and she had practiced phrases like "Marc and I are coming home for Christmas" and "Here's a picture of Marc and I biking on Nantucket" long, long before she had any business saying them to anybody and she had waited her turn and now she caught her breath just as the buoyancy of being liked by somebody carried her above all the plodding and the everyday.

And she wished Shelly would just shut up.

It was the strangest thing, Shelly prattling away at Marc. Shelly had known him all her life, yet never aimed her coy little glances at him until now. But some people just needed a thumb to suck, and Shelly's was: *Who can I get to follow me around today?*

Ginni leaned against the cold window. This was turning in to the longest 532 miles ever.

"Do you want these olives?" Shelly asked Marc. "I can't stand them."

"Sure. No problem. Hey, wait, not *that* many!"

Ginni felt him flinch. His arm went away. "Did you just put that one down my shirt!" he said.

Shelly laughed.

Ginni stared out the window at the shadows of scrubby trees. Concentrated, actually, the better to block out the wrestling match that had just broken out between Shelly and Marc. It was enough to rock the car.

Teresa's eyes flashed in the rear-view mirror. "Cut it out, both of you."

But the giggles and the rocking just wouldn't die.

"You really don't fight fair." Giggle, giggle.

"Comes from growing up in a big family." Rock, rock.

Ginni felt something dark and ugly growing in her. The conditions were certainly right for it, as right as a damp towel in a dark and steamy locker.

Then his arm was back around her again.

And why, if that arm was there, did Ginni feel a small hiss of air leaking out of her mood? Was it petty for her to wish she had all of his attention? Couldn't she be like Marc, the child of the big family, used to sharing every little thing? Couldn't she be like Shelly back at that dance with Will? All the younger boys had hung around, flipping their ties and tossing their shoes, and yet Shelly never lost her cool.

Couldn't Ginni be just as smooth?

Teresa leaned toward the radio dial, snatching music out of the dark desert air. A truck passed, looming against them, its trailer outlined in orange lights. Ginni's unfinished burrito sat in her lap, growing cold and greasy.

April stirred in the front seat, wadding her parka against the window.

Teresa looked over at April. She turned the radio down. She glanced over her shoulder, taking in Shelly, who nodded off, and Marc, who stared into space. Turning back to the road, she watched Marc in her rear-view mirror. "What's this? Arms around two girls?"

"Just practicing. In case polygamy comes back," Marc laughed.

Teresa's eyes locked on the mirror.

Suddenly, she steered the car over to the shoulder, bounding over rubber tire bits and gravel, grinding to a stop.

April awoke, blinked, looked around.

Teresa jammed the gears into park. She turned around. "Guys like you should just…" her jaw muscles pulsed, "should just … go pee on an electric fence!"

"Whoa!" he said. "Your nachos go down wrong or something?"

"No, but if you want to get all pioneer-y on me, you can get out and walk."

Ginni's mind teetered like a knocked glass of water. Teresa, all blazing eyes and flaring nostrils, turned back to her steering wheel. The smirk frozen on Marc's face twitched at the corners. Some parka fabric, somewhere, schussed against itself.

"Way to go, smart boy," said April.

A muffled beat struggled out of the radio. Ginni exhaled. The car lights turned away from the scrubby desert bushes. The road rumbled beneath them all again.

Shelly stirred. "If I don't get this kink out of my neck …" she said. "That's what comes from riding on a bus for three days. Oh, that feels good. Yeah, try it over here, too. Oh! Don't stop!"

Ginni reached for Marc's hand behind her. Lifting it over her head, she dropped it back into his own lap. Then she crumpled the paper around her half-eaten burrito and stuffed it into her Taco Bell cup.

NOTES

"The Gilded Door" appeared in the Fall 2008 issue of *Dialogue: A Journal of Mormon Thought.*

"'Atta Boy" appeared in the Summer 2005 issue of Dialogue. In 2006, it won the Association for Mormon Letters' award for Short Fiction.

"Gypsy Holiday" won honorable mention in the 2006 Irreantum fiction contest, appearing in the combined 2007/2008 issue.

"Follow Me, Boys" appeared in the Summer 2007 issue of Dialogue and won a "Best of the Year" award for Fiction.

ACKNOWLEDGEMENTS

I would like to thank a lot of people who shared their expertise with me:

Sylvia Hunt, a tireless supporter of the arts in my hometown, shared her stories of women's music clubs. Shelley Brown, Jesse Galle and the late Vic Kumma of the State Theatre in Easton, Pennsylvania, shared their behind-the-scenes memories. I learned about pigs from Joel Geiger and Brian Fugate. I was thrilled to stumble on to Eric Green's vast website, http://www.civildefensemuseum.com/. And thank you, Elvin, the custodian who gave me a tour of the old fallout shelter at my county courthouse.

Jay Reed taught me about boats. Jon Aki kept from going too far astray on medical emergencies.

Merrilee Meacham advised me on runaway teens. Tom Royer shared his passion for muscle cars. Thank you, Greyhound Bus Lines, for finding my luggage.

Special thanks to Robert Rebein, the professor who taught me to 1) aim for the big world out there and 2) make it fun for the reader.

Thanks to Becca Tippets for editing.

Finally, thanks to my writer friends at Troubadours in Woodstock, Illinois; the Lehigh Valley Writer's Academy in Allentown, Pennsylvania; and the gang at the Indianapolis Writer's Center that still hasn't gotten around to naming itself.

About the Author

Kristen Carson was born in Idaho. She has lived in Utah, Texas, Illinois and Pennsylvania. She currently resides near Indianapolis. She and her husband are the parents of four adult children. Carson's stories and articles have appeared in *Chicago Parent*, *Indianapolis Monthly*, and *Dialogue: a Journal of Mormon Thought*. Visit her at www.kristencarsonauthor.com.

www.ingramcontent.com/pod-product-compliance
Lightning Source LLC
Chambersburg PA
CBHW021950170626
46808CB00001B/98